THE LION RAMPANT

THE LION RAMPANT

William Paul

Macdonald

A Macdonald Book

First published in Great Britain in 1989
by Macdonald & Co (Publishers) Ltd
London & Sydney

Paul, William 1955–
    The lion rampant
    I. Title
    823'.914[F]

    ISBN 0-356-17558-8

Typeset by Leaper & Gard Ltd, Bristol
Reproduced, printed and bound in Great Britain by
Hazell Watson & Viney Limited
Member of BPCC Limited
Aylesbury, Bucks, England

Macdonald & Co (Publishers) Ltd
66-73 Shoe Lane
London EC4P 4AB

A member of Pergamon MCC Publishing Corporation plc

For my two boys...

Breathes there the man with soul so dead
Who never to himself hath said,
This is my own, my native land.

Sir Walter Scott

CHAPTER ONE

Andrew Wallace, leader of the resurgent Scottish Nationalists, is our undisputed choice as man of the year.

He has wrought something akin to a miracle in his own land by reshaping a previously dormant party and bringing it to within a whisker of gaining real political power. The British Government is at a loss over how to deal with somebody who has taken them on at their own constitutional game and is beating them all ends up.

Who is to say now that Scotland will not secure independence after almost 300 years in the shadow and in the control of neighbour England? Exiled Scots have been responsible for running countries the world over. Perhaps the time is ripe for them to take charge of their own.

Time Magazine

The kangaroo hit the windscreen of the truck just as the final movement of Beethoven's Seventh Symphony was reaching its climax. Behind the steering wheel Murray Tarrant was rudely shaken out of a pleasant daydream, jerking his head backwards so that the stereo headphones were dislodged and fell down round his neck. The constant, hammering roar of the giant diesel engine intruded into his senses. At the same time he imagined he had heard the dull crack of breaking bones and the hollow slap-thump of the big 150-pound carcase thudding against the toughened glass.

The animal's body and neck were strangely twisted. Its pointed face was directly in front of Tarrant's. One bulging eye stared at him through the insect-smeared glass, weeping a clear liquid that rapidly turned pink. Its top lip was wrenched back, exposing a tight curve of splayed yellow teeth that vibrated sharply against the smooth surface as if the thing was trying to bite its way through to get at him. 'Sorry, sport,' he said, regaining his composure. 'Can't stop.'

The kangaroo stuck in that position in front of him for several seconds, held there by the forward momentum of the truck, flattened against the glass so that the texture of the reddish-brown fur was all whorls and loops. Then it began to slide slowly off to one side, leaving thick and thin trails of orangey-red blood like a crudely-drawn road map. The shattered body momentarily flapped like a torn flag at the side of the speeding truck, its head caught between the corner of the windscreen and the upright exhaust pipe. The claws on its hind legs swung round to scrape against the door window. Then it was gone, to be swallowed in the rolling clouds of red dust behind. Tarrant watched it disappear in the side mirror. Sorry, sport, he repeated to himself. Can't stop.

He had seen it coming all the way, he now realised. His mind had been coasting in neutral while he had watched with casual disinterest as the trembling grey blob emerged out of the heat haze and grew steadily into a full-grown buck kangaroo bouncing in long, lazy arcs through the sparse salt-bushes and scrub at an exact right-angle to the Stuart Highway thirty miles north of Barrow Creek in the Northern Territory. The haze made distances hard to judge with any accuracy. The endless row of telegraph poles at the side of the pot-holed road were as good a guide as anything. All around him the desert seethed and swelled like a solid sea; the 'roo, a hairy dolphin jumping and diving. Tarrant did not once slacken speed below seventy miles per hour or even attempt to brake when he realised, at the last moment, that they were on a collision course. It would have been too dangerous with two hundred head of livestock behind him in the three trailers that he was hauling south. He did not even bother to blast the horn. He had run down plenty of kangaroos before, and sheep, and cattle. He had squashed a million rabbits, and snakes, even the occasional crocodile in the far north, and once he had sideswiped a wild camel. They made as much impression on the huge Dodge truck as the winged insects that were like a growth of moss all over the steel surface at

8

the end of each two-thousand-mile trip between Darwin and Adelaide. The wheels crushed them or the heavy 'roo bar over the radiator simply battered them out of the way. It never ceased to amaze him how the stupid beasts managed to co-ordinate their lives in all that endless emptiness of the outback in order to wander in front of his truck at the exact moment he happened to pass by.

The 'roos usually came out to feed around dusk, then were mesmerised by oncoming headlights, standing motionless in the road, sniffing the air, watching death bear down on them with intense fascination. But this one was different, this one was special, because it was early afternoon and it must have decided it wanted to die spectacularly. A kamikaze kangaroo.

The top of the bar had caught the kangaroo at the very peak of a bound, so instead of brushing it aside, the animal was flipped up into the air to come thumping back into the windscreen. Tarrant had heard of this happening before but had never seen it. He had been lucky the glass was tough enough to take the impact and the 'roo had not crashed right through, to wrap itself around his neck. He had known one man who had been killed that way in his car. It hadn't happened to him this time, though. Not this time. We live to fight another day, he thought. Maybe the kangaroo was some kind of omen. Good or bad?

He looked past the blood streaks, down the arrow-straight road to the far horizon where the flat land and sky met in a crooked line as if the joint between the two had slipped. He lifted a hand sticky with sweat from the jolting wheel and squirted the washer-jets onto the windscreen before the greasy blood hardened. It took several sweeps of the wipers to clear it properly. When he was satisfied, he moved the displaced earphones back onto his hears. He rewound the tape and the loudness of the engine was drowned by the music. He turned up the volume and began to whistle through his teeth in time to the music. The tuneless whistling was a habit he had when he was nervous.

It was Tarrant's second day on the road, and his fourth return trip in just under a month. He was exhausted. He had not slept since leaving the town of Katherine, and it was only the pep pills that were keeping him awake and upright. He

9

felt like a coat hung on a hook. But he had to keep going. He was three hours late because of having to mend two punctures. It was roughly ten miles to the meeting place. Then he would run on to Alice Springs, and there perhaps he could afford to take some rest.

The dust penetrated the air-conditioned cab and got into his hair and his eyes and his throat and the pores of his skin. His blond hair was coloured red by it. He was drenched in sweat. His yellow vest and black football shorts were sticking uncomfortably to his bare skin. Miles and yards seemed interchangeable in this flat, featureless landscape. Sometimes he thought he could see for hundreds of miles; at other times the road seemed to run into a blank wall just a few hundred yards ahead.

A web of fine cracks had appeared on one side of the windscreen. The glass would probably hold together for now, but it would need to be replaced soon. The incident with the kangaroo had produced a surge of adrenalin inside him that gradually dissipated. He opened the door of the ice-box built into the passenger seat beside him and drank from one of the bottles of carbonated water. Then he took a handful of ice-cubes and rubbed them over his face and chest before pushing them down the front of his shorts and leaving them there to melt. That helped a little.

An approaching truck loomed suddenly in front of him, lights flashing, horn blaring, flinging out a cloud of whirling sand. Tarrant's reactions were too slow for him to react before it was past. All he got was an impression of green and white and the slatted sides of the trailers before the cloud hit him and he was just as quickly out the other side and all alone again. He waved a hand in front of his face. 'Hi, pal,' he said too late.

The other truckies thought Tarrant was pretty strange. He didn't mix with them much. He wasn't really one of them, having been in the job only a couple of years. He had his reasons for keeping himself to himself.

The usual method of carving up the huge distances into manageable chunks was to travel between landmarks, marking out the journey in short lengths so that you didn't go insane thinking about how far you still had to go. Tarrant

10

used music instead. He travelled by individual songs and LPs and recorded concerts, knowing exactly how far each would take him. He went through phases in the type of music he liked to use. At the beginning of the year it had been rock music, plain and simple and as loud as possible. Then in the summer he had briefly developed a taste for the twanging chords of Country and Western. But at some point in September that had changed over to classical music, and he quickly found that he could not get enough of the full orchestral sound. Now he was travelling by symphonies, long concerts, and short, snappy overtures, transported by Herbert von Karajan and the Berlin Philharmonic. Beethoven's Seventh, barring accidents, carried him about forty-eight miles along the way. Today it would be nearer sixty by the time it finished because he was replaying the last bit. And as the music played he dreamed about arriving home, stocking up from the local bottle shop and climbing into bed with the delectable Donna to celebrate Christmas in style.

The tape had just run to its end for the second time when he saw in the distance the old, disused wind-wheel standing back from the road. He was instantly alert, snatching off the hissing headphones and easing his foot off the throttle to begin pumping the brakes gently. He had the delivery ready for them. There was no problem about that, but back in Port Darwin he had been told that they wanted to speak to him about another job. That was what was making him nervous.

He drove off the road onto the softer sand at the side and skidded a little as he applied the air-brakes with a little too much force. The truck came to a halt and the dust settled around it like smoke round a dying fire. Tarrant killed the engine and the silence hummed in his ears. He took a swig of cold water to clear his throat before jumping down from the cab. His back was stiff, his muscles sore from sitting so long in one position. The sweet smell of hot rubber came from the chest-high tyres, mixing with the smell of the restless cattle moving in the trailers. His hands trembled as if they were still gripping the shuddering steering-wheel. The searing heat of the desert was like a blanket thrown over his head.

There was a white van parked in the shadow of the rusty derrick that supported the motionless wheel. Three men got out and stood beside it as he approached. Two were relatively young, big and muscular with wide shoulders, loose-fitting clothes and wrap-around sunglasses. The other was a thin, elderly man, scorched brown by the sun, with wrinkles as wide as dried-up riverbeds round his eyes and mouth. He was wearing an open-necked shirt, a pair of kneelength shorts, sandals, and a leather bushman's hat tied under his chin. Tarrant recognised Luigi Fachetti immediately, although he had only met him once before. Legend had it that Fachetti had decided to retire from a long career in the Sicilian Mafia to run a sheep ranch in Australia, but had quickly got bored and set up a sideline bringing drugs in through Darwin for distribution in the big cities of the south and east. Tarrant had been recruited as a soldier two years ago, during one of his periodic bouts of unemployment when he was in the middle of a fierce drinking binge. Fachetti had personally promised to get him a job as a truck driver if he would drop off any stuff he was given at a stated rendezvous point. Tarrant had jumped at the chance and coined in the money, making double the wages of the average truckie. He was being remarkably disciplined in salting most of it away to save up to buy a share in his uncle's prawn boat working the Spencer Gulf out of Wallaroo. His uncle said the chance was there if he wanted it. He reckoned it might take him another year to make it.

'G'day, Mr Fachetti,' Tarrant said. 'Long time no see.'

'You are late and you don't answer your radio, Murray my son. Tell me, what is the point of having a radio if you are not going to answer it?' He had a high, whining voice, like a young teenage boy.

'Sorry, Mr Fachetti. I had the 'phones on. I wouldn't hear.'

The two young men walked past Tarrant without acknowledging him and he turned to watch them go to the first trailer. They bent down and opened the catches on a rectangular, underslung box, taking great care not to dirty their clothes. Inside were a dozen bulky nylon sacks. They picked out three sacks which were tied with yellow binder twine, cut open the top of one and poured a few nine-inch squares of rough cattle cake onto the ground. Fachetti, too, walked past Tarrant, who turned and followed a few steps behind.

12

'I had to sit here for many hours waiting for you, and it is the hottest part of the day,' Fachetti said over his shoulder, taking off his hat and mopping his brow with the crown. His hair was grey but encrusted with the red dust. 'They tell me at Tennant Creek that you have passed, so I have to sit here and wait. All day I sit, roasting like a chicken, waiting for you.'

'Sorry, Mr Fachetti. I had a couple of punctures. I got here as soon as I could.'

The blocks of cattle cake were a faded red colour like dried blood. One was broken open. The red colour inside was much deeper. It was held up so Fachetti could pick out the clear plastic bag that was packed into the hollow centre. He examined the bag carefully, pressing it with his thumbs. Then he nodded and the three sacks were dragged towards the van. The cattle bumped and scraped restlessly against the sides of the trailers. They were missing the cooling draught caused by forward motion.

Tarrant stood with his hands in his pockets, whistling softly. The bags contained high-quality cocaine channelled in through Bangkok and Djakarta. It had taken him eighteen months to pluck up the courage, but for the last six months he had been stealing an occasional bag to supplement his income. An old mate in Sydney had a friend who had contacts willing to pay a healthy price for one of the fat plastic bags. They did not seem to miss it. There were too many links in the chain for it to be traced back to him. There was so much of the stuff they probably did not even realise. He had not tampered with this consignment, though, because he knew he was being met by the boss himself.

'You do a good job for us, Murray my son,' Fachetti said, wiping his fingers.

'I drive the truck.' Tarrant shrugged. 'My main problem is remembering which cakes to feed the cattle. If I pick the wrong sack I could send the herd a mile high. They would probably reach home before me.'

The sun was a shimmering orange eye watching them over the desert, sliced into quarters by strips of dark blue cloud. The shadow of the wind-wheel seemed to lengthen by the second, like a hand closing round the white van. There was not a breath of wind. A lizard scampered out of sight around the corrugated-iron casing of the derrick.

'How you like to go somewhere a little cooler than this?' Fachetti asked, squinting up at Tarrant's six-foot frame and flapping the hat in front of his face.

'You got a different job for me?'

'You know when I do personal visits I got special jobs. Otherwise I send letters. You interested?'

'Sure am,' he said, pretending eagerness when he knew there was, in effect, no question of him refusing. 'I could do with a little adventure in my life. The joys of trucking begin to pall after a couple of years in the saddle.'

'Your passport up to date?'

'Sure is. Got a new one for a trip to the Philippines last year.'

'Good. As I say, this is a special job. You've been selected because of your good looks, Murray my son.' Fachetti grinned as he put one hand on his waist and the other over his head to do a few shuffling dance steps, stirring up the dust around his feet. When he stopped he was breathing heavily. 'We want you to do a little lady killing.'

'Lady killing,' Tarrant frowned, suddenly alarmed. 'I'm not into violence, Mr Fachetti, you know that. I'm a message boy. You've got better soldiers than me for that kind of thing.'

Fachetti bit the back of his hand and laughed quietly. 'You misunderstand me, Murray. We don't want you to do any hurting. We want you to do some romancing, some sweet talking.'

'Ah,' Tarrant said with relief. 'That kind of lady killing. You want me to seduce a sheila.'

'Yeah, that kind of thing. That's close enough. You game?'

'Who is she? What's she like?'

'You'll find out soon enough if you take it on. I can tell you she's not bad looking, though. All the right equipment.' Fachetti modelled a female shape in the air with his hands and then kissed his fingers. 'You game?'

'What exactly do I have to do with her?'

'If you enjoy yourself you'll be doing fine.'

'I'm your man, then.' He hesitated, grinning ingratiatingly. 'It's an offer I can't refuse.'

Fachetti smiled hugely, his mouth opening so wide there seemed to be nothing to connect his chin to the rest of his face. He stepped forward and reached up to put an arm round Tarrant's shoulders. 'I knew you would say that, Murray my son. I picked you myself when I heard about the job. You've been doing some good work for us.'

'It's been two years, Mr Fachetti. I thought you'd forgotten about me in my obscurity here.'

'I never forget, just like the elephant. Come the hour, come the man, eh, Murray? You always were a ladies' man, they tell me. You're perfect for this job. And there will be a fat cheque waiting for you when you get back.'

'Get back? Where am I going?'

'The other side of the world, Murray my son. Europe. It's winter. It's snowing there. You'd better take an overcoat. And we want you on your way as soon as possible.'

'I've never been to Europe. How long for? Where in Europe?'

'A couple of months, maybe more. All expenses paid. Your air ticket will be delivered to you soon, and you will find out where then. We will book you into a hotel over there.'

'What about my job?'

'Going to Europe is your job.' He spat in the palm of his hand and held it out. 'Deal?' he asked.

Tarrant took a hand out of his pocket and slapped the upturned palm. 'Deal,' he replied, excited and curious at the prospect, and only a little apprehensive.

Fachetti climbed into the van and nodded to the driver, who started up the engine. He leaned out the window. 'Good luck, Murray my son. There will be two of you on this job.'

'Who's to be my mate?'

'You will meet him in Europe. He will come to your hotel. He will be the boss. You'll do what he says. He is a good man.'

'What's his name?'

'It's a foreign-sounding name. I can't get my tongue round it. Russian, I think it was originally.' Fachetti scratched his nose, enjoying a private joke. 'We call him the Demon.'

'Sounds a fun bloke.'

'You just save your strength for the lady in question, Murray my son. Let the Demon do all the worrying. He's

15

been told to take very good care of you.' The van reversed and swung round to the east. 'Enjoy yourself,' Fachetti shouted, raising a boney fist in a farewell wave. 'Enjoy.'

Tarrant watched the car drive away down the narrow track scratched almost invisibly across the surface of the desert, hidden among its own smokescreen of dust. On the horizon a tall whirlwind, fattening itself on sucked-up sand, appeared to be chasing after it.

A two-year gap, a two-minute conversation, and life takes a sudden turn for the better, Tarrant thought gleefully. The kamikaze kangaroo had been a good omen after all. His mind buzzed with excitement. There were so many questions about the job he should have asked Fachetti, but they were only occurring to him now. Europe was a big place, bigger than Australia. The land of his forefathers. He would have to buy an atlas. Maybe he would get the chance to do some sight-seeing. He wondered what the woman looked like and what she had done to deserve attention of this sort. Blackmail it would be, probably. He would have to get her to pose for some pretty pictures. If so, he hoped she was as nice as Fachetti said.

He walked back to the truck. A trip to Europe would do him a lot of good, blow away the cobwebs. He needed a change, and it was time to dump Donna anyway. This would be a good excuse. Whatever happened, it was better than truck driving. He was still physically tired but the different possibilities queuing up to present themselves to his imagination meant there was no chance of sleep for the time being. He was still a day and a half from home. A long way to go. He decided he would force himself to rest at Alice Springs.

He climbed up into the cab and started up the engine. He chose a tape at random and was pleased to see that it was Mendelssohn's Third Symphony, one of his new-found favourites. It would break the back of the next two hundred miles. He slotted it into the deck and adjusted the head-phones. The tyres spun in the loose sand, and took hold as he engaged the lowest of the ten gears. The truck rolled back onto the road. The music swelled in his ears. *Andante con moto.*

16

CHAPTER TWO

The British Government has been severely embarrassed by the outstanding success of the Scottish Nationalists in their latest propaganda drive in the US and Canada.

Prime Minister Black is known to be angry with the deference and respect shown to Nationalist leader Andrew Wallace in Washington, despite fears in the White House about the future of American bases in any independent Scotland.

Wallace's popularity is riding at an all-time high and he has a further opportunity to enhance his status as an international statesman when he opens the debate on national self-determination at the United Nations in New York next month.

International Herald Tribune

The converted cottage was situated about fifty yards back from the road on a small hump of ground on one side of Glen Halkston in Argyll. High above its flaking whitewashed walls and black slate roof a vertical face of exposed rock rose from the heather and coarse grass, like the forehead of a giant about to emerge from underground. The steeply sloping land in between was littered with random streams of frost-gouged scree boulders and scored across by straight sheep tracks among the faint traces of ancient cultivation. A small burn of tumbling white water had cut a deep scar round one side of the rockface and down past the croft before turning sharply to flow at a more sedate pace along the edge of the road, following the line of wooden poles supporting a thick power line in long drooping curves. A clear, shallow river occupied the floor of the U-shaped glen. The wide strip of water

17

meandered carelessly from side to side, and spread itself even wider in one place so that it could almost have been called a loch. Little clumps of bare bushes crouched in the sheltered curves of its banks. Forest had encroached on to the hillsides where the two-mile long glen dipped and narrowed at its eastern end, lining both sides with geometric patches of trees. There was another house at that end, a larger one, on the opposite side of the river. It was situated well away from the trees, tucked into a sheltered fold with the hills towering over it.

A gale-force wind was whipping along the length of the glen.

Inside the cottage, Mrs Kirsty MacPherson was sitting by the small-paned window with her feet resting on a cushion on another chair, idly flicking at the glossy leaves of a tall rubber plant with a duster in one hand and stroking the head of her big crossbred Alsatian, Breck, with the other. She was a large, elderly widow greatly troubled by fluid in her limbs. She knew just the right pace to do the housework to avoid over-taxing her legs and starting off the agonising pains that kept her awake at nights. It required frequent rest periods with her feet up to let them recover. Hers was a circulatory problem, the doctors said. But with plenty of rests she managed to get through what work was required of her, not that it was a great deal because the place was kept clean and tidy without her anyway.

She first noticed the big red car as it came over the two-mile distant horizon and dipped down into the glen. She watched its progress through the fancy wrought-iron window bars, losing sight of it for long stretches as it approached on the undulating road. She was not surprised when it drew to a halt at the foot of the driveway, because visitors occasionally turned up unannounced. But she was surprised when the driver got out and went round to open the bonnet. He studied the engine for a few moments, then straightened up and turned to the croft. He began to walk towards her, head down, arms tight in against his body, leaning sideways to balance himself against the tremendous force of the wind. She looked up at the sky and the unbroken covering of dirty white clouds like the underside of an overstuffed pillow. 'Snow soon,' she said quietly to herself, sniffing as if she could smell it.

She got painfully to her feet and hurriedly tidied her hair

in front of the mirror. She ordered Breck to sit as she took off her flowery housecoat and crammed it into her bag out of sight, before smoothing down the blue woollen dress she wore underneath. The outside door opened directly into the corner of the living-room. There was an interior glass door back to back with it. She pulled open the first one and waited for the man to knock before pushing the second one outwards. The wind immediately caught it and the hinges creaked with the strain. The constant howl of the wind whistling through the heather all around them filled her ears. The stranger had his face virtually hidden in the hood of his padded anorak. He was almost blown off his feet as he started to speak.

'Would you have any water?' he asked politely. 'My radiator is dry.'

Mrs MacPherson smiled when she heard the merest hint of a foreign accent in the voice. She liked tourists, especially foreign ones. When she had been younger, she and her husband had run a guesthouse, and for nine months of the year the dining-table had been a rich babble of competing languages every night. She liked tourists to come to her country to see the wonderful scenery. She liked to imagine how impressed they must be by it all. It was unusual to see them in December, though.

'Of course, of course,' she said, moving out of the doorway. 'But don't be standing out there in the cold. Come away in, man.'

He had to help her push the door shut against the insistent force of the wind. Breck growled threateningly. The black and brown hairs of his coat bristled. She tapped him on the muzzle to shut him up as she shuffled over to the sink at the back window on her treetrunk legs to search in the cupboards for a suitable container, finally deciding that a green plastic watering-can was the best thing for the job. She filled it from the rainwater tank. When she turned round the man was standing in the middle of the room. He had lowered the hood to show a head of jet-black hair and swarthy features. He was watching the dog warily. Very foreign, she thought. Eastern European, she guessed. Learned his English from Americans.

'Will this do?' Mrs MacPherson asked.

'It will be excellent. It seems to be the radiator overheating. I stopped here because it seems to be the only house for miles and I don't want to get stranded out here, if I can help it. The forecast is for snow, I believe. I hope you don't mind?'

'Not at all. Not at all. It's not often we see strangers around here, especially at this time of year. You're sightseeing, are you?'

'That's right. I was in Scotland on business so I though I would take the opportunity to drive around a bit to see the scenery.'

'Yes. They're a great worry.' She nodded, but his face was a blank — he did not understand. 'Cars, I mean. They're a great worry. My wee one is parked outside. It is always in and out of the garage.'

'I will let the hire company worry about it once I get back.'

'Where are you from?'

'Italy. A visitor to your lovely country.'

'Your English is excellent but I can always tell. I knew you were a foreigner the moment you spoke.'

He nodded to concede the point. 'Thank you for the water,' he said. 'I'll just go and fill her up.'

'It's freezing cold out there,' Mrs MacPherson said. 'Would you not like a cup of tea to warm you up a bit before you go on?'

The man stopped at the door. 'If it is no trouble?' he said.

'No trouble at all,' she assured him.

'Then I would be delighted. I will be back in a few minutes.'

The howl of the wind rose and fell as the door opened and closed. She watched him go down the hill to his car. Breck was quietly growling after him, so she dragged him across to shut him in one of the bedrooms before busying herself putting the kettle on to boil and laying out a plate of biscuits. The man re-entered the house and came straight across to return the watering-can. They talked about the weather as he stood warming his hands on the oldfashioned kitchen range with the oven and hotplates to one side of the fireplace that was stoked with sweet-smelling peat and crackling logs. She felt a faint twinge of unease, making her begin to wish she had not invited him in. There was something about him, something unsettling, but she was not exactly sure what it was. Perhaps it was the way he talked without opening his mouth properly. She took the tray and balanced it on a small table in the centre of the room and sat down beside it.

'You won't mind if I sit down,' she said. 'It's my legs. They give me terrible bother if I stand for too long.'

'Please, do sit down,' he replied.

'I thought you were my son Tommy at first,' she said quickly. 'His car is the same colour as yours and I am expecting him any moment.'

Tommy lived in Canada but Mrs MacPherson didn't want her guest to think she was completely alone. She was suddenly regretting shutting Breck up. His presence in the corner of the room would have been reassuring. She didn't want this man to get any funny ideas. His face registered no change of expression when she told him about her son. Perhaps she was just being paranoid.

The stranger took tea straight from the pot with no milk or sugar, and a single plain biscuit. He walked round the room, examining everything carefully. Like a browser in a bookshop, she thought. It was not something she would have done in somebody else's house but she had always been prepared to make allowances for foreign habits. His footsteps clicked sharply on the varnished wooden floor. He stopped by the mahogany bookcase and fingered the key in the lock.

'You have a very nice place here,' he said, but his face remained expressionless.

'Mercy me,' Mrs MacPherson laughed. 'This house disnae belong tae me. I'm just the cleaning lady who comes in twice a week tae keep the dust back a bit.'

'I see.'

'No, no. To tell ye the truth, they dinnae really need me but they keep me on to give an old woman a job. This place belongs tae the Wallaces.' She held her head up proudly at the mention of the name. 'Perhaps you'll have heard of Mr Wallace? He's a well-known politician in Scotland. A Nationalist, of course. Always on the telly. Always has his picture in the papers. That's them there in that picture on the shelf on the wall. They're abroad at the moment.'

The visitor sipped his tea and stepped onto a rug to bend

21

forward and look at the picture. His face betrayed not the slightest sign of recognition. Ah well, Mrs MacPherson thought charitably, she herself wouldn't have known any foreign politicians either.

'This place was a ruin when they bought it,' she explained. 'It didnae even have a roof. They have done a lot of work to turn it into this. There are four bedrooms and this room of course, and the toilet, which is a bit primitive, but they are having a new one put in. It's at the back there.' She indicated a door in the far corner. 'The builders had difficulty installing the new septic tank — kept hitting rock, so they got caught out with the bad weather this winter. The new toilet just has plywood walls covered in thick polythene at the moment, but it will be nice when it's finished. They restored the kitchen range and its fire heats the boiler that heats the whole house. Marvellous things, those ranges. I used to have one myself but not now. It's all double-glazed and there's a wee diesel generator in the lean-to at the side when they want it, beside where they store the peats and the logs, but they've got mains electricity as well, though it often gets cut off out here, especially at this time of year when the snow brings the lines down. They don't need much electricity really, just enough to run the heating pump and the lights and the record player. Very fond of her music is Mrs Wallace.'

'I see they also have the phone.'

'Yes. Mr Wallace being who he is, the phone company ran a line all the way out here on the electricity poles. He couldnae survive out here without his phone, couldn't Mr Wallace. Him being a politician like he is. Mind you, when the electricity goes down so does the phone line, but he always has one of those radio phones in his car.'

'And you live nearby?'

'Nobody lives nearby, dearie. You winnae find another house for five miles in any direction you care to try, apart from the Fowler place along the glen. I look after that as well, but they live in London and only use it maybe a couple of weeks in the summer, otherwise it's always lying empty, though they do try to let it out.'

'Do they now?'

'Oh yes. There was a Frenchman a few months ago. He

22

claimed to be an artist, but I never saw him painting any pictures. But most of the time it just lies empty. It's a pity, because it is a nice house.'

'Who would one contact about taking the place for a time?'

'Beveridge and Stewart. They're a big firm of Glasgow solicitors. Are you interested then, Mr ...?'

'I'm definitely interested.' He took a small notebook from an inside pocket and wrote on the first page. 'I just don't know if I could afford the time away from my work.'

'Aye, of course. It's Mrs Wallace who likes her solitude. She's a physicist, works on lasers or something equally scientific at Heriot-Watt University. She tells me it helps her tae think mair clearly to be out here. They have a big flat in Edinburgh as well, and spend most of their time there.' Mrs MacPherson thought it was rather impolite for him to push open one of the bedroom doors and peer inside but she did not mention it. Breck started barking in the other room. 'No,' she went on. 'I live in Halkston village myself. That's over the hills to the south a bit, about fifteen minutes' drive.'

'This room must be a cosy place in the winter.'

'It is that. You're lucky. I never usually light the fire when I am here, but it was so cold I just had to today.'

He walked back over to the bookcase again. 'Wallace, you say. A politician. Perhaps the name does sound familiar somehow.'

Mrs MacPherson nodded wisely. 'You'll have read about him. I guarantee it. He's never out o' the papers. Foreign papers as well.'

'All Scots are Nationalists these days, from what I hear.'

'Aye, that's right.' She had voted Conservative all her life but had finally decided to vote for the Nationalists at the next election.

'Well, thank you for the tea,' he said abruptly. 'I must go now.'

'Going back home for Christmas, are you?'

'Yes. I had better get back to my hotel before the snow comes.'

'I hope you have a happy Christmas, then,' she said.

'You also. It was nice meeting you.'

He zipped up his anorak and gave a little bow. His mouth

23

twitched a little but he did not return her smile as she showed him to the door.In fact he had not smiled once since coming into the house. Maybe that was what was bothering her about him, she thought.

She resumed her seat by the window and watched him go down the hill to his car for the second time, crouching into the wind then turning and walking backwards so that he was looking back at the house. She waved to him from the window but he did not seem to notice her. Breck started barking from the bedroom again. Queer chap, she thought, as he drove away, heading east instead of west. She shook her head, thinking that she should have explained to him. Then she looked up at the sky. Definitely snow soon, she said to herself.

CHAPTER THREE

Scottish Nationalist Party leader Andrew Wallace flies
home tomorrow at the end of a gruelling North American tour, well satisfied with what he has achieved.

The charismatic figure has been a sell-out attraction
wherever he has spoken, and has convinced many more
thousands of people that his dream to restore independence to one of Europe's oldest nations is within his
grasp.

Mr Wallace (47) spent the weekend holding private
talks with White House officials. Last night he emerged
in public again as the guest of honour at a special
performance of *Macbeth*, at the Folger Shakespeare
Library in Washington.

Washington Post

Andrew Wallace was dozing peacefully, not quite asleep, not
fully awake. His eyes were half open, reducing the room
around him to a luminous blur. He was in bed, propped up by
a nest of pillows with the sheets bundled at his waist. The
warm air from the heating system spilled luxuriously over his
bare shoulders and chest. The first editions of the day's newspapers were spread out around him. His meeting with the
Majority Leader of the Senate was mentioned in most of
them. The only complaint he had about the stories was that
they had all, without exception, got his age wrong. Since
midnight he had been exactly forty-eight years old.

He was exhausted but was trying to stay awake to take the
expected phone-call from his wife back home in Scotland.
The tour had dragged a bit since she had left him to return to
work almost two weeks before. It had not been nearly as
enjoyable as the time in Australia earlier in the year when she
had been constantly by his side, but it had been just as worth-

while. It had been non-stop travel, two or three speeches a day, endless media interviews, nightly formal receptions and dinners, gallons of whisky and acres of tartan. The purpose had been threefold; to build Scotland's image abroad; to make useful political contacts; and to raise money for Party funds. Overall, it had been another huge success. It was amazing the number of people who were desperate to prove the authenticity of their Scottish origins by contributing to the cause. Scots ancestry was chic. And every scrap of publicity, every dollar and every cent helped to keep up the pressure on the London Government back home. Press coverage had been extensive and obligingly uncritical, despite American fears on defence implications. Even the overtly hostile London papers had felt obliged to run some pictures and stories. He could not be ignored, now or in the future.

Wallace had enjoyed his night out at the theatre too well. He had eaten too much and drunk too much in premature celebration of his return home the following afternoon. Senator Macrae's lovely daughter had sat beside him during the play and had deliberately kept bumping her knee against his. She was young — younger than his wife — and pretty and fairly obviously available. If he hadn't been a respectably married man with a vested interest in avoiding any hint of scandal he might have responded. Instead, he pretended not to notice the signals she was sending and confined himself to a chaste kiss on the cheek and a knowing smile into her disappointed eyes when they ran him back to the Embassy Row in their limousine.

Then there had been the barman, when his publicity manager Graham Turnbull had uncharacteristically pleaded fragility and gone to bed. Wallace stayed for one last drink on his own. The barman was a big, black man called Luther Mackay, who told a wonderful story about one branch of his ancestry being burned out of their croft in Strathglass during the Highland Clearances and emigrating in the 1830s, and the other branch being captured in the Gambia as slaves for shipment across the Atlantic about the same time. Somewhere along the line these two lines had come together to produce him and his brother, the only red-haired Negroes in the world.

'There can't be many like us about, eh?' Luther said, leaning on his elbows and holding his chin in his hands as if the big, grinning mouth was too heavy for his face. 'Scotch blood and Gambian blood make some unique cocktail, don't they, now?'

'Ospreys,' Wallace said.

'Ospreys?'

'Yes. Ospreys. They are a kind of fish-eating eagle, spend the summer in the Gambia and the winter in Scotland.'

'Is that a fact now, Mr Wallace? No kidding?'

'No kidding. Beautiful birds of prey they are.'

Luther thought about it for a while. 'Well,' he said finally, 'I think I'll call myself Osprey Mackay from now on, and eat nothing but salmon.' He capered behind the bar flapping his arms like wings.

Wallace sat in bed and tried to recall the whole tour, day by day, to keep his mind active. Instead, his thoughts kept leaping forward to the United Nations speech, and to the next election that would make or break him. It was so easy in the heady atmosphere of a Scottish-American banquet in a place like Toronto, with five hundred fervent exiles willing him on, to imagine that it was going to happen, that Scotland was going to regain her independence after almost three hundred years. His confidence was unshakable on occasions like that. He hated being alone because it was only when he was alone at night that the doubts began to creep into his mind. He worried that it was all going *too* well, that it was all too painless and too simple. But those were private doubts that he never shared, that he never allowed to see the light of day. In the morning he knew that his confidence would return.

Wallace thought he heard a noise in the adjoining room. He opened one eye and looked across at the connecting door. There had been nobody in the room earlier that day. Perhaps it was somebody booking in late. The door was locked. It didn't really matter.

He pushed the newspapers onto the floor, wriggled down under the sheets and turned onto his side with his face close to the phone. He reached up to the control panel built into the headboard and switched off the lights. He could speak to Helen in the dark. It would not be long now, he hoped.

The noise came again. There *was* somebody next-door. The sound of a key turning in a lock was unmistakable. Wallace rolled over and opened his eyes, rubbing the tiredness out of them. The hotel room was big and spacious. The door was at least ten yards away, level with the foot of the bed, and it was opening. He could see someone backing into the darkened room, the long legs of a woman pushing the door inwards with her backside, face obscured by tumbling hair. She was wearing one of the hotel bathrobes and carrying something held out in front of her. Oh my God, Wallace thought. The Senator's daughter.

He sat up, desperately trying to decide what to do. She must have put the wrong interpretation on his farewell smile. It hadn't been disappointment in her eyes. It had been lust. Now he was trapped. He could not move out of the bed because he had nothing on. The sight of him naked might not shock her but it certainly wouldn't help to calm her down.

He fumbled blindly for the light-switch as the figure turned and seemed to be cut in half by a narrow band of flickering flames. The door swung slowly shut behind her. He found the switch and blinked as the room abruptly flooded with light.

'Helen,' he said in astonishment. 'It's you.'

'Expecting somebody else, were you?'

'No, no.' He looked round at the phone, staring stupidly. 'But you are supposed to be in Scotland. I was waiting for you to call.'

'Surprise.' She held up the birthday cake and approached the bed. 'I couldn't let you have your birthday without me. What kind of wife would do that?'

'So you flew all the way across.' Wallace felt suddenly alert as if he had put his head under a cold shower. He relaxed and a smile broke across his face like ice cracking. 'Did Turnbull know about this?' he demanded.

'Graham arranged everything. The plane was late and he even came to fetch me at the airport.'

'So that was why he abandoned me in the bar. I don't believe it. This is great.'

'He told me all about precocious young Priscilla, the Senator's daughter, as well.'

28

'Sorry about that, Helen. But you know I can't resist younger women.'

'I'm young enough for you,' she said. 'A twenty-year age-gap is quite sufficient. Any more and you wouldn't be able to cope.'

'It's a twenty-one-year gap as of today.'

Helen began to sing: 'Happy birthday to you. Happy birthday to you. Happy birthday, dear Andrew. Happy birthday to you.' She bent down and put the cake on the bedside table, then leaned over and kissed him on the forehead. 'Happy birthday.'

'Why twelve candles?' he asked.

'The number of days we have been apart.'

'Very appropriate. You're not really here, are you? This is all a dream.'

He took a deep breath and blew out all the candles at once. She stepped back as he made a grab for her waist, and her loosely-curled auburn hair swung as if it had been caught in a gust of wind.

'Uh-uh,' she said teasingly. 'First things first. I've got a little birthday present for you. I had it specially made at huge expense.'

She reached in the pocket of the robe to bring out a long chain and dangle it from two fingers to show a small object attached at the end, spinning rapidly so that it was a golden blur. Wallace reached out and steadied it with the palm of his hand. He saw that it was a lion standing erect on its hind legs, clawing at the air in front of it. Its mane was cast in relief. Its eye was a tiny diamond, glinting in the light.

'A lion rampant,' he said softly. 'It's so beautiful.'

'You like it? I designed it myself.' She opened out the chain and put it over his head. The golden lion lay on the fair hair covering his chest. 'I want you to promise me you will never take it off until we have the independence. And I will do the same.'

'You have one, too?'

'Of course. It's identical. They are two of a kind, just like us. Do you promise?'

'I promise.'

'Want to see mine?'

Wallace looked up and watched as Helen untied the belt of her robe and let it slip from her shoulders all the way to the floor. She was wearing nothing at all apart from the lion necklace hanging between her breasts.

'And now,' she said, snatching away the sheets in a single movement, 'it looks like you're expecting your other present.'

He lay back as she climbed onto the bed and knelt above him, leaning on her hands. Her necklace hung down and the two lions tangled together. Her breasts hung down and brushed his chest. She lowered her head and kissed him on the lips.

'Happy birthday, darling,' she said in a hoarse whisper. 'Happy birthday to my very own flesh-and-blood rampant lion.'

The trees on the shore beside the wooden jetty were bare apart from a few shrivelled leaves stuck in the tangled branches like old flies caught in the strands of an abandoned spider's web. The blustery wind slapped them back and forth so that they creaked like old chairs. The grey clouds threatened rain. Tom Seneca untied the rope and stepped down into the stern of the rowing boat. He balanced himself as it rocked from side to side, and sat down with a leg on either side of the fishing gear. Barrett Coleman waited with the oars angled out over the water as the boat drifted clear of the jetty.

'Where to?' he asked.

Seneca unbuttoned the fur-lined flaps of his cap and tied the cord under his chin. He looked round the small kidney-shaped lake and clicked his tongue against the roof of his mouth.

'Over there,' he said, pointing.

'Is that where the fish are biting?'

'Never mind the fish. That's where we'll get the best shelter.'

Coleman dug the blades of the oars into the water, and grunted with the effort of fighting the inertia of the heavy boat. The rowlocks grated loudly as they turned, scraping themselves clean of accumulated rust. Coleman was a large man, enveloped in a green, poncho-style waterproof cape.

The red and white bob-hat he was wearing made his face look triangular, with his chin as the base and the bobble as the peak. Silver-grey hair poked out from underneath the hat along the line of his forehead. His eyes were small and round behind glasses misted by the humidity. He had a flat nose and hardly any neck. He was sixty years old and had been Director of the CIA for just under two years. He was glad of the excuse to enjoy a pre-Christmas outing fishing in the Catskills. They could talk freely here. There was no chance of being interrupted or overheard. The only bugs around were wriggling in the bait box.

Tom Seneca was fifteen years younger than Coleman. He was just as tall but much more slightly built, with a head that seemed too large for his body and a mouth that seemed too big for his face. He, too, was wearing one of the capes, but the head-hole was so large that his shoulders almost came through it. Like Coleman he was an ex-Navy man, turned academic, turned Government servant. They had been coming across each other in various guises and roles for twenty years, and had struck up a mutually beneficial relationship. It was not that they liked each other all that much, not that they even trusted each other, but they did understand each other. Seneca had been appointed National Security Adviser at the White House the same week Coleman had been promoted from Deputy Director at Langley. He had arranged the fishing trip so that the two of them could sound each other out on the latest issues. Their wives were back at the cabin preparing a big evening meal.

Coleman leaned back to pull on the oars, and the boat cut through the wind and the water. The little waves whipped up by the wind tinkled against the hull, and some spray blew in over the sides, spattering on their capes and running off to pool on the boards at their feet. Seneca picked up one of the rods and began to check the reel for freedom of movement.

'How come the old man gets to do the hard work?' Coleman asked.

'That's okay, Barry, I'll be picking the fish out of the water.'

'Watch your back, then. There must be some whoppers down there from the stories you tell about your fishing trips.'

'The biggest ones always get away. They often sacrifice their little brothers, though.'

Coleman stopped rowing and shipped the oars. The boat began to drift slowly with the wind, about two hundred yards out from the rocky shore. He scrambled over to the seat at the bows. Seneca handed him a rod with the hook already baited.

'Take starboard,' he said. 'I'll take port.'

They sat in silence for a while, fishing out of either side of the boat, hunched against the cold, each concentrating on the spot where their lines disappeared under the choppy surface. The swirling wind reddened their cheeks and the points of their noses. The rain began to fall steadily. The pools of water in the bottom of the boat gradually deepened. Coleman took off his glasses and balanced his rod between his legs while he searched for a pocket under his cape to hold them.

'What do you make of this Wallace character then?' he asked without looking up.

'He's some guy,' Seneca replied. 'I met him at the White House earlier this week. Now I believe all I've read about him.'

'What's his selling pitch?'

'Can't really say, but he has managed to sell himself to a whole bunch of people. I guess there is a bit of the Messiah about him.'

'Yeah. Kennedy in a kilt, that's what I'm told.'

'We had trouble persuading the President to keep out of it. We didn't want to give the meeting more weight than we could help. London was a bit on edge about it.'

Coleman shifted his position and the boat rocked gently. 'He gets along fine without our help. Wallace carries his own political weight. *Time* magazine did that big cover story on him the other week. Man of the fucking year, for Chrissake.'

'He's the man of the moment.'

'Will he really kick us out of Scotland if he takes over?'

'That's not his Party's policy but he was keen to explain that any independent Scots Parliament would take the final decision. He was hinting that maybe the clamour to close the bases would not be so great if the Scots could negotiate their own terms to let us stay. Myself, I reckon his influence might be enough to win the day.'

'Can we take the chance anyway?' Coleman asked. 'At least we know where we are with old boy Edwards and his cronies running the show from London. The Holy Loch is the only deep-water anchorage suitable for our subs in that part of Europe. Without it, the whole strategic balance changes for the worse from our point of view, especially since we negotiated away our Cruise missiles in Europe.'

'I know all the defence arguments,' Seneca said wearily. 'The brass hats are on to me endlessly. If Scotland did not exist, it would be necessary to invent it. How many times have I heard that? The country is at one end of the Greenland-Iceland-UK gap. Take it away, and the red subs can pour through there in their hundreds without us knowing a thing about it.'

'And the Scots might just pull the plug. The question is, what can we do about it?'

'I'm not listening, Barry. I got the impression that Wallace wants us to stay, but if he does get independence, and his people tell him different, then that's the way it is going to have to be.'

'There's integrity for you. I always hated democrats.'

'Don't forget there are those among us who want to leave the Europeans to run their own show anyway. Let them live in the real world.'

'Not me,' Coleman said, shaking his head. 'If we ever have to take on the Russkies, let's make it on those guys' front doorstep, not ours.'

Seneca propped his rod against the side of the boat and reached into the middle to open the lunch bag. He took out a flask of thick vegetable soup and poured some into two cups. Coleman leaned forward, pulling off a mitt to accept the soup.

'You know I started up a one-man station in Edinburgh when the Scots started making serious noises,' Coleman said. 'I was worried it might end up like this. Had to pass over everyone with a name beginning Mac or anything like that, and finally sent over a promising young buck called Sheahan. Irish descent he is, like my grandmother. The first few sitreps he sent back were so favourable to Wallace, I thought he must be exaggerating. You know what I mean: carried away

33

by his first overseas posting, under the spell of their romantic history — Mary Queen of Scots and all that.'

'That is the trouble with these ancient countries, they have so much bloody history you never know what will be turned up next. A couple of years ago we Americans all thought Scotland was just another part of England. You know, the cold bit at the top. Now we know different.'

'We sure do, Tom. It's easier in a country like ours. You can just about get all our history into one book. Across there they have more history than they know what to do with.'

Seneca poured more soup into his cup, shaking the flask to coax out the lumps. 'History is bunk, according to a famous American.'

'Maybe so, but it's working for Wallace. I was convinced that my boy Sheahan was way over the top, but everything he has been saying is coming true now. He said support for the Nationalists would snowball, and it has. He said Wallace was hot stuff and would cut a dash on the international scene if he was given the chance, and he has. It rather confirms my assessment of Sheahan as well, by the way. So when he says Scotland will achieve independence, I have to sit up and take notice. The British Government has to call an election sometime soon, and Sheahan says that will be the watershed. If the Nats take more than half the seats they contest, it will be cut and dried. He says they will walk it.'

'Another little bit of history to add to their never-ending saga.'

'Coleman flung the dregs of his soup over the side and reeled in his line to check that the bait was still on the hook. 'Jesus, Tom, Scotland ain't no size at all. We've got at least a dozen states with a bigger population than them, and the folk there don't want to go it alone as far as I know. As I said before, what can we do about it? What does the President think?'

'What do you want me to tell you, Barry? The President believes in democracy. We're not dealing with some hairy-assed guerilla leader here. In this case we can't supply arms to the opposition and hope a stray bullet solves our problem. If Wallace gets in, he will be voted in, and become a fully paid up member of the family of nations.'

34

'So was Hitler.'

'What?'

'Democratically elected. Well, according to his own rules. The world would have been a better place if someone had put him out of his misery before he started his little game.'

Seneca sucked at his top lip and tasted the bitter rain. 'Don't get the wrong idea, Barry. The President says he wants us to stand back and watch — take it as it comes. It stops at politics.'

'What the President says and what the President wants are not necessarily the same thing. You're an old enough hand at this game to know that, Tom. Besides, where does politics stop?'

'No coded signals, Barry. No hidden instructions. This President doesn't sleep during his briefings and I'm with him all the way. He knows what is going on around him. Nobody farts without his say-so.'

'Excuse me while I send a memo.' Coleman lifted one leg and screwed up his face before noisily breaking wind.

'Besides, making a martyr of Wallace would only aid his cause,' Seneca continued. 'There is a big organisation behind him that would carry on to independence on the sympathy vote. Then we would have a relatively unknown leader in charge. He might throw us out the next day. Wallace is guaranteeing us at least ten years.'

'Yeah, I know. That's the way my boy Sheahan reads it as well. He says the next in line is a guy called Shand. Tubby guy, more of a rabble-rouser, more to the Left in British terms. Doesn't have Wallace's personality or presence. He couldn't make it on his own, but he could if someone blazes the trail ahead of him and sets it all up for him to take over.'

'That's not going to happen.'

'Isn't it? Must be a possibility.'

'Wallace is too tough-minded to be used like that. He's nobody's fool.'

'It's still a possibility. I admit that Sheahan rejects it as well, but he could be getting a little too close to the subject. I've submitted a report to the President today. I'm keeping an eye on things over there, too.'

'An eye on things? Isn't that your code for drawing up contingency plans?'

35

'I am duty-bound to have contingencies available to meet every emergency. Nothing wrong with that. But the President will have to make a decision.'

'Decide what?'

'If we are to keep the Holy Loch and all the other bases in Scotland.'

'I told you it's not as clear-cut as that, Barry.'

Coleman shrugged and scattered the raindrops from his cape. 'Better the devil you know, Tom. That's my motto. Let's keep the world safe if we can. If the Scots get their way, then what is to stop the Basques in Spain, the Tamils in Sri Lanka, the Sikhs in India, the Kurds in Turkey, the Abos in Australia and every bloody tribe in Africa. The list is never-ending, for Chrissake.'

'I'm not listening, Barry.'

'I'm not saying anything, Tom. At least, nothing I haven't said before a thousand times. Let's keep the world a safe place, I said. How can anyone argue with a sentiment like that?' Coleman sucked up the saliva lying in his mouth and spat out over the water. 'We're certainly keeping it a safe place for the fish in this bloody lake.'

Seneca wiped the rain from his eyes and began to bale out the water in the bottom of the boat, using an empty baked beans can which had half its label still attached. He noticed that they had drifted more into the centre of the lake, blown by the wind. The trees on the banks were waving furiously, looking like a crowd of people desperately trying to attract their attention. Coleman's body suddenly tensed as his rod bent in a smooth curve and the tip nearly touched the surface.

'I've got a bite,' he shouted excitedly. 'It feels like a real beauty.'

CHAPTER FOUR

The political year in Britain has again been dominated by a figure who rarely bothers to walk the corridors of power in London.

Nationalist leader Andrew Wallace has not spoken at Westminster since the Scottish Assembly opened on Calton Hill in Edinburgh just over three years ago. And yet it is his voice which the whole of the UK wants to hear.

Opponents in Scotland who said he was mad to accept reduced representation in the London Parliament — 72 MPs down to 50 — in return for the Assembly have been proved utterly wrong. Mr Wallace's mesmeric hold over his own countrymen grows ever stronger, while the Tory Government's grip on the nation — or the two nations — becomes progressively weaker.

Guardian

Sir Archibald Ballantyne was more and more convinced he would live to enjoy some of the twenty-first century after all. At the age of fifty-eight, he had now come through two successful heart operations and was feeling robust and healthy for the first time in many years. He had adopted a policy of moderation in all things, and these days spent most of his time reading or walking the dogs on his small estate outside Anstruther in Fife. He had taken early retirement from the law firm because of his illness, and relinquished all his directorships except for a couple of sinecures. He had reduced his weight from a corpulent sixteen stone to just over ten, but his former lifestyle had left its mark. His face was heavily lined and pitted, like a withered peach, and the skin all over his body seemed to be one size too big for him. He lived comfortably off his investments, and had never felt better.

The measure of Drambuie set in front of him by the waiter was his second one of the evening. Together with the single glass of wine he had drunk during the meal, that was his quota. They had moved through to the lounge of the New Club from the restaurant and now occupied a table by the window. Ballantyne stifled a yawn and looked across at the floodlit shape of Edinburgh Castle. Ice sparkled on the vertical rockface below the walls. The castle's outline stood out clearly against the grey snow-laden clouds that had their undersides bathed in reflected moonlight. The forecast was for more snow. A new fall seemed imminent. He would like to be on his way home to Fife soon, before the road conditions began to get worse. He decided he would make a move as soon as politeness allowed. He picked up his glass and smiled over at his companion.

'Cheers, Suds,' he said, sipping at the sweet, sticky liqueur.

The small man opposite smiled back, showing unnaturally white teeth, and returned the gesture by drinking from his glass of soda-water. There was not a wrinkle on a face that was the colour of polished oak. His close-cropped hair was like a covering of moss on his head. His name was Saoud Abdulla Sembawa, but they had called him Suds for short at Gordonstoun. He and Ballantyne had been close friends at school, with Ballantyne adopting the role of father-confessor for the frightened foreign kid. They had gone on to different colleges at Oxford and kept in touch after that, always meeting up for at least a weekend every two years at the regular class reunion. Sembawa had become an uninhibited, outgoing type at school, happy-go-lucky, everybody's friend. But later his personality changed as he grew older. He became more introverted, more inflexible in his attitudes, more suspicious of the motives of people around him. Ballantyne had never fully understood what Sembawa's exact social standing was back in his home country. He was not a full-blown sheikh or anything like that, but he did inherit enormous wealth from his family about ten years after leaving university. The change set in around then, when he and Ballantyne were still in regular contact. It was a common trait in people who did not have to work for their money. He just was not the same old Suds.

Sembawa made himself into one of the biggest landowners in the western Highlands, buying most of his estates during the late Seventies and the Eighties, and knitting them together into one huge tract run as a commercial sporting estate that he visited perhaps two or three times a year for short periods. He was acutely sensitive to charges of being an absentee landlord — and tried a few years ago to sue a Sunday newspaper which had described him as just that. The case went to court and he had lost, in a welter of publicity. Ballantyne found it difficult to feel sorry for him at the time. Sembawa also owned land in Spain and the Bahamas.

At their last reunion in October, Sembawa had arranged the private dinner with Ballantyne because he said he wanted some guidance on the prospects for an independent Scotland in the future. Since then he had twice postponed it because of pressing business. He had phoned Ballantyne from Paris that morning, and said he had just crossed the Atlantic and would by flying into Edinburgh with a business colleague in the late afternoon. He apologised for such short notice, but would it be possible for them to dine together? Ballantyne accepted at once. He wasn't doing anything else.

The colleague turned out to be an American, who introduced himself as Ted Gentry and hardly spoke another word all night without being prompted. He was from Texas, he said. An industrialist thinking of setting up an electronics factory in Scotland — just checking out the prospects. The quiet American, Ballantyne silently christened him. He had iron-grey hair and a square face with a tiny pink birthmark like a fingerprint above the corner of his right eye. There was a large gap between the bottom of his nose and his top lip, giving him a haughty, superior expression. When he did say something, you had to listen very carefully because his voice was very soft and low. He sat between Sembawa and the window, rolling a glass of Southern Comfort between his hands.

'The castle is looking at its most impressive tonight, is it not, Archie?' Sembawa spoke in perfect English, each word clipped and groomed, like a show poodle, before it left his mouth. 'Now, to finish our conversation, I would like you to explain to me again this divestiture principle. I must go soon, before the airport closes.'

'Home to the glen tonight, is it, Suds?'

'Down to London, I am afraid. Business.'

'I see. Well, land divestiture is quite straightforward. If Wallace gets his way, foreigners like yourself who own large swathes of land in Scotland would only be able to sell it to Scottish nationals, like myself, for instance. If no national wanted it, the new independent government would step in and buy it for the nation.'

Sembawa leaned forward earnestly. 'Is this not the very stuff of Marxism?' he asked, nodding in answer to his own question and glancing sideways at Gentry.

'It's certainly one of the more controversial of Wallace's ideas, but that's what it is, just an idea. It's not Party policy. Besides, it would only apply to very large holdings of land, not individual houses, as I understand it. It is more likely to be applied to indigenous industries and companies, to prevent foreign takeovers. That type of divestiture is a fairly common practice in other countries.'

'I bought my land in good faith, as an investment. I am entitled to sell it to whom I like, am I not?'

'Under divestiture, not if one doesn't live here and pay taxes here.'

'That cannot be fair. Do you think it is fair, Archie?'

Ballantyne wrinkled his nose and shrugged his shoulders noncommittally. 'Maybe not,' he said.

The evening had been one long process of Sembawa picking Ballantyne's brains for all the information he had on Andrew Wallace, with Gentry the American an interested observer. Ballantyne had first come across Wallace when he was a fresh-faced youngster trying to make a name for himself in the Scottish boardroom jungle after a short spell as an economist in Brussels. Wallace had branched out on his own and had been conspicuously successful on the European stage, backing his intuition in a variety of risky fields to achieve millionaire status within the space of a decade. Ballantyne had always remained principally in the legal profession, plodding along sedately by comparison. He had set up his own firm and had never burned his fingers when he dabbled in business deals. He had never made the millionaire class, never would now, but he greatly admired those who did make it by their own efforts. He went into local politics, got himself elected to the City Council, and spent two happy years as Lord Provost before retiring gracefully. That was where the knighthood came from. He regularly met Wallace at various functions organised by the Edinburgh establishment.

Their friendship dated from 1979. Wallace had joined the group campaigning for a *Yes* vote in the referendum asking Scots if they wanted an Assembly. Ballantyne was on the *No* side. The two were allocated as rival speakers for a public meeting in some village where only three people turned up but had hurriedy left again in embarrassment. There was nothing for it but to retire to the pub and have an argument between themselves. The whole idea of devolution was just a needless and costly administrative burden which would sap the strength of people who should be devoting their energies to the creation of wealth, Ballantyne said. Control of your own affairs was a fundamental principle from which all other benefits would flow, Wallace countered. Thinking back, Ballantyne was sure he had noticed a few flashes of the latent charisma and persuasive powers that were then hidden just beneath the surface. In the end, the result of the referendum was a narrow vote in favour of the Assembly, but not by a big enough margin to make it a reality.

Ballantyne was getting more and more radical in his old age. He had voted for the new Assembly just formed, and was becoming increasingly sympathetic to the demands for full independence coming from the Nationalists. He considered himself a dyed-in-the-wool Conservative, and if Wallace could talk him round, then the rest of the country was at his mercy. He finished his Drambuie and licked his lips.

'You know Wallace, Archie — is the man a Marxist?'

'No. He's not even a mild-mannered Socialist. In fact, he is probably a Tory who just happens to be a Nationalist. That, the nationalism, comes before everything else for him. Don't try and classify him in traditional British terms. He is creating a new politics to suit us here in Scotland.'

Ballantyne wondered if Sembawa would pick up the mention of 'us', indicating approval and compliance. But he

41

didn't seem to notice. He was not really listening. He sat on the edge of his seat, staring out at the castle and rubbing his thumb vigorously into the palm of one hand. All through the meal he had seemed preoccupied, and gave the impression he already knew the answers to all the questions he was asking. It was not just politics he was interested in, either. There were plenty of searching personal questions thrown into the melting-pot. It obviously was not the first time he had enquired about Andrew Wallace. And Gentry, the American, sat quietly taking it all in, occasionally exchanging what were supposed to be covert nods and winks with his host. When another prejudice was confirmed. They didn't seem to like Wallace all that much.

'I own my land,' Sembawa said. 'I have paid for it. Surely I cannot have it taken away from me?'

'They are not taking it away. Some of them would love to do that, but all Wallace is saying is that if you want to dispose of it you have to sell it to a Scot, or to his government. That is what compulsory divestiture is all about.'

'And what price will they give me?'

'The going rate.'

'Which will be determined by them, take it or leave it.'

'I'm afraid so, Suds. The land is sacred, you see. I remember Wallace telling me that as a young man he had this nightmare vision of the Russians taking over the country simply by buying up all the land that came on the open market. To this day there is nothing to stop them. It would not take them very long to own most of the country, and it would be a lot cheaper than invading by force. So we have to keep the land for ourselves.'

'Is it not racist, this discrimination against foreigners?'

'You could argue that, I suppose. But, remember, if I wanted to flog my couple of hundred acres in Fife, I would be restricted in who I could sell it to as well, if it fell within the limits.'

'Hmm, I see.' Sembawa stroked his lips as if he was trying to remove a hair from his mouth. 'And you think this is a real possibility, Archie?'

'Divestiture? If the Nationalists get independence it will be pretty high on the agenda, I would think.'

42

Actually, Ballantyne didn't think the idea had much chance of getting through the inevitable legal minefield that would be laid to destroy it. But he felt replete and relaxed, and in the mood to wind Suds up.

'And what about things like membership of NATO?' Sembawa gestured towards Gentry beside him. 'Will the Americans be thrown out?'

'I've already said that is a possibility, although Wallace himself is soft on it. Personally, I think there is a lot of fellow-feeling in Scotland for the American these days. Don't be fooled by the people who shout the loudest. It's usually the people who don't shout at all who have the final say.'

Gentry pursed his lips. 'Amen to that,' he said.

'And independence?' Sembawa continued. 'How likely is that to happen?'

'If there was a vote tomorrow, it would happen.'

'But there is no vote tomorrow, is there, Archie? What are the long-term prospects.'

'Wallace has got everything going for him. It will be his fault if he fouls it up now.'

'How could he foul it up?'

'Complacency?' Ballantyne suggested. 'Cold feet from the voters? Sudden discovery of a forgotten love-child? Sex scandal? Over-eagerness amongst the troops?'

'There have been stories in the papers of Wallace and his women. It has not hurt him.'

'He admits it all — adds to his credibility. But he's a married man now, and it's different. Since the marriage he has managed to keep his nose clean, as far as we know.'

'His wife is very attractive,' Gentry interrupted. 'Maybe she has a past?'

'I was a guest at the wedding. A nicer girl you couldn't find. She was hardly old enough to have had a past when he married her.'

'A blushing virgin?' Sembawa grinned unpleasantly.

'Perhaps not quite that, but I doubt if there are any credits for blue movies in her bottom drawer.'

'I have heard there is a possibility of some scandal,' Sembawa said slyly, narrowing his eyes.

'I don't believe it,' Ballantyne replied simply.

43

Sembawa rubbed his hands over his face as if he was washing it, and quickly changed the subject. 'So you think there is to be independence, then?' he asked.

'I'm resigned to it. Barring accidents, of course.'

Sembawa suddenly stood up. 'Accidents happen all the time. Perhaps things will remain as they are.'

'I wouldn't bet on it, Suds.' Ballantyne was enjoying frightening his old school friend. 'If you are thinking of selling, I would do it before the next election, or as soon after it as you can, before they get a chance to change the law.'

'That may not be necessary, Archie, but thank you for the advice. I must go for my plane now. We must get together again soon.'

'Any time, Suds.'

'It was nice meeting you, Sir Archibald,' Gentry said. 'It has proved most interesting. Most interesting indeed.'

'What about your factory, then?'

'I reckon there could be worse places to set up shop.'

Ballantyne stood up and shook hands with both men as they took their leave. He sat down again and watched them weave through the scattered tables on their way to the exit. He called across a waiter and ordered another Drambuie. Just one more would not hurt. He transferred his attention to the street outside, looking down on the people hurrying past, huddled against the bitter wind. It was starting to snow. He would have to head for home soon.

Peregrine Edwards, Prime Minister of the United Kingdom, had made up his mind to escape from the family Christmas party as soon as possible after the traditional lunch was over. His over-excited grandchildren had given him a terrible headache, and he was glad when they were distracted from demonstrating their noisy new toys to sit silent and openmouthed in front of the afternoon's Walt Disney film. His wife and daughter-in-law settled down to snooze in front of the fire. Edwards beckoned to his son Christopher and picked up the port decanter. Together they retreated from the room and went to the private study on the other side of the house.

Father and son were physically very alike. Both had dark eyebrows, long noses and square chins. Edwards recognised a lot of himself as he was thirty years before in the relatively unlined features of the younger man in the golf-club sweater and the sheepskin slippers. He had been a backbencher then, too, painfully ambitious and desperate to make his mark. Now he was at the top of the tree, and it was an awfully long way down.

He went to the window and looked out over the snow-covered lawn. A strong wind was rippling the smooth, powdery surface. A single set of footprints made by one of the children cut across from one side, described a loop in the middle, and disappeared off to the right. It was already dark and the snow was tinged blue where the driveway lights were sunk into the lawn's edge. The occasional snowflake flashed into and out of the vertical beams. His son had only recently bought this house in Kent, fulfilling a long-standing pledge to live in his new constituency. Edwards closed the curtains and stuck his hands in the pockets of the new woollen cardigan that was drooping towards his knees. He turned away and began to examine the books on the ceiling-high shelves.

'Well, Father?' Christopher Edwards said from behind the vast Victorian desk. 'Have you enjoyed your Christmas, then?'

'Ask me again once it's all over.'

The Prime Minister accepted a generous glass of port and went over to lie out on the chaise-longue with its ancient bare-leather surface polished as smooth and warm as an animal's fur. He lay with his head propped up on the round cushion at its end and his glass balanced on his stomach.

'You know, son, I think this Government might just have to go to the country again before the next year is out. We seem to be losing our authority. There is a torpidity in the air. We need a new mandate.'

'Nonsense, Father. Go to your full term. You've got the majority — stick with it. You've taken all they can throw at you and are still standing proud.'

'We'll have a new majority and a new mandate when we get back. There is no problem about that.'

'I just don't think the time is right, Father.'

'Maybe, maybe.'

Edwards needed his son's cosy compliments to boost his ego, because he was well aware that the knives were out for him. A leader going nowhere and taking everybody along for the ride: that was what they were saying about him. And he wasn't too sure about the party actually winning an election anyway. The majority certainly looked safe enough, but the fickleness of the voters was one element he had learned to respect. The Tories had been in power an awful long time, almost the entire last quarter of the twentieth century. Maybe it was *too* long. Things got stale, people got complacent. And if *he* was thinking like that, how much easier must it be for the man in the street to decide the other side deserved a chance. The professional analysts changed their minds about the political climate on an almost daily basis. The Government bumbled ineffectually along and the country carried on regardless.

'When I became Prime Minister there were a hundred things I wanted to do,' Edwards said. 'I'm the boss now, I thought, and there will be a few changes around here. It must have been sitting in on Maggie Thatcher's Cabinet meetings that conditioned me to think like that. Maggie could get away with it, bless her, but once she was gone the natives got slightly more restless. Life suddenly got a lot more complicated. Enemies and friends seem to be interchangeable these days.'

Christopher Edwards had been elected for the first time at the last election, after making a considerable fortune from a brief career as a merchant banker. He drained his glass of port and held it upside-down by the stem between two fingers, tapping the base against a gold signet ring. Edwards stretched his neck to see what the noise was, then turned back to resume looking up at the dust caught in the crevices of the room's elaborate cornice.

'It was a mistake, you know, Father,' the son said after a while.

'What was?'

'Giving the Scots that bloody Assembly. It's getting all the credit for the general economic upturn and the increase in North Sea oil production. It's got nothing to do with it at all.'

'Try telling that to the Scots. They're like young Chris and Trixie were this morning with their new toys.'

'We should have imposed an extra tax to finance their Assembly. Made the bastards pay through the nose. Made the thing unpopular from the start. As it is, up there they seem to think they are getting something for nothing.'

'Wallace was wise to that trick,' Edwards said. 'I must admit that when he spoke at his Party conference and got them to endorse the reduction in Parliamentary constituencies I thought he was knocking the nails into his own coffin. But he was right, wasn't he? What was the point of making all the noise in London? They were irritating enough, but it was not that difficult to ignore them, really. You know that, Chris. But shift the focus to Edinburgh and your own people sit up and take notice and begin to think for themselves. They used to call it consciousness raising. Wallace took a big risk, but he got exactly what he wanted. And now he has gone over our heads and wangled this appearance at the United Nations, despite everthing we tried to do to stall it. Goldman will have to go. He's useless. You have to hand it to Wallace, though. He's nobody's fool.'

'Scotch git. He'll get what's coming to him soon enough.'

'Now, now, Chris. Personal abuse will get us nowhere. Credit where credit is due. He has played his cards supremely well, and whenever we call the next election he'll be ready for us.'

'You think he can achieve full independence, Father? Surely not. I just can't imagine it happening. Customs posts at the border? It's ridiculous.'

'You've seen him operate, and we're all Europeans now with no customs posts to divide us. Would you bet against him?'

'Yes, I would.'

'Your privilege, Chris, but the Scot Nats have got eighteen of the fifty Westminster seats and eighty-three of the two hundred Assembly seats. At the last by-election up there they romped home with sixty per cent of the vote in an inner-city constituency. Even a modest projection suggests that they could take around thirty seats and easily more than fifty per cent of the total votes. If that happens, and Wallace demands independence, what do we do? Send in the army to stop him?

47

'The army is full of Jocks. They would probably join him.'

'Anyway, it's a constitutional question. England and Scotland are supposedly equal partners in the Treaty of Union and if one partner decides to end the union, the other can't legitimately stop him. Wallace has got it all worked out. It's perfectly legal.'

'Barring accidents,' Christopher Edwards said.

'Of course, of course. But Wallace seems to have a charmed life. He can do no wrong. He has had a colourful past and admits it freely, so Fleet Street's finest are at a loss for muck to rake. Then he goes and marries a lovely girl twenty years younger than himself, and an Englishwoman as well, just to prove he isn't parochial.'

'That was smart. He gets the male vote for having something they would dearly like to have, and the female vote for having something that she obviously likes. But it's just not natural.'

'What isn't, Chris?'

'For a politician to be as popular as he is. It's just not natural.'

'Ah, but they don't see him as a politician up there in Scotland. They see him simply as a leader. All present ills can be blamed on dear old England. He stands apart from all responsibility unless he chooses to accept it. It's black and white, goodies and baddies, Jerries and British.'

'It's all a bit like a cargo cult, with the dumb natives convinced the promised land is going to appear. It will be a different story if he ever actually has to run the bloody godforsaken country. It should be avoided at all costs, you know, Father, the break-up of the UK.'

Edwards swung his feet down onto the floor and sat up, with his elbows on his knees and his full glass dangling from his fingers. He looked across at his son and frowned. Secretly he coveted the idea of founding a political dynasty, but he wasn't sure if Christopher was the type of person he wanted to carry the family flag. He had had to take him aside and instruct him to resign from the British Unionist Forum, a reactionary body that was formed soon after the creation of the Assembly in Edinburgh, and which preached the retention of the status-quo by whatever means might prove neces-

48

sary. It was all right for cranky backbenchers to support such wild organisations, but it was poor judgement for any politician with aspirations to future office to associate himself with the kind of people responsible for the BUF. The personal link had made it doubly embarrassing for the Prime Minister. Christopher had resigned, and Edwards had weathered the storm, but he remained suspicious about his son's attitude. He had been extreme in his own youth, of course — so had to make allowances. Even so, his younger son Gerald might have been a better prospect. But he had gone into the diplomatic service and didn't seem at all interested in politics. A pity.

'At all costs?' he said quietly.

'We have to do everything we can to stop Wallace. Don't you agree?'

'What do you suggest, Chris? A bullet in the brain? A knife in the back?'

'I'm being serious, Father,' he answered disdainfully. 'Wallace is enjoying power without responsibility just now. The bubble is bound to burst sooner or later.'

Edwards nodded and smiled and sighed. 'You know what Wallace once said to me? He said: "Never mind, Perry, once we're gone you'll still have Northern Ireland to look after." "Thanks very much," I said.'

'It should be avoided, Father, the break-up of the UK.'

'You're repeating yourself, Chris. Wallace has made himself into an international figure. He goes globe-trotting and dazzles everyone he meets. I hear the American President was seen down on his knees peeking through the keyhole of a room at the White House just to get a look at him. Wallace has charisma, he was credibility, he has stature. I wish the bastard was on our side.'

'I know all that, but he is willing to throw the whole defence of Europe into a state of confusion. They want to kick out the NATO bases and send the Americans home.'

'Maybe. Wallace himself wants them to stay. The official policy is that the Scottish Parliament would make up its own mind in its own time. The Americans drooled over him, despite that threat.'

'They can't do it. Where would it leave us? So much uncertainty can't be healthy. It would be destabilising.'

49

'The point is, they can do it.' Edwards gulped down his drink. 'Wallace is a revolutionary with the ultimate weapon on his side: democracy — and he knows it. In our civilised society it's far more powerful than any terrorist campaign. He doesn't use guns, he uses votes. He's a past master at that. You can't abandon the principles of reasoned argument just because the people are listening to him instead of us. Have you been up there recently? There can't be a poster site that doesn't have that bloody lion rampant sticking its tongue out at passers-by. They are beginning to appear in London, as well.'

'There must be a way of stopping him.'

'Look, Chris. *We* don't want it to happen because we think they belong to us. The Americans don't want it to happen because it might mean them losing their bases up there. The Russians don't want it to happen because Scotland with-drawing from the UK might cause stirrings among the more ungrateful Soviet Socialist Republics. But Wallace wants it to happen, and he may have convinced a majority of Scots that they want it to happen, too. If he has, we can shout all we like and Mr Wallace will not take a blind bit of notice of any of us. Then again, it might never happen at all.'

Christopher Edwards began to tap out an insistent Morse-code message with his glass on his signet ring. *Dot-dot-dot, dash-dash-dash, dot-dot-dot* — SOS. He frowned and his eyebrows were pulled into a single, unbroken line. His father wondered if he realised what he was doing.

'I'm not exaggerating, Chris,' he said in a low voice. 'I'm not going to say it outside this room, but I think we have to face up to the fact that Scotland may be a lost cause. I'm not going to make it easy for him, though. He will have to fight every inch of the way. Besides, you know, there is a strong feeling in the Party that we should cut Scotland loose anyway, let them stew in their own juice for a while, run up a few unhealthy debts and things like that, and then graciously take them back under our wing in a new Treaty of Union they would never get out of.'

'It's not right, Father. It's just not right. Britain is too inte-grated. You can't just wipe out three hundred years of history. Christ, Wales will be next, and then Yorkshire. Where will it all end? We can't allow it.'

'It doesn't have to be right. It's constitutional. It's democratic. Wave bye-bye to the United Kingdom, Chris,' Edwards said mischievously, snorting with laughter. 'Remember, it means independence for England as well, when the union is dissolved.'

CHAPTER FIVE

The new Scotland, emerging from England's shadow as the United Kingdom crumbles, may jeopardise the long-standing defence plans of the NATO Alliance in western Europe.

Andrew Wallace, the high-profile leader of the Nationalists there, tried to assuage fears recently during his visit to the US, but the future of the American military presence in Scotland, particularly the strategic Holy Loch submarine base, must be in serious doubt.

Wallace himself says the US bases will stay for at least ten years. But it is the men behind him, the dim figures in the lee of the coruscating political phenomenon, that give cause for concern.

The desire to be *maîtres chez nous* can make blood run hot. We should remember that, for all his sincere assurances, Wallace remains just one man. Given independence, anything could happen.

Reuters

The freezing mist filled the valley that straddled the border between Luxembourg and West Germany. It lay motionless like a huge concave lake, clinging a little higher up the sides of the containing hills on both sides, and sinking lower in the centre over the invisible houses and the river. The château floated on the calm lake. It emerged majestically from the opaqueness below. The windows shimmered as if fires were burning behind the glass. The frosted whiteness of the walls and the tiles on the steeply-pitched roof sparkled in the reflected rays of the cold early-morning sun.

Renzo Demionscuk sat waiting in the warmth of the soft leather seats of his cream-coloured Porsche. Its engine was idling in near silence in the lay-by high above the village of Vianden.

It had been a good Christmas. He had returned from Scotland weighed down plenty of presents for his young daughters and expensive jewellery and clothes for his wife Barbel. He had not looked forward to joining the teeming thousands in London for a last-minute shopping spree before his flight out, but he soon began to enjoy himself, and had quickly filled three big Harrods carrier-bags. Things had gone well for him in the north. Everything was in order. He was ready to begin whenever they wanted him to. Even the small scrape he found on the wing of his car in the long-stay section at the airport when he returned to it had not ruined his good mood.

Demionscuk was a powerfully-built man with black hair and dark eyes. When he smiled, only half his mouth moved, making it look more like a sneer. When he talked, his lips hardly seemed to move at all. That was because the whole of the left side of his face and the upper part of the right was affected by muscular paralysis, the legacy of a childhood illness. It was not immediately noticeable. It was only after some length of time in his company that people usually became aware of the lack of movement there. It gave his face a curiously blank, expressionless quality, as smooth as a mask, with lively eyes looking out from behind the unchanging surface.

There was little sense of feeling in the skin either. When his daughters kissed his cheeks the contact was like something tapping against foam rubber. Barbel knew to kiss him on the eyelids, the most sensitive part of his face. She had done it that morning as they said goodbye in the hallway of their flat in Grand-Rue in Luxembourg city centre, going up on her toes and putting her arms round his neck to pull him down to her. He had felt the damp warmth of her tongue, rough as sandpaper. Go carefully, my Cossack, she had whispered to him as he got into the lift.

It had been a good Christmas, a real family Christmas. The girls had been a delight. Barbel, her hair newly bleached as a surprise for him, had been a joy. No guests had outstayed their welcome when they came for dinner.

'*Moïen*, Renzo,' she had greeted him on his arrival. 'It's good to have you home again. How was Scotland?'

'Cold,' he had replied. 'But not as cold as here.'

'All done?'

'For the moment.'

The moment had now passed. It was time to get back to work. He had left the almost deserted city that morning with the cold nipping at his ears and filling his throat and lungs. There were only a few pedestrians around, fattened for the Christmas season by the thick padding of their winter clothing. The pavements had been cleared of snow and he was able to walk quickly until he reached the park, but there had to slow down and pick his way more carefully along the icy pathways. His car was parked in its usual spot at Place Churchill. He had set the engine running and then gone round scraping the frost from the windows. For some reason he had decided to go out of his way and drive past the flat in Grand-Rue before heading out of the city on the empty roads, travelling north.

Now, waiting in the lay-by above Vianden, Demionscuk noticed something poking out from underneath the passenger seat. He reached down and pulled out a colourful paper bag. It contained two cheap wooden puzzles, intended as Christmas presents for the girls, but forgotten in the excitement of all the other things that had been showered upon them.

He left the bag lying where it was, and straightened up. As he did so, he caught sight of the red Mercedes in his side mirror as it turned off the road and lurched over the ridge of compacted snow at the edge. It rolled to a halt, level with him. He pulled the yellow lambswool scarf up over the point of his nose. There was an electric whine as his window glided open. Tiny droplets of ice formed in the soft material as his breath froze instantly on contact with the outside air. The passenger window of the Mercedes opened halfway. Demionscuk saw the profile of one man under a fur hat, the brim pulled right down, the small circular birthmark above his right eye glowing like a hot spot on his fair skin. Beyond him the face of the driver was lost in the high collar of an anorak. Neither looked in his direction.

'Cold, isn't it?' Demionscuk said in English, and his breath

54

billowed out across the gap between the cars.

'I've known it hotter,' the man replied in an American accent, turning his head so that his eyes were framed between the broad band of his hat and the top of the window glass.

'When is it to be, then?'

'Next month.'

'We have a suitable subject?'

'Yes. An Australian. He has been recruited.'

'What is he being told?'

'He will be sent to you. You can tell him what you like.'

'Where in Australia is he from?'

'Adelaide.'

Demionscuk nodded. His eyeballs felt as if they were pressed up against a lump of smooth ice. His ears were tingling. 'When?' he asked again.

'He will be here on 4 January. You will have two or three days to get to know each other, then you get down to work.'

'Is there a deadline?'

'Be ready as quickly as possible. That is all. We will tell you when.'

'Good. I have already made some preparations.'

The window of the Mercedes was opened to its full extent. The man in the passenger seat rubbed his nose with one hand as he handed over a large, bulky envelope with the other. Demionscuk took it and laid it in his lap.

'You will find fifty thousand francs for general expenses while you remain here,' the man said. 'There is also one thousand pounds sterling to be used in England. Your fee will be as agreed. Regular payments into your bank account will continue.'

'What is the Australian called?'

'Tarrant. He will be sent to the Hotel Cravat.'

'He will have to use his real name.'

'Of course.'

'We're all set then, at last.'

'Yes.'

The Mercedes reversed back onto the road. Demionscuk closed his window and watched it go down the hill and turn a sharp bend, before disappearing towards the village. The trail of exhaust fumes was left behind like a thread torn loose from the blanket of mist. He pulled the scarf away from his mouth and tucked the envelope away in an inside pocket of his coat. He sat still while the heater poured more hot air into the interior, to replace what had been lost. The warmth flowed like a liquid round his eyes and ears. He looked out at the château and saw that the rock beneath it was just becoming visible. Beyond it he could see more of the hills a few hundred yards inside West Germany. The lake of mist was gradually subsiding, soaking into the land.

The last time he had been in Vianden he had travelled up from Luxembourg for the annual nut festival on a pleasantly warm October day. The narrow main street leading down the hill from the castle, made narrower by the stalls on either side, had been so packed with people that the marching band had been unable to find a way through, and had marked time on the same spot all afternoon. He had sat at a shaded table by the bridge over the river and sipped cold beer, while Barbel and the twins joined the crowds and bought helium balloons and Bratwürst. He had listened at the time to the project as it was explained by the soft-spoken American in the midst of all those people. He had accepted the contract there and then. It was more elaborate than the tasks that were usually required of him, not a straightforward hit-and-run but perfectly workable. If that was what they wanted, that was what he would give them. He rather enjoyed the prospect of not being on his own for once. It would make a pleasant change.

A bird flew high above the mist, its shadow racing over the surface and up the sun-washed walls of the château. He had another week before beginning, then — another week with his family. Demionscuk slipped the car into gear and prepared to drive south.

Sandy McInnes slipped the almost empty half-bottle of whisky into his jacket pocket and rose unsteadily to his feet. He leaned too heavily on the kitchen table in front of him and pushed it away, toppling the stack of crumpled beer cans to clatter and bounce erratically over the floor. The noise of the legs scraping across the hard vinyl was like fingers being dragged across a tight balloon. He grimaced and held his hands up to his face to try and shut out the sound. With his eyes closed he lost all sense of balance and staggered backwards, knocking over his chair as he half-turned, his hands groping to find some support. The edge of the worktop slammed into his side at kidney level and he doubled over in pain with his face only inches from the dirty dishes crammed into the greasy water of the sink.

'Forbidden to go out o' m'ain house, am I?' he groaned as he struggled to breathe properly. 'Ah'll show Mr high-and-fucking-mighty what he can do wi' his fucking master plan.'

The tap was dripping slowly on the back of his neck, the cold water providing a soothing, not unpleasant sensation. He stayed where he was with his head down, and the dizziness that made him afraid to move for fear of falling over gradually left him. When he opened his eyes he could see out the window over the rim of the sink. Lights were on in nearly all the tenements opposite. He could hear people passing in the street below, shouting and singing. The whole of Pollokshaws was on the move. The snow fell silently.

'Okay, Sandy' he said to himself as he straightened up and rubbed his neck dry. 'Let's show General George that his one-man army is on the move too.'

McInnes was a wiry, sallow-faced man with sloping shoulders and the suggestion of a pigeon chest. He had been drinking continuously since the morning. He had originally agreed to the rule about not leaving the flat if he was to be allowed to drink, but as the day wore on it got to seem more and more ridiculous that he could not go out and visit his friends. He had twice been physically prevented from leaving by his house guest, the first time at around eight o'clock and the second time two hours later. After that he had shut himself up in the darkened kitchen and finished off his supplies of alcohol.

He hated himself when he got so drunk. He retreated into his shell, becoming morose and uncommunicative and totally lacking in self-respect. He watched the glasses or the bottles or the cans rising to his lips with objective contempt, but welcome relief. When he was sober, people would order him around and tell him what to do and what to think, and he never answered back because he couldn't articulate his thoughts well enough. He had his own opinions but words did not come easily to him, so he always spoke slowly and hesitantly and deferred to other people because he didn't like being made to look a fool. It had started at school, with bullies who beat him up and teachers who ridiculed him when he was unable to reply to their questions. They had told him how stupid he was, and how useless, and all he could do was stare back sullenly, absorbing all the abuse they heaped on him because he wasn't big enough or smart enough to fight back. And there had been the girls as well, laughing at him behind his back, giggling at his thin, unattractive body. Then, when he began working, it was his workmates who mocked him and scoffed at him. Even his best friends, he knew, tolerated him rather than liked him.

When he was drunk, from the safety of his protective shell, he had the consolation of imagining that when he sobered up it would all be different. That was why he drank. It was a form of self-defence. When he sobered up, it would be him making fools out of everybody else. They would discover the real person under the skin. Next time.

McInnes crushed an empty beer can and imagined his hand was round the neck of the Englishman. The thin metal folded easily. But McInnes knew he was no match for him, not in the state he was in, even though the bastard was old enough to be his grandfather. Still, it was worth one last try to make a break for it. The previous New Year and the two before that he had been in prison, nearing the end of a four-year sentence for armed robbery He would have been out in October if they had not given him an extra six months for spitting on one of the screw's boots. He had tried to explain that it had been an accident but they wouldn't listen to him. Now he was in a different sort of prison. It just wasn't fair.

He waded noisily through the scattered beer cans and out into the dark hallway. A strip of bright light showed along the bottom of the living-room door. Before he had a chance to do anything the door opened and he was dazzled by the avalanche of harsh electric light. He held up a hand to shield his eyes and could just make out the jagged-edged silhouette looming in front of him.

'Where do you think you are going this time, Sandy?' asked a deep voice that seemed to make the whole flat vibrate.

'First footin',' McInnes said quickly, leaning wearily against the wall, knowing that he wasn't going anywhere. 'It's an auld Scottish tradition we hae up here.'

'Well, why don't we let your fellow countrymen indulge themselves while we stay here at home? Is that not a better idea, now? What do you think?'

'You dinnae understand. Not to go first footing can mean bad luck fur the whole year. Ah'm only thinking o' you and your plan, so ah am.'

'Is that so, Sandy?'

'Aye. Ah need to go out tae bring you good luck. Don't you see? It could spell disaster if ah stay here the night.'

'You're staying.'

McInnes tried to stand up straight but only succeeded in falling against the opposite wall. 'Who the fuck are you tae tell me whit ah can dae and whit I cannae dae?' he said aggressively.

'I'm the man who is paying you to do a job.'

'Aye.' McInnes shaded his eyes and peered ahead, momentarily sober and thinking clearly. It seemed a very long time since he had been approached with the offer. It had been on the Larne to Stranraer ferry after the summer marching season, when three drunken days at his cousin Liam's home in Londonderry had been a complete blank to him. General George must have been watching him them, measuring him up. God alone knew what he had done to attract his attention in the first place. McInnes didn't have to think about the offer for long before accepting it outright. Anything was better than going back to erecting scaffolding during the winter. Besides, he was flattered by the approach. It was good to feel wanted.

'You're paying me a'right, ah know that,' he said. 'But who's paying you? That's whit ah'd like to know. Who's pulling your strings?'

'You know what the deal was, Sandy. If you drink you stay here. No two ways about it.' The voice dropped to an even lower register. 'Time for bed,' it said.

McInnes felt his arms being grabbed and he was lifted up

59

till only the tips of his toes remained in contact with the ground. He was marched into his bedroom and thrown roughly onto the bed beneath the big colour picture of the championship-winning Rangers team on the wall and the six-foot-long Union flag pinned to the ceiling. The door closed almost at once, leaving him in darkness. The alcohol inside him seemed to slosh all at once down to his feet and then back up to his head, bursting round his brain like a wave round a rock at the edge of the sea. He could still feel the pressure of the grip on his upper arms, as if he was being pressed down onto the mattress. He fumbled in his pocket for the whisky bottle and clumsily unscrewed the top. He misjudged the position of his mouth so that he poured the liquid onto his chin and cheeks.

'You'll be sorry,' he murmured. 'You should hae stuck to selling carpets.' He kept repeating the last few words over and over in a slurred refrain until they tailed off into silence as he fell asleep.

The man McInnes knew as General George Cumberland stood listening outside the door until he was satisfied that McInnes was not going to reappear. His real name was Major George Mortimer. He returned to the living-room and picked up the fat cigar he had been enjoying. It had gone out, but he put it in the side of his mouth anyway as he sat down behind the portable typewriter on the table. He balled his hands into fists with the forefingers pointing out like the barrels of guns, and began to punch at the keys.

There was already a pile of a dozen letters on the table. Each was identical, apart from spelling mistakes. The top of each page had three overlapping letter Ws drawn on it in red and the first letter of the first three words in the typewritten message below was also handwritten in red. The message read:

We're With Wallace and we're not going to let you forget it. The time has come for us to act to ensure that Scotland does break out from under the yoke of English oppression.

You cannot stop us. We are too strong. Independence is ours for the taking. We will now be making sure. Soon we will demonstrate our strength and you shall realise we must be taken seriously. We shall not be deprived of our rights. It begins in Glasgow and there will be four blows for freedom.

If people must die then so be it. Remember, it is not for glory, nor riches, nor honours that we are fighting, but for freedom which no honest man gives up but with life itself.

Mortimer chuckled to himself as he laboriously typed out the words, pausing frequently to scratch at the ragged beard he had started growing as soon as he left his daughter's home. He was not used to whiskers on his chin and could not shake off the irritation caused by the unfamiliar feeling.

It was a suitably crackpot letter. He had given a lot of thought to what it should contain. It seemed to have just the right combination of threats and romantic nonsense to make people remember it, even if they did throw it in the bin immediately afterwards. He was particularly proud of the last sentence which had been a late addition. It was a quotation from the Declaration of Arbroath, an affirmation of independence signed by the Scots in 1320. Much good did it do them then, as well, Mortimer thought. He had noticed it on a tea-towel in the window of a shop in Argyle Street.

He finished the last sheet of paper and pulled it out, sliding the typewriter to one side. He laid it flat and drew in the large capital letters at the top with a red felt pen, then sat back to admire his handiwork. It certainly was a striking feature. The same motif could be seen spray-painted on a hundred walls and road signs across Scotland. McInnes was an efficient worker when he was sober. He had not been idle over the last month or so. He had single-handedly launched the We're With Wallace campaign.

Mortimer stubbed out the cigar he was smoking, put his hands behind his head and yawned. He had a list of the addresses the messages were to be sent to, but decided he would type out the envelopes later. He would have liked a strong drink but he was disciplined enough never to drink when on duty, so he restricted himself to orange juice. The cigar was the only concession to the time of year which he permitted himself. There would be plenty of time for celebration once the job was successfully completed and he was back home. He did not want to make any mistakes. The organisation he worked for had a lot of anonymous but influential people, and no lack of money behind it. Personally, he had no doubts or qualms about what he was being asked to do. It was much more positive than writing speeches or sending out leaflets. Andrew Wallace had to be stopped. The break-up of the UK had to be avoided. A desperate situation called for desperate measures.

He rose from the table and went through to his bedroom. He had left his home in Buckinghamshire on Christmas Eve, stopping off at Manchester on the way up to spend Christmas with his grandchildren. He had taken a plastic machine-gun for Simon and a doll for young Maggie, both wrapped in paper decorated with green holly and Santa Clauses on sleighs. He had brought other presents as well, four packages the size of thick paperback books and neatly wrapped in red Christmas paper with robins and snowmen all over it. He bent over a small cardboard box and stroked the edge of one of the packages, partially concealed in a sea of white polystyrene balls. It would have been a disaster if the two sets of presents had been mixed up.

It had been good to finally get moving. He had spent so many years pottering around his little garden and putting on his magic shows at children's parties, content to let the world pass him by. He was long over his grief at being widowed. Now, he was keen to earn his new status as an active patriot. It excited him that he was actually going to do something he would never have dreamed of doing only a few short years ago. He might have talked about in the past, grumbled about it, but he would never have put himself at such risk while Margaret was still alive. Now, at last, he had the freedom to indulge himself, and the motivation to put his theories into practice. It created that old-time thrill, that racing of the blood, which he remembered so well from his army days just before an operation got properly underway, even if those had always been exercises and he had never seen any real action. There was soon going to be plenty of real action, now. He was glad to get the opportunity to use his skills again. The struggle to keep his ageing body in trim had been made worthwhile. He was sixty-two but had the strength and energy of a forty-year-old. Life was too short to miss a chance like this.

He turned his attention from the box to an old brown leather suitcase lying on top of the bed. It had the words Major Magic embossed on the lid in faded gold letters. He opened the lid carefully, almost as if he expected something to escape from inside. From the jumble of items he picked out a hollow cylinder of stiff black cardboard. Using two fingers, he withdrew an identical white cylinder from its inside, and from that he took another cylinder, this time of thin paper, and unrolled it. There was a single paragraph, written in flowery, copperplate script: *Major Mortimer, England expects you to do your duty whatever it may entail. We are all behind you. God Speed.*

The personal message was signed and dated three weeks previously. For the thousandth time since receiving it at the final briefing session in London, Mortimer felt the rush of blood to his face and neck, and his chest again swelled with pride. He lightly traced his finger over the letters of the signature. With men of such substance behind him how could he fail?

It had been a small piece of deception to retain it, instead of destroying it as he had been ordered. He had found it simple to switch the piece of paper when they demanded he should burn it in front of them, simpler to fool them than a roomful of sceptical children. He was, after all, an accomplished magician. It was wrong, he believed strongly, to destroy such a precious document. He would keep it in a safe place. It would never leave his side. He could guarantee confidentiality. History would be glad of what he had done, in the future.

Mortimer replaced the sheet of paper and the cylinders and closed the lid of the case. He went into the hall and listened outside the other bedroom door. McInnes was snoring loudly. He had allowed him to get hopelessly drunk beacause he knew it would be simpler to control him that way. He had the measure of the man. Drunk, McInnes was slow-witted and predictable; sober, he had a sort of dull intelligence and could be annoyingly curious. That curiosity was acute and insistent. It would probably not take him long to discover Mortimer's true identity. It was fairly obvious he did not believe his real name was General Cumberland. Of course, it didn't really matter. McInnes was sound, and came highly recommended by Unionist contacts in Northern Ireland. He wasn't likely to give the game away. Still, he was a surly partner in crime and he could be dangerously careless when he had a drink in him. He had to be handled sensitively. Mortimer was permitting him to go to the traditional New Year Celtic-Rangers match at Parkhead. No drink was allowed at football matches. He couldn't get too outrageous, and it would cause more trouble than it was worth to try and keep him away.

Mortimer re-entered the living-room and stood beside the electric fire. He rummaged idly in his pocket and found a couple of Clydesdale Bank pound notes. Curiously he examined the drawing of Robert the Bruce among his soldiers at Bannockburn, which was printed on one side. Not this time, boys, he murmured. Not this time, boys, he murmured. Not this time.

With exaggerated gestures he pulled back his sleeves and rolled one of the notes into a tight cylinder before sliding it inside his closed fist. He crouched down to push it through the guard rails of the fire until it was hard against the glowing orange bar. It smouldered and burst into flames. He used it to light his cigar, then watched, smiling, as the flames rapidly turned the burning banknote to crumbling ash that fell apart and drifted slowly down into the fireplace, like flakes of black snow. When it had all disintegrated except for the very last corner, which he dropped when the flames reached his fingers, he opened out his hand and a creased but untouched note lay unfurling on the palm.

CHAPTER SIX

Name two aspiring new member states of the European Community which have been members since 1973.

The answer to the riddle is Scotland and England, two countries which seem destined to split apart after almost three hundred years of interdependence.

The former will join as a newly independent nation and the latter will probably have to reapply for membership because the London Government originally signed on behalf of the United Kingdom, which will no longer exist, as such.

Bureaucrats in Brussels are already scratching their heads trying to ascertain what forms will have to be filled in to deal with such an unprecedented situation.

Andrew Wallace, the forty-eight-year-old leader of Scotland's Nationalist Party, has made it clear he wants his country to remain part of the European economic structure if full independence is granted. He should be made welcome.

Der Spiegel

The snow was falling steadily on Edinburgh. The fat white flakes drifted slowly out of the dark sky and past the windows like shoals of fish, down onto the people packed shoulder-to-shoulder in the High Street and round the Tron Kirk. The restless crowd was far from silent as it repeatedly hushed itself in anticipation of the bells about to ring out from the church-tower, wet hair and upturned faces shining under the streetlights. The bells sounded their prelininary notes. Then there was a brief pause before the first stroke of midnight. An impatient murmur from the waiting audience suddenly changed into an answering roar to greet the official arrival of the New Year.

In the warmth of the flat high above the crowd, the same scene was displayed soundlessly on a television screen ignored by everyone round about it. They were all watching Andrew Wallace instead. He stood in the centre of the L-shaped lounge and raised his whisky glass in front of his face. All the hands in the room copied the movement. The booming sound of the first toll rang out. He grinned broadly and raised his glass even higher.

'Happy New Year,' he said loudly, and the words seemed to be magnified by the explosion of noise from outside.

'Happy New Year,' the assembled company replied as one, drinking the toast, and immediately beginning the traditional round of handshakes and kisses.

Wallace turned to Helen. She was wearing the close-fitting black cocktail dress with the single shoulder-strap which she knew he liked a lot. The gold chain round her neck disappeared between her breasts. Her hair was held to the side by a light-blue ribbon, and she was smiling up at him in that intimate way she had, in the most public of places, of shutting everybody else out of their own private relationship. She put her hands on his arms and stood on tiptoe to stretch up and kiss him gently on the lips.

'Happy New Year, Andrew darling,' she whispered. 'It's the last year of the century. What are we going to do with it?'

'Well, Hanson,' he said, using her maiden surname as a term of endearment, 'my first resolution is to get rid of all these people as soon as possible and get you into bed.'

'A worthy cause if ever there was one.'

'After that I intend to lead my country to independence and become the first Prime Minister of the world's newest sovereign state.'

'That's all right, then. From a personal point of view, I'm glad you've got your priorities right.'

'You can be my first lady.'

'I'm not interested in being anything else. See you later.'

Then they were separated as different groups pressed forward with New Year congratulations. Wallace entered into the spirit of things. He was among friends. The flat contained forty of his closest colleagues, all of them sharing the same ideal. He shook hands, slapped backs and kissed glowing cheeks enthusiastically. It had been a good Christmas and it was going to be a very happy New Year, he decided. There was no room for doubters and faint hearts at this party. Outside, some people started singing the new Assembly-approved Scottish anthem, 'Auld Lang Syne', and it was quickly taken up by the rest of the crowd. Wallace hummed the tune to himself as he went over to the buffet table to treat himself to another whisky and some food. He found himself beside Dave Sheahan, the US Consul-General, and the only non-Party member — apart from the French Ambassador from London and an Italian film star — to be invited to the party. The Sheahans had taken him and Helen out for a fare-well dinner a couple of days previously.

'Have we done the business?' Sheahan asked. 'I've shaken so many hands I can't remember who they belong to.'

'I believe we have, Dave. But I suppose we had better make sure.'

They shook hands. Sheahan was moon-faced, with a pale complexion that made him look permanently unhealthy. He was wearing a cream-coloured suit that seemed a little small for him. Beside him his wife, Sally, grinned infectiously from under her cloud of bubble-bath blonde hair. Wallace leaned over to kiss her.

'We'll miss you, Dave,' Wallace said. 'Monday, is it, that you leave us?'

'Yes, sir. Life goes on,' Sheahan replied. 'They say it is promotion I'm being recalled for. I must have been doing a good job.'

'You sure did, Dave. Keep in touch.'

'Good luck with your country.'

'Thanks.'

The doorbell rang and everybody hurried to form two rows on either side of the door as they waited for the host to answer it. Wallace excused himself, left his glass and plate of food on the table and walked through the avenue of people. Helen joined him. He made a big show of pulling the door open to reveal the tall, stooping frame of Hamish Henryson on the doorstep, whisky bottle in one hand and a slice of black bun wrapped in a napkin in the other. 'Happy New Year,' everyone sang in chorus before he had a chance to say anything.

'We'd forgotten about you, Hamish,' Wallace said. 'It's been five minutes since the bells. Did you get lost out there in the corridor?'

'My watch must be slow and your sound-proofing must be too good. It's as quiet as the grave out there. I didn't hear a thing.'

'In you come, anyway. Bring in the good luck.'

'I must be about the last to wish you a Happy New Year, Andrew,' he said as he entered. 'With the accent on the *happy* and the *new*.'

'Likewise, Hamish. A new year, a new beginning.'

'That's what we want, and that's what we are going to get. Ready for the UN, Andrew?'

'Give me the audience and I'll sing them the song.'

The two men shook hands and then embraced before being separated as others gathered round. Helen and Wallace went back to the buffet table.

'Tall and dark he may be,' Helen whispered, 'but hardly handsome.'

'He is going deaf as well,' Wallace added.

Henryson was an ugly man with coarse grey hair, puffy cheeks and watery, bloodshot eyes, made worse by the amount of alcohol he had consumed. The veins stood out as blue ridges on the backs of his hands. He looked as if a puff of wind would blow him away, but his physical frailness belied an enormously tough mind. He had been Wallace's mentor from the early days. He was no leader of men himself, but he had shaped Wallace's personality and carefully groomed the now famous charisma to transform the Scottish National Party into a potent and irresistible political force. The potential had always been there, Henryson believed passionately. All that was missing was the leader to realise it. Wallace was that leader.

'Remember the New Year party we were at before the Assembly was set up on Calton Hill?' Henryson came up beside them. He talked in short bursts of words as if his lungs could not hold enough breath to produce a whole sentence at once. 'It was Graham's flat in the New Town. You and Helen were still in the first flush, and you went crimson when the boys lined up to claim their kisses from her.'

Wallace laughed and handed Henryson a glass of whisky. '*Slainte*,' he said. 'I've a very protective nature.'

'We got our Assembly, Andrew,' Henryson said more quietly. 'We'll get our independence. The English have already given away too much ground. We're unstoppable.'

'You don't have to tell me. I'm in there at the sharp end.'

'Private doubts are healthy enough, Andrew. Public certainty is what we need. This is our year. Believe it.'

'I believe it, Hamish. I believe it.' He nodded and then lowered his voice. 'It's just sometimes I get the feeling that they won't allow it to happen, whatever we do. Know what I mean? I look ahead and I can't help being just that little bit frightened.'

'"Thou art blessed compared wi' me. The present only toucheth thee: But och, I backward cast my e'e on prospects drear. An forward tho' I canna see I guess and fear."'

'I'm a man, not a mouse.'

'You are. Shake off that feeling, Andrew. We're playing them at their own game and we've got them running round in circles. After the next election we'll be free men once more. Believe me.'

Wallace shrugged and straightened up. 'You're a romantic, Hamish. Besides, I kept getting the same feeling before the Assembly opened. I'm sure it's a good sign. I believe you.'

Henryson smiled, showing crooked teeth. 'Don't make the mistake of over-estimating the English, Andrew.'

'I married one, didn't I? I would never do that.'

Helen turned from where she was just ending a conversation with someone. Wallace let his arm slide round her back until his hand rested on her hip. He turned his head and kissed the top of her ear.

'You'll never do what?' she asked.

'Forget to wash behind my ears,' Wallace said.

Robert Shand, the Party's deputy leader, grabbed Wallace by the elbow and pulled him away. 'Come on,' he said insistently. 'Your public is calling you. Let's not be selfish up here.'

The noise from outside had evolved itself into a slow chant of the two syllables making up Wallace's name. He crossed the room, after Shand's barrel-shaped figure, to the five large windows which faced two ways — onto North Bridge and the Royal Mile. Shand unlocked the window facing the Tron Kirk's tower and pushed it up as far as it would go.

'Look how many friends we've got, Andrew,' Graham Turnbull said.

'It's bloody cold out there,' Wallace complained, tucking his shirt into the waistband of his trousers.

'There are a couple of camera crews, too,' Turnbull said, taking away the whisky glass with one hand and shoving him towards the window with the other. 'Let's give them some good pictures.'

The snow was falling more lightly as Wallace poked his head out. The air was freezing cold after the dry heat inside. He looked down on the heaving mass of people below him and held out his hands in a stiffly formal wave. Two huge St Andrew's flags appeared, unrolling on the surface as if they had bobbed up from under water. The chanting of his name changed into a swelling roar of approval that gradually died away to be replaced by a spontaneous chorus of the folk song 'Flower of Scotland.'

Other heads appeared from windows in the same building, and from other windows in the tenements facing onto the Royal Mile. Wallace stayed where he was until the song reached its end, looking through the snow past the church tower and the city rooftops to the statue of the Golden Boy — symbol of unlimited potential — pointing at the sky on the dome above Edinburgh University's Old College. The grey storm-clouds shifted just enough to let through a single shaft of moonlight that picked out the boy, making him incandescent for a lingering moment before the clouds moved again and he was covered by the darkness.

The wind rose with sudden, unexpected force, driving the falling snow into slanting lines that fused into a white wall to obscure the statue. The snowflakes settled in Wallace's hair and slid over the skin of his face. He looked down and shivered as he smiled.

CHAPTER SEVEN

It was one of the world's most famous Scotsmen who wrote: 'The best laid schemes o' mice an' men gang aft agley', meaning never count your chickens until they are hatched.

Robert Burns put his finger on it rather stylishly, and his countryman Andrew Wallace would do well to heed the warning.

At this point in time it must seem to Wallace that nothing can stop him and his Nationalist Party from achieving the independence of Scotland.

The Scottish lion may indeed be rampant but it should remember another useful saying: 'You never know what is round the corner.'

Economist

The brilliant whiteness of the squash court hurt Lord Fairchild's eyes when he pressed the token into the meter and turned the handle to flood it with light. He entered through the glass door and began to knock up by himself, batting the ball gently against the wall with the racquet and swinging his arms to loosen his unwilling muscles. He was a short, portly man aged less than forty, in white shorts and a yellow T-shirt already stained with sweat under the arms before he left the locker-rooms. His hair was cut very short and his glasses were tied with a cord at the back of his head like a swimmer's goggles. He began to hit the ball harder, making himself run about the court. He puffed and panted as his lungs struggled to cope with the unaccustomed bout of exercise, and he rubbed his chest where a fluttering pain came and went spasmodically. After a few minutes he fell over trying to retrieve a difficult ball, and remained sitting on the floor in the corner with his back against the wall and his head drooping down between his raised knees.

'You're out of condition, Arthur,' Christopher Edwards said as he stepped into the court, dressed in dark blue shorts and vest.

'New Year resolution, Chris,' Fairchild gasped, sucking in great mouthfuls of air. 'Got to get fit for the battles to come. Got to get some of this weight off.'

'I wondered why it was squash today of all days. Usually your idea of an energetic ball game is snooker.'

Fairchild grinned as he clambered awkwardly to his feet, still panting. 'All that walking round and round the table tires me out. There isn't so far to run on a squash court.'

Edwards picked up the ball and bounced it on the strings of his racquet. 'Okay, Arthur,' he said seriously. 'Tell me where we're at. I haven't got long.'

'The way I'm feeling, I doubt if I've got that long either.'

They played one set. It didn't last long. Edwards won easily without dropping a single point. The sound of the ball thumping against the back wall echoed through the near-empty club. The other five courts were all in darkness. There was no one at all in the snooker room, but a few keep-fit enthusiasts were working out on the weights in the gymnasium. Two elderly ladies with caps decorated with plastic daisies floated on their backs in the pool. The attendant in the entrance area was busy braiding her long chestnut hair into a ponytail.

Edwards had arrived at the club a little late, just as Fairchild was tying his laces in the locker room. They had not been able to talk because somebody else was changing on the other side of the row, so Fairchild had gone out to wait on the court. This meeting had been arranged well in advance. The first week of the New Year had been chosen the previous February, when the British Unionist Forum had supposedly been disbanded. Only it had not been disbanded at all. It lived on with Christopher Edwards as its leader, Lord Arthur Fairchild as his trusted lieutenant, and about half a dozen other carefully selected people making up a close-knit executive. Precautions were taken: the organisation had no written records; it was never even mentioned by name; its meetings masqueraded as social occasions. But radical plans had been formulated and set in motion. Those plans were now being drawn towards a conclusion by the momentum of their own inexorable logic.

Edwards was aware of an intense, almost sexual thrill whenever he attended the clandestine meetings of the forum in Fairchild's dockland flat. He was defying his father the Prime Minister, defying his wife and family, defying all his best advisers from whom he normally took counsel. If his continued involvement became known, his political career would be totally wrecked. He was in no doubt about that, because his participation in the original foundation of the Forum had caused a lot of damage to him, set him back a great deal. Even so, he had never been clearer in his own mind about what he should do. He had no hesitation about placing his whole future at risk. It was simply something that had to be done. A risk that had to be taken. And he enjoyed doing it.

Fairchild was on his hands and knees. Sweat dripped from his forehead and the point of his nose. 'Mortimer is in position and waiting for the word,' he said, snatching breaths between each word.

Edwards stood over his playing partner and glanced up at the balcony behind the court to check that no one was there. 'Any problems?'

'None. It has all been as smooth as clockwork.'

'How was Mortimer? Did he get my letter?' Edwards had missed the final briefing session because he was on an unavoidable Parliamentary trip to Brazil.

'Eager,' Fairchild replied. 'A good man, Mortimer. A reliable man. He has a proper sense of history and tradition.'

'And my letter was destroyed?'

'Of course. He burned it in front of us. He went north at Christmas. Everything is ready for the first phase. When do you want it to begin?'

Edwards felt the familiar thrill of excitement take hold of his body; the tightening in the groin, the weakening of his legs, the warm rippling along his spine. He smiled and slammed the ball as hard as he could against the back wall of the court.

'Well? When?' Fairchild persisted.

Three times Edwards managed to return the ball before it

73

bounced out of his reach and hit the floor.

'Three days,' he said. 'Begin in three days from now.'

Murray Tarrant flew in from Rome to a city that looked from above — when they emerged from the low ceiling of cloud — as if it was trapped inside a cocoon of frozen air. He had to wait twenty minutes for a taxi, and had never experienced cold quite like it. In the darkness of the morning at Rome he had not ventured outside the airport building and had not appreciated just how cold it was. Now in Luxembourg he stood surrounded by his suitcases in the murky daylight and shivered as his stiffening bones ached so much he feared they might shatter like brittle glass. The blustery wind jostled him like an invisible crowd passing by. The sub-zero temperatures were totally alien to him. He clenched his teeth tight to stop them chattering. The cold fastened itself to him like a leech, sucking out his body heat, threatening to turn his blood into solid red ice. He could no longer feel his nose, his fingers, or his feet. His lips were so cold he could not shape them to form a whistle. He had been warned about this, of course, and he had found time to buy a thick overcoat and a fur hat at the stopover in Singapore, but they hardly seemed designed to cope with such extremes. And he had forgotten to get himself a decent pair of gloves. Why did people choose to live in such a hostile climate? Why didn't they all just uproot themselves and move to the sunshine and warmth of Australia?

At last a taxi arrived and he huddled in the back with his hands stuffed deep into his pockets and his head sinking well down between his shoulders. After a few minutes there was a sharp prickling in his fingers and ears and he thought he was just beginning to thaw out when the taxi reached Grand Hotel Cravat on Boulevard Roosevelt. The cold swooped in again as the driver opened the door and took his arm to help him out. Tarrant pressed a couple of notes into his hand as payment and rushed across the few yards of open space, abandoning his luggage to the uniformed porter. A heater above the door blew a powerful down-draught of warm air over him, and he tilted his face up to receive it. The receptionist warmed him up a little more with her welcoming smile when he introduced himself, but his hand was so clumsy he barely recognised his own signature when he registered. She handed him his key and an envelope with his name on it. The porter led the way to the lift and then up to the second floor and along a wide corridor to his room. His footsteps made no sound on the thick carpet; neither could he feel his feet touching the ground as he walked.

It was not that long since Luigi Fachetti had given him this job at the rendezvous in the outback. He had looked forward to the journey to Europe, even though he was still not certain exactly what was expected of him. All he knew was that it involved contacting this guy nicknamed The Demon and then seducing a sheila. Some kind of blackmail remained his best guess. He didn't want to tell his girlfriend Donna where he was going, but that didn't pose a problem because she had walked out on him after a blazing row in the alcohol-induced haze sometime between Christmas and New Year. The day after that, the travel tickets were delivered and he discovered all the arrangements had been made to send him to Luxembourg. They had even supplied some local currency. He had already bought an atlas, and the tiny country — when he eventually located it — seemed not much bigger than the Spencer Gulf where his uncle worked the prawn boat.

Inside the hotel room he paid off the porter and stood over the radiator while his whole body tingled with the gradual return of sensation to the extremities. The radiator gave off a good heat, a dry heat, a desert heat. His muscles unknotted and slackened. After five minutes he was able to remove his coat and hat. He stretched his arms and rolled his neck to relieve the stiffness in the joints. Only then did he really begin to notice and appreciate his luxurious surroundings. He had never stayed in such a high-class hotel in his life. He bounced on the edge of the bed and wondered if the rest of the job and the mysterious sheila he was destined to meet would be up to the same standard. Fachetti had promised him a real honey.

He remembered the envelope the receptionist had handed to him, and retrieved it from the pocket of his coat. His name was handwritten on it in large unconnected letters. Inside he found a single sheet of paper with the same kind of writing on it covering almost the whole page with half a dozen lines. It told him succinctly that he would be collected and taken for a meal the next night. The signature was illegible.

Tarrant lay back on the soft bed and closed his eyes, suddenly realising how weary the long journey had made him. Tiredness jumbled his thoughts into a confused blur. His skin glowed warmly all over as his body temperature over-reacted to compensate for its failure to combat the cold outside. By tomorrow night, he hoped, he would have recovered enough to have all his wits about him. He had the feeling he was going to need them.

CHAPTER EIGHT

The marriage five years ago of sultry Helen Hanson to Scottish Nationalist Andrew Wallace appeared not to be a match made in heaven.

He was a rising political star in his mid-forties with ambitions of taking over a country all for himself. She was a 22-year-old science undergraduate yet to venture out into the big bad world. And she was English to boot.

They said she was too young and too gullible and had stars in her eyes. They said he was an old fool who should know better. They said an awful lot of things about how it would all end in disaster.

They were all wrong. Five years on, the couple are closer than ever. 'When Andrew saw me he knew he wanted to marry me straight away,' Helen said. 'He has a happy knack of getting exactly what he wants.'

Cosmopolitan

A row of people sitting at the long table in front of Andrew Wallace in the Edinburgh Sheraton looked rather like figures posing for a remake of The Last Supper. There were a dozen of them, and the thin man in the middle was on his feet, making expansive gestures with his hands as he spoke at length, while the others adopted various attitudes as they listened to him, apparently concentrating on every word. There were eight men and four women, all very smartly dressed and turned out. The youngest man was in his twenties, babyfaced and with a rash of spots under the collar of his shirt. The youngest woman was probably in her thirties, definitely a few years older than Helen, but not that many. She was long-legged, dark-skinned and raven-haired. She would write something on the pad of the hotel notepaper and

77

then use the pencil to hook the flowing hair back behind her ears. In the old days he would have made special arrangements to have her sit next to him at the dinner he was hosting in the evening. Not this time, though. Changed days indeed.

Wallace smiled benevolently at the curving line of City of London investment analysts and feigned interest in the rambling, convoluted question that was being asked. Changed days, indeed, he thought again. Three years ago there had been no takers when he had first suggested the idea. Now independence was a clear possibility, and things were very different. There were to be four one-day sessions in the next two months to satisfy the demand for places. It began with a lecture, then questions and answers, lunch, tour of the sites, and a formal dinner — courtesy of Party funds — to round it all off. Not a very demanding itinerary, but one that was sufficient to get the message across. Wallace was to attend every one of the sessions because it was him they really wanted to see. He was the moving force, the Party's prize exhibit, and he was more than capable of putting on a positive display. They wanted to be reassured on the economic stability of an independent Scotland. He would reassure them. The fact that the majority of them had no direct involvement in Scottish business was unimportant. They had contacts who were — and friends who might be — in the future. Business confidence was mainly a matter of whispers and impressions. The seminar was a long-term investment for the Party.

Graham Turnbull sat a little apart from Wallace on the same side of the table. A tape-recorder stood on its end beside some empty coffee cups on the polished wooden surface. The two spindles were towards Wallace, rotating slowly under the transparent cover like clownish eyes. The tiny red recording light above them was a comic nose. The thin man stopped speaking abruptly, and sat down. Wallace had anticipated the sense of the question from the beginning and had his answer ready.

'Mr Kuypers, under that philosophy it makes no sense for the clutch of countries on the European mainland to maintain independent governments. Should Belgium and Holland unite just because they have common borders? Or France and Germany? Or France and Italy? Or France and Belgium?

They already co-operate in the EEC, but no one suggests they should compromise their national identities by uniting under a common flag.'

'But these countries you mention have long histories of self-government,' Kuypers interrupted, jumping to his feet again. 'The UK has a long history, too. You want to change that, radically and drastically, do you not?'

'I do indeed desire to change that.' Wallace leaned forward onto his elbows. 'Scotland is one of the oldest nations in Europe. We have not had our own Parliament for a long time, but then, as my mother used to say, just because something has been happening for a long time does not necessarily make it right or, for that matter, the best way of doing things.'

The youngster to the left of Kuypers spoke, pointing his finger across the table like a pistol. 'You are prepared to upset a mature society and established economy to impose your own vision of how it should be governed?'

'What is upset, Mr Mills? We are pledged to a ten-year period when all personal and business taxes in Scotland will be decided in joint agreement with Westminster. We will still be living next-door; we just want to run our own house. Is that not a reasonable ambition?'

Wallace fielded a few more questions, almost without having to think, enjoying himself immensely. He liked head-to-head sessions like this because he knew he was good at them. He could argue the hind legs off a donkey — as his primary teacher had once told his parents — and have the donkey believing it was in its own interests. He had never yet met anyone who could better him in an argument, and sometimes he had to be careful not to get too cocky and cause offence.

'Tell me, Mr Wallace,' said the dark-haired woman hesitantly as she looked up and brushed her hair back. 'Why is it that your brand of nationalism is not associated with the violence that has been a typical feature of nationalism in so many other countries?'

'A very good question,' he replied, crossing his legs and holding his knee in both hands. 'And there is a very simple answer. You see, it is a fact that most nationalist movements emerge among peoples who are a minority in a larger country.

They and their culture have generally been subsumed into a larger unit, but they want to create their own country, their own state; and violence springs from the frustration of that minority being unable to impose its will on the majority. The Basques in Spain are, as you know, an ideal example of this. Or the Tamils in Sri Lanka.

'The essential difference with Scottish nationalism is that the Scots already have their own country, and they are in the majority in it. We are formally linked to a larger neighbour, but through choice, not force. The only obstacle to us taking control of our own affairs, it we want to, is lack of self-confidence. To achieve it we only have to vote for it on the time-honoured democratic manner. Nothing could be simpler. We already have the means, and therefore do not have to resort to bombs and bullets. We do not have to advance with a rifle in one hand and a ballot-box in the other. We can have both our hands on the ballot-box, because it is our most powerful weapon. My Party's frustration lies only in the long failure to convince the Scottish people that they should take control of their own country. Violence has no part in our attempts to persuade them.'

She smiled earnestly. 'A failure that you are now changing to success?'

'Hopefully. You see, Scotland is in a unique position. It had then the only sovereign Parliament in history to vote itself out of existence. That was in 1707. The possibility that the Parliament should vote itself back into being has always been there. I hope that possibility will become a reality soon.'

'And the last three hundred years count for nothing?'

He sat forward, and would have liked to reach out and pat her hand. 'More than three hundred years of history preceded the Union of the Parliaments. There were those that argued then to retain the status quo. Our political opponents today would probably be against such a radical move as that very union. It is not the principle they oppose, it is because they just don't like too much change. They are afraid of the unknown. Better the devil you know — that is how they think.'

'You admit, then, that independence would be a step into the unknown?'

'Of course it is. It has to be. Not exactly the unknown; the untried would be a better description. But we are mature adults in Scotland, not irresponsible children. We can look after ourselves if we choose to do so. In my opinion, dignity and self-respect demand that we make that choice.'

She sucked the end of her pencil and thought for a few moments. 'Can you identify the point when the SNP really began to win the support of the people?'

'It was a gradual accumulation of things that turned the tide in our favour. Most significant, perhaps, was the increasingly offhand and arrogant attitude of both the Westminster Parliament and the London Government to the situation up here. At the 1987 election the Tories won in the UK but were massacred in Scotland. Despite that, there was no dilution of Tory policy, no recognition of a different identity and state of mind. At that election we only returned three MPs, while Labour had fifty, more than two-thirds of the total number of Scottish MPs, yet Labour were powerless to do anything because they were thirled to the UK organisational base of their Party. We called it the Doomsday result and it certainly was for Labour. They huffed and they puffed, but their impotence in trying to protect Scotland was displayed for all to see. They were unionists, playing by unionist rules so they could not claim special treatment for Scotland. They had been found out. We won Govan at a by-election in 1988 and at the next general election we stormed back to win ten seats and made the big breakthrough into Labour's heartland in central Scotland. Since then we have not looked back.'

'Why did you agree to reduced Scottish representation at Westminster, Mr Wallace?'

'In order to get an Assembly. The other parties didn't really want it to happen because, as I said, they were unionists at heart. That was why they made such a fuss about the reduction, because they hoped that conditions would prevent the Assembly happening. I am a realist and the truth was that seventy-two Scottish MPs are never going to impose their will on the six hundred and more in London, even if they all thought alike. They can shout and scream, generate a few headlines, but they cannot achieve anything. They may be tolerated, they may even be listened to politely at times, but

81

they are never going to have real power. Seventy-two or fifty. The numbers never really mattered.'

'Does your Assembly have so much power, then?' someone asked.

'Limited power as yet. We have made a fairly good start.'

The thin man spoke again. 'Is it really necessary to break up the United Kingdom to achieve your goals, Mr Wallace?'

'I can see no other way, Mr Kuypers, but I don't think that should be too serious a stumbling-block. If a company was not performing well, would you not try to restructure it to improve its performance?'

'Yes, but I would question if the UK performance was sub-standard in the first place.'

'That is a value judgement, Mr Kuypers. And one made very much from the perspective of the south of England. Anyway, I am a nationalist by conviction, as well as by economics.'

'Is there sufficient governmental experience in Scotland to carry out such a task?' somebody else asked.

'We already have our own civil service. All it lacks is domestic political control.'

'And your revolution,' Mills interrupted, firing the question across the table. 'You think it will ultimately be successful?'

Wallace spread his arms wide. 'Do I look like a revolutionary, Mr Mills?' he asked. 'I call it a facing up to responsibilities. We're not going to collectivise the farms on independence, or line the intellectuals up against the wall. Life will go on. The Queen will be our Head of State. Business will continue to make profits. Money will be made.'

'Life could go on without independence, then?'

'Of course it could. Life could go on without investment analysis as well, but where would that leave you?' He paused for the laughter to die away. I'm too old to have many illusions left, but I'll never lose my vision of the future.'

Wallace sat back and smiled, switching on the full force of his charm. Opposite him, the twelve faces all smiled back without exception. He had them eating out of the palm of his hand. By the end of the evening, he knew, they would be on his side.

★ ★ ★

82

Helen Wallace was the only person in the large, spartan laboratory. The seasonal holidays meant that the university was virtually devoid of staff and students. Occasional figures could be seen wandering among the snow-wreathed buildings like survivors of some terrible holocaust that had snuffed out the human population but left the bricks and mortar untouched. There was a huge puddle taking up most of the car-park outside the window, and ice had formed round the edges, making a jagged circle which looked as if it had been shattered by something dropping from the sky into the water.

Her last-minute decision to fly to Washington for Wallace's birthday just before Christmas had put her well behind in her work and, what with parties and receptions and official dinners, she had not had much opportunity to catch up since then. She was determined to do so as soon as possible, and that was why she was fiddling with the electronic guts of one of the new medical lasers the department was developing, while all her colleagues had still had to get back from their holidays.

The lab was a single, square room with several little partitioned cubicles off it. The walls were bare except where they were lined by filing cabinets or notice-boards or bookshelves, and the ceiling was supported by a circular pattern of exposed metal beams. Pieces of equipment, large and small, lay haphazardly about the floor and on the numerous scattered tables. The heating was always on because of the delicate machinery, but it was still cold enough for Helen to wear a thick sweater under her white coat. With nobody else around, it was quiet, too quiet. She kept thinking she was hearing noises and would cast suspicious glances over her shoulder, annoyed with herself because she knew there was nobody about. She did not want to start getting paranoid again.

The day had started early for her, and she had worked right through without a break for lunch. There was a pain at the base of her spine, caused by sitting in the same position so long, and cramped muscles along her shoulders. She got up from the experimental apparatus and walked round in circles, massaging the small of her back with her hands while she looked out over the frozen landscape. Her particular speciality was the development of flexible infra-red optical fibres capable of transmitting a carbon-dioxide laser beam which was already in widespread use as a surgical scalpel. A properly flexible fibre delivery system would provide more sensitive control and feedback for any surgeon using it. Her experiments had increased the tolerable curvature by a fractional amount, but she was convinced she was close to achieving some significant results. Six months, maybe, and she would know if she was on the right track. The computer was going to process a lot of important data for her over the next few weeks. Meanwhile, she planned to head north tomorrow morning to do some uninterrupted reading. She grudged having to give up the time she could otherwise be spending with her husband, because it was rare these days for them to be able to snatch more than a couple of consecutive nights together. But there was always tonight after the dinner at the Sheraton, and he had promised to join her on Friday night, come Hell or high water. She reckoned she could survive for two nights on her own. They needed the rest anyway. They had not slept apart since the night she had surprised him on his birthday in Washington. Now he was complaining that he was too tired to pay proper attention to his work during the day. Long may it continue, she thought, smiling down on her reflection in the glass-topped table. Another two hours to finish this and back into the city to ensure that it did continue, for another night at least.

Helen realised she would inevitably lose him when he began his travels again. It was to be New York first; then it would be back into the routine of his itinerant lifestyle. It saddened her to think of all the lonely nights she faced in the future. If she got bored, it was simple enough to use the Edinburgh flat and to gather some lively friends round her, but she really preferred the solitude of the remote glen and their little cottage there. The outside world could not intrude there when they were alone together behind the defensive rampart of mountains. They often walked for miles without seeing another living soul. Like the animals around them, they were part of the land, part of nature. It was the same when she stayed there by herself. Only sometimes did the isolation become so oppressive that she just had to flee south to seek human contact. Just before Christmas she had suffered from wild ideas of being followed and watched all the time, both in Edinburgh and then in Glen Halkston. She had refused to let her delusions intimidate her and had stayed on, but was finally glad of the excuse to escape to Washington. By the time she was safely in her husband's arms she did not even bother to mention them.

It was a long time since she and Andrew had been alone together, just the two of them, at their croft. More usually they would have a guest, or two or more guests; people whose support Andrew was courting or whose experience he wanted to tap. He never stopped working and she did not blame him. She actively encouraged him. They couldn't hide from the rest of the world. That was the way it had to be.

The obvious solution to their frequent separations was for her to give up her job to become a professional wife and follow him around everywhere. They had talked about that when they married, but she wasn't ready to do it yet. Her research work on medical lasers was important too, and she was not far away from her doctorate. It would not be long before she wanted to settle down and raise a family — she could feel the maternal pull already — but until then she would carry on as she was.

A phone started ringing on the far side of the lab, the bell clattering loudly across the empty space. She hurried across to the departmental secretary's desk to answer it.

'Hold on a moment, Mrs Wallace, I have your husband for you,' said a familiar female voice.

Helen waited until Wallace was at the other end, then spoke excitedly before he had a chance to. 'I was just thinking about you.'

'Likewise, Hanson. I thought I'd phone you up to see if you had anything new to report.'

'We must have a telepathic link. I was going to do the same. What are you doing?'

'Sleeping with my eyes open. These investment analysts are a pretty boring lot, but we've dispatched them to do their tourist bit now, so I don't have to see them again until tonight. I just wondered if you were free for dinner tonight?'

'Just you and me?'

'And twelve analysts in the background. I've set them up;

all you need to do is knock them dead.'

'I'll wear my most powerful perfume.'

'Then I reckon I'll be in sore need of somebody to warm my feet on tonight.'

'You know that I am an excellent foot-warmer.'

'Good. Everything all right in the lab?'

'A few small steps for mankind.'

'Don't be overdoing it. Save your strength for tonight. Got to go.'

She replaced the receiver, stood for a few seconds looking down at it grinning foolishly, and then went back to the laboratory to finish her work as quickly as possible.

CHAPTER NINE

The successful Nationalist movement in Scotland, which has brought the Party to the very brink of achieving outright independence, is a remarkable story.

Without a single drop of martyr's blood being shed, Mr Andrew Wallace may be about to defeat the formidable power of the English Government and the massed ranks of vested interests that tried to warn him off.

No bombs. No bullets. Instead, Mr Wallace has employed a method which other, less accountable nationalists in other areas of the world might like to consider: persuading people to vote for him.

If democracy is proved to be a more effective force than the gun perhaps it will even replace the arms trade as a currency between nations.

La Stampa

The knock at the door came while Tarrant was standing at the window looking down on the frozen, near-deserted streets. He had not been outside since arriving the previous day. His head snapped round to stare in the direction the sound had come from and his nervous, breathy whistling died on his lips. He had been pacing restlessly about the room for hours, half listening to a classical-music channel he had found on the radio, measuring the minutes by the music he recognised. He turned it off as he moved quickly over to the door. He had expected the call to come much earlier. He had not known what to wear and had finally opted for a plain jacket and trousers. He thought a tie would be obligatory, and had had to buy one from the hotel shop. It felt strange round his neck. He had not eaten since lunchtime and his stomach was cramping with hunger pains.

'Murray Tarrant?' inquired the stocky man standing in front of him.

Tarrant nodded, taking in the dark hair, the dark eyes, the bright yellow scarf round the thick neck that gave an impression of great strength. A teardrop was clinging to his cheek. It suddenly slid down and out of sight below his chin.

'Allow me to introduce myself. I am Renzo Demionscuk'

'Ah,' Tarrant said involuntarily. 'The Demon.'

'A play on words from my name,' he acknowledged impassively. 'I know of it but I prefer not to be called that, if you don't mind.'

'It was Mr Fachetti told me the name,' Tarrant stammered, instantly regretting having blurted it out. 'He never told me your real name, you see. He just said you were known as that. I'm sorry.'

'No need. It is a small thing. Fachetti can call me what he likes as long as I do not hear it from him.' Demionscuk stroked the corner of an eye with his fingertip. 'Or from anybody else. As long as I do not hear it.'

'I'm sorry,' Tarrant repeated.

'Call me Renzo. Renzo Demionscuk. I will call you Murray. We must work together. We must be friends.' He held out his hand and Tarrant took it, returning the strong pressure and smiling into the expressionless face. 'Are you ready now? I have a table waiting at a restaurant. It is very cold. You should wrap up well.'

Tarrant went to collect his coat and hat. Demionscuk turned in the doorway as he came back and led the way along the corridor to the lift. They descended in silence, buttoning up their coats. A taxi was at the front door, its engine running, the driver stamping his feet on the snow-dusted pavement. The cold slapped Tarrant viciously in the face. His eyes watered in a blast of icy wind, and he wiped away the tears with the flat of his hand. He had thought he would be ready for it but the shock of it filling his lungs made him catch his breath. He stumbled over the mound of frozen snow at the edge of the road and dived into the comparative warmth of the back seat to escape the cold.

'It is not far,' Demionscuk said. 'Nothing is very far in Luxembourg. It is a small city, a small country.'

'Is it always as cold as this, Renzo?' He spoke the name tentatively, uncomfortable in its use.

'By no means. We are in the middle of a very harsh winter.'

'Yes. Well, I'm used to hot weather. The only snow I had seen before arriving here came out of a spray can. I feel as if I'm shut in the bloody ice-box.'

'We'll get some strong drink and hot food inside you. That should warm you up.'

Tarrant watched the darkened city pass by. There were very few people about. The car stopped at a junction and rocked from side to side as it was buffeted by the wind. They started moving again. He glanced sideways at Demionscuk, seeing his profile appear and disappear against the flickering screen of background lights.

'Are you from Luxembourg, Renzo?' he asked, just to break the silence.

'No.'

'Mr Fachetti said yours was a Russian name. Are you Russian?'

'My grandparents were Ukrainian. My parents were born in Italy. I was born in America and then brought up in Italy.'

'You're an American?'

'Perhaps. I am many things.'

Tarrant thought he saw him smile but realised it was just a fleeting shadow passing over his face. 'I'm an Australian,' he said. 'Dyed in the green and the gold.'

'I know. Here is the restaurant.'

Once again the bitter cold rushed at him, attacking the exposed flesh of his cheeks and hands as he stood on the pavement waiting for Demionscuk to pay off the taxi driver. He screwed up his eyes and looked up at the many-coloured haloes round the streetlights, but had to look down quickly because there was hail in the wind and the hard particles stung against his face and bounced on the roof of the car.

Entering the restaurant was like stepping into a warm bath. The place was quite large and very busy. All the tables seemed to be taken. Conversation hummed alongside a gravel-voiced singer whispering from the hidden loud-speakers. The smell of freshly cooked food provoked Tarrant's hunger and made the saliva pour into his mouth.

The waiters wore red waistcoats and over-starched white shirts that crackled as they moved. The two men left their coats in the alcove by the door, and Demionscuk, in a grey business suit, led the way to a table in the far corner, separated from the rest of the diners by a head-high partition.

'A drink first? Or shall we just order a bottle of wine straight away?'

'I could do with a whisky to take the chill off,' Tarrant said, accepting a menu offered by a skinny, bald-headed waiter with a pointed face, who looked like a greyhound standing on its hind legs. The thing was all in French. He couldn't understand it.

Demionscuk ordered two whiskies as well as a bottle of wine. 'You'll like the food here. It's all red meat — steaks. You cook it yourself at the table.'

'Cook it yourself? Why? Don't they have a chef?'

Demionscuk laughed. At least, Tarrant assumed it was a laugh. It was a strange sound, like a rattle in a hollow iron pipe. One side of his mouth curled up, lifting the lip a little like a dog beginning to snarl. The rest of his face was a death-mask, smooth and unmoving, apart from the eyes. Tarrant swallowed the saliva that had gathered at the back of his throat. Christ, what a weirdo, he thought. I'm glad the mongrel is going to be on my side. I think I could get to like him.

'You'll see,' Demionscuk said. 'You *do* like steak? You're not a vegetarian or anything like that?'

'Steak's great.'

'I think I'll start with the pâté and then a nice piece of sirloin with roast potatoes and a selection of fresh vegetables.'

'That sounds good. I'll have the same,' Tarrant said, folding the menu and putting it down on the table.

The greyhound waiter was back with the whiskies and a bottle of white wine in an ice-bucket. Tarrant finished his whisky while Demionscuk was tasting the wine and ordering the meal. He grabbed the waiter's bony wrist as he was about to leave, and pointed at the empty glass.

'Another please,' he said.

The waiter fetched one within a minute. That was quick, Tarrant thought. Living up to your name you are, like a greyhound out of the trap.

'No need to be nervous, Murray,' Demionscuk said.

Tarrant imagined his name was spat out the side of the twisted mouth like a grape pip. 'Who's nervous?' he replied, pressing his tongue against his top teeth and resisting the strong urge to whistle.

The first course was served. Demionscuk launched into a lesson on the history of Luxembourg. The pâté and the bottle of wine were soon finished. A replacement bottle was brought and offered to Tarrant to taste this time. Then in front of them were placed wooden platters with large chunks of raw meat on one side and inset rectangles of grey stone in the centre. Tarrant held out his hand and felt the intense heat radiating upwards. Demionscuk licked his index finger and tapped it against the stone. The moisture vaporised with a sharp hiss. His lip curled in the friendly snarl.

'Slice off a piece of meat and prepare it to your own preference,' he said. 'You've only yourself to blame if you don't like it.'

Blood ran out of the meat as it was carved, filling the shallow grooves in the platter. They ate more or less in silence, transferring the cooked portions to an ordinary plate as they were ready. The heat given off by the stone and the sizzling meat made Tarrant start to sweat. He removed his jacket and loosened his tie. A third bottle of wine was opened. That loosened his tongue. When his hunger was satiated and his plate was empty he sat back and watched Demionscuk finishing his meal.

'What's it all about then, Renzo?' he asked confidently. 'You haven't brought me halfway across the world for a cooking lesson.'

'What did Fachetti tell you?'

'Not much. He promised me some fun with a goodlooking woman as part of a serious business venture. Blackmail, I suppose.'

Demionscuk put his knife and fork together on his plate. The greyhound waiter moved in immediately and cleared the table. They both declined dessert, and ordered coffee. Tarrant asked for a malt whisky as an afterthought. There were still a couple of glasses of wine left in the bottle. Neither of them spoke again until the waiter had returned with the coffee and the whisky.

'You have just eaten some prime Aberdeen-Angus steak, product of Scotland. What do you know about Scotland?' Demionscuk said.

'Scotland? Not a lot. My grandfather came from there originally, or so my granny always said, but the bastard abandoned her when he found out she was pregnant with my mother.'

'Ever heard of Andrew Wallace?'

Tarrant thought about it and shook his head.

'Or, more to the point, his wife Helen?'

'Should I have heard of these people? Who are they?'

'Wallace is a successful politician, leader of the Scottish Nationalists. Helen Wallace is his wife.'

Tarrant grinned and poured himself another glass of wine. 'And you want me to sleep with her to create a scandal and ruin his career?'

'You already have.'

'I have?' Tarrant frowned and raised his eyebrows. 'Did I enjoy it?'

'Immensely. You had a brief, passionate affair with her last summer when she and her husband visited Australia as part of an overseas tour.'

'It must have been pretty brief. I think I missed it.'

'Two nights only. That was how long they stayed in Adelaide. She went out bar-crawling and picked you up, told you all sorts of things — like how she liked to have a different man in every city she visited.'

'She told me that?'

'She did. She is a real nymphomaniac.' Demionscuk spoke in a flat monotone. 'Her husband just can't keep up with her. He's a bit past it, you see. She is far too young for him.'

Tarrant poured his whisky into the wine and swilled the mixture round. He tasted it and grimaced. Demionscuk took out his wallet and handed a newspaper photograph across the table.

'Nice,' Tarrant said admiringly. 'I'm sure I must have enjoyed it at the time. Do I get another shot?'

'We already have the scandal. All we have to do now is sell it to the British Press. I have already made contacts to begin

92

that process. We will need pictures, and I have a reasonable look-alike lined up.'

'Naughty pictures?'

'Nothing too blue. Holiday snaps you took, just for the memory.'

'So I don't actually get my leg over at all in this scenario?'

'You can screw around as much as you like, Murray. But you'll have to find your own. You're being well paid. You can afford it.'

'Not Helen Wallace, though? Pity — she's a real stunner.'

'She's a happily married woman. What would a woman like her want with a Casanova like you?'

'Careful, Renzo. That was almost witty. Your face might crack if you were to smile.' Tarrant tried to out-stare him but lost the battle and dropped his eyes to pour himself another glass of wine instead. 'Why me?' he asked. 'Why bring me all the way for this? Of all the joy-prongs in all the world why does it have to be mine?'

'Fachetti found you. We needed someone who happened to be around at the same time she was. Adelaide is as good a place as any. If the reporters check up on you, they will find you have a certain reputation as a ladies' man. Your neighbours will testify that you bring different women back to your flat all the time. They will be impressed, and put two and two together. Of course, we will already have supplied the answer to the equation, but *they* can take the credit if they want.'

'Maybe I was on the road when she was there? When was it?'

'June. You were just back from a trip, and on the first date in question your neighbours called the police to a rowdy party in your flat in the early hours of the morning.'

'Hey, that's right. I remember that night.' He frowned, thinking of a difficulty. 'Why didn't they arrest her, then?'

'They didn't arrest anyone, just asked for the music to be turned down. She hid under your bed.'

'Naked?'

'If you like.'

Tarrant rubbed his thumb over the photograph. 'I like. You've really got the story all worked out, haven't you?'

'I'll be going over it with you in detail before we meet the great British Press.'

'You think I can convince them?'

'Having talked with you tonight, Murray, I'm sure you can.'

'Shouldn't be too hard. I'll just use my imagination and it will all seem totally real anyway.' He closed his eyes and put his head back for a few moments. When he moved it forward again the alcohol made the room spin crazily. 'What's your job, Renzo?'

'Management. I am setting it all up.'

'No, no. I'm a lorry-driver, Renzo. What's your job?'

'I am a consultant.'

'And what do people consult you about?'

'Things they want done.'

'And you do them?'

'If the price is right.'

'I'm not going to ask who wants this job done?'

'Good.'

They were getting up to leave. Tarrant got unsteadily to his feet. He talked to himself inside his head. You kill people, Renzo, don't you? That's why they call you The Demon. You're a killer and you'll kill me if I don't go through with this. You would already have killed me if I hadn't measured up to your inspection. I don't have any choice in the matter and the joke is, Fachetti, you old bastard, that I don't even get to seduce the bloody sheila after all.

The greyhound waiter helped Tarrant on with his jacket, and fussed around them as they walked to the door to collect their coats. The restaurant was almost empty. Outside, the wind was as strong as ever but the hail had changed to sleet. A taxi was waiting by the kerb. Its back door swung open as they appeared.

'The cab will take you back to your hotel,' Demionscuk said.

Tarrant nodded, bracing himself against the wind. 'You're not coming?'

'I prefer to walk home.'

'In this?' Tarrant gestured at the sky.

'I'm used to it.'

'When do we leave for bonnie Scotland, then?'

'Tomorrow — but not to Scotland. We will travel to

94

London to conduct our business. I will collect you from your hotel in the morning.'

'You're the boss.'

Tarrant climbed into the rear of the car and pulled the door shut. For a few moments he saw Demionscuk's face looking down on him through the window, distorted by the streaming water on the glass, like a fat blob of melting wax. A demon, he thought. A true demon. A demon who never smiles. He started whistling tunelessly through his teeth as the car carried him away into the night.

Helen Wallace lay on her side with her leg resting casually over her husband's knees and her hair pressed softly against the side of his face. The fingers of her left hand traced wavy lines on his shoulder, then picked up the golden lion rampant and made it march over his chest. She brought over her own identical piece of jewellery and made the two lions kiss.

'I really must be going,' she said dreamily.

'Uh huh,' he replied without opening his eyes.

'This is just so decadent. Do you know what time it is?'

'All time is relative.'

'It's after ten. The day's half over.'

'Let it go. There will be plenty more.'

They had made love the moment they came in the door of their Edinburgh flat the previous evening, almost before they could get their clothes off, not bothering with the bedroom. It was short and sweet, and then afterwards when they did it again it was in bed and it was long and languorous. The dinner at the Sheraton had been pleasant enough, but they drifted away as soon as politeness would allow so that they could be on their own. Outside, the sounds of the living city at night had continued all around them. They could not have been more isolated if they had been at the Argyll cottage. They went to bed and slept deeply. They rose early to a breakfast of orange juice and toast and the news on the radio, then went straight back to bed to make love again.

'Hey, lover,' Wallace said as Helen moved away from him and swung her feet down onto the floor. 'Where are you going?'

'Far away,' she said. 'Otherwise I'll never get any work done.'

'Not too far, I hope.'

'All distance is relative.'

She went through to the bathroom and he heard the shower running. He was sitting up with his arms folded when she came back, rubbing herself dry with a large white towel. He watched as she began to get dressed.

'Hanson, did I ever tell you that I knew I was going to marry you from the moment we first met?'

'Frequently.' She pulled on a pair of pants and snapped the elastic against her stomach.

'Mind if I tell you again?'

'Not at all. I think it was one of your better decisions.'

'It's true, you know, Hanson. I get this strange feeling sometimes and then I just seem to know what is going to happen.'

'You mean our eyes met across a crowded room?'

'No. It's not like that at all,' he said seriously. 'It's hard to explain. I just know.'

Helen lay on the bed beside him and wriggled into a pair of tight jeans. 'Wishful thinking, perhaps?'

'In your case it turned out to be true, didn't it?'

'Fond memories, then?'

Wallace shook his head and bit his bottom lip. 'No. It's a definite feeling I get. It's not an obvious thing. I didn't suddenly hear wedding-bells ringing in my head. It's much more subtle than that. It's just an impression, an idea that lodges there.'

'Maybe you've got the second sight. Like that auntie you were telling me about.'

'She wasn't my auntie, and maybe I do have the second sight. I've never told anybody except you, but I've used it a lot in the past. You know, for business deals and that kind of thing. When to sign and when to back off. When to sell and when to buy. I cashed in an awful lot of investments a few days before the crash of 1987, just because I had a funny feeling things were about to go on the slide. My friends then thought I was mad to bale out of a rising stock-market — but the rest is history. It's been pretty useful for making tricky political decisions, too. It has served me well up till now.'

'Other people call it talent, darling.' Helen fastened her blouse and pulled a high-necked jumper over her head, fluffing out her hair once it was on. 'And how do I rate as business deals go?' she asked.

'You're a bargain and a half.'

'Glad to hear it.' She bent down to kiss him on the tip of the nose. 'Now I really must be going, and you had better shake a leg or they'll have search parties out for you.'

'That's all right. I warned them I would be a little late this morning because of our efforts on behalf of the Party last night.'

'How did we do?'

'I think I did fairly good. How about you?'

'Me too.'

'Wait a minute and I'll walk you down to the car park. Carry your books for you?'

'No thanks. The rate you're moving at this morning, we'd be lucky to make it before dark. See you on Friday. Don't be late. I'll keep the bed warm for you.'

She collected her bags and her bulging briefcase and left the flat. Wallace sat in the bed for a few minutes before getting up. He dressed hurriedly, wondering if he was being foolish. He really did believe that he knew he was going to marry Helen the very day he met her. It was at a lunch at her Cambridge college, when she was a beautiful, shy 21-year-old student. They had been seated together by chance, and had hit it off straight away. Then, again, maybe he was reading too much into it. Everybody who got married had to meet for the first time at some stage; and presumably they were attracted to each other or they wouldn't bother seeing each other again. It was a bit much to claim the second sight for something like that. And, it had to be remembered, not all his business deals had been roaring successes. So how did he explain that away? It was true that he had an ancestor, a Mackenzie from the Black Isle, reputed to have the second sight. But *he* was burned in a barrel of tar for witchcraft, and surely he should have seen that coming.

Wallace knotted his tie in front of the mirror and combed his hair back with his fingers. He had been troubled by a vague feeling for some time. It was a bad feeling, a black feeling that lay like a shadow over another long-established belief that one day he would win independence for his country. Bad vibes they would have called it way back in the Sixties. It had started about a year ago, and quickly faded. Then it had returned sometime before Christmas, during his North American tour. It had left him for a while again. Now it was back. He had wanted to share it with Helen but he didn't want her to laugh at him, so when she did not immediately take him seriously, he was ready to turn the whole thing into a joke. But he should have told her. The feeling had not gone away.

The House of Fraser carrier bag which Sandy McInnes held as he walked slowly among the morning shoppers in Glasgow's Sauchiehall Street contained one package wrapped in red Christmas paper decorated with robins and snowmen and sealed with sellotape. McInnes discreetly held the bag out from his leg to prevent it banging. He had walked the length of the street twice, deliberately avoiding stepping on the joints between the paving stones. His mouth was dry. A nervous tick jerked at one eyelid. His time was running out. This time he had to go in.

Earlier that morning he had watched in open-mouthed fascination as General George had produced the packages from their nest of polystyrene and unwrapped one to demonstrate how the bombs were to be handled. They were black rectangular boxes containing ten pounds of Czechoslovakian Semtex plastic explosive completely enclosed inside thick polythene; vacuum-packed in fact, he said, so that no telltale traces of explosive were left at the storage sites, nor could they be detected by sniffer dogs. The timing and detonation mechanism was Dutch-made and simple. It had ten individual push-switches, activated by pressure through the protective polythene, each controlling a thirty-minute unit which gave a choice of setting detonation from between half an hour and five hours. Each little switch glowed a dull yellow when activated, like square goldfish swimming underwater. There was a larger master-switch at the bottom of the row of lights. It went red when clicked down to load the programme into the timer and set it running. If it was turned off, it wiped the memory of the whole mechanism and prevented detonation. Cumberland had set the timer for three hours, six fat yellow lights, and operated the red switch. They were highly accurate, these electronic devices, he told McInnes laughingly in his plummy voice. You could set your watch by them.

McInnes looked at his digital watch. Fifteen minutes to go. He entered the jeweller's shop and went straight to the steps at the rear to climb to the first floor where the tea-room was situated. He walked round the display stands and up another flight of steps to reach the entrance. He stood there for a few moments looking round the pattern of tables and high-backed Rennie Mackintosh chairs. He counted fourteen people: one group of four old ladies in cardigans and hats leaning inwards over their table like the sides of a pyramid; three even older women in outdoor coats and headscarfs just settling down; a young couple in the corner watching passers-by in the street below; and five individuals including a tall thin woman sitting by herself sipping tea with her little finger crooked in the classic fashion. Twelve minutes.

'Table for one, sir? Can I take your coat?'

The waitress appeared at his side, dressed in white blouse and black skirt, smiling solicitously. He moved the carrier bag away from her. All his answers were ready.

'Just by myself, yes,' he replied, putting on as refined an accent as he could manage. 'I'll keep my coat just now, if you don't mind. Just till I warm up a bit.'

'Of course, sir. It is cold outside, isn't it? Nice and warm in here, though.'

She led him to a table by the window and waited until he had quickly read the menu and ordered Indian tea and a scone and jam. He put the carrier bag against the wall and rubbed his hands together to get the circulation going. Ten minutes.

The Willow Rooms was an excellent choice of target to begin the campaign, General George had lectured him. The deaths of a few harmless old ladies in these elegant surroundings would seem pointless and barbaric. The outrage would shock the public. That was exactly the intention. McInnes didn't seem to be able to get enough air to fill his lungs. He began to breathe through his mouth.

A round-faced lady from the group of four at the next table leaned back and nodded politely to him as their eyes met. He returned the gesture and looked away, hearing a quiet 'Good Morning' reach his ears like a whispered confidence. He had never actually killed anyone before. The thin woman seemed to stare straight through him. Eight minutes.

The young couple got up to leave, paying their bill at the door. He was cutting it fine so that the customers who saw him would be the ones caught in the explosion. The waitress served his tea and scone. He poured himself a cup and tasted it. He cut the scone in half and buttered it. He looked out the window and wondered if General George was somewhere outside watching him, checking that he followed the detailed instructions to the letter. Six minutes.

McInnes got up, feeling in his pocket for the small can of paint spray. He walked to the door and back along the corridor to the men's toilet. He went in and saw himself in the mirror, supremely calm now, breathing slowly and deeply. This had to be done the first time, just the first time, so that there could be no case of mistaken identity. He twisted off the top of the can and sprayed the letter W three times on the shiny white tiles. The red paint ran in thin vertical streaks down from the fat overlapping lines. He snapped the top back on and put the can back in his pocket. Four minutes.

He left the toilet and turned unhurriedly to go down the stairs. Nobody called after him. The young couple who had left just before him were standing looking at a display of suitcases. He hesitated for a second but had no time to spare. They did not look round as he went past them and down to the ground floor and out into the street. The cold air greeted him. Two minutes.

He turned right, heading towards the city centre, losing himself in the bustling crowds, careful not to hurry too much and barge into people and thus make himself too noticeable, reluctant to go too far and miss the crucial moment. He wondered if the waitress would have realised he had gone by now. Perhaps she was standing over the table looking down at the cooling tea and the uneaten scone, trying to decide if she should find somebody to go into the toilet to see if he was all right. Perhaps the old ladies at the next table were worried about him. Perhaps their smiles had turned to frowns as they thought how he had been away for such a long time. For the first time he thought how the one who had smiled at him looked like an old primary-school teacher who had once belted him for stealing a pear from a girl's bag. He had never borne her a grudge about it, though.

The alarm on the watch on his wrist gave out a high-pitched squeal. The explosion behind him was deafening, hitting McInnes like a slap in the back of the head. Everybody around him stopped abruptly and turned to stare. He did the same. There was a rising cloud of black smoke with yellow flames licking round its base. Windows had been shattered all along the street. Broken glass pattered down onto the ground like crystal raindrops. People were lying on the ground. Others were staggering to their feet. Suddenly there was a single piercing scream and then a furious storm of shouting and crying. People began to run back along the street. Somebody said that there might be another bomb, and some people changed direction. McInnes slipped up a side street and kept heading for the city centre.

CHAPTER TEN

A bomb explosion killed at least eight people and horribly injured many more in the centre of Glasgow this morning.

Pedestrians in Sauchiehall Street were showered with flying glass when the front wall of the Willow Rooms, a famous first-floor tea-room and meeting place, disintegrated in the powerful blast.

A fire started in the building but was quickly brought under control by firemen who ignored the risk that other bombs might have been planted.

Detective Superintendent Bryan Leslie of Strathcylde Police said soon afterwards: 'We have reason to believe this incident was a deliberate act. These people were murdered.'

Glasgow Evening Times

Maria, the young Portuguese femme de ménage, had taken the girls out to play in the snow. That gave Renzo Demionscuk and his wife Barbel the freedom to have a belated breakfast in bed and as long a lie-in as possible. It was part of their farewell ritual whenever he was due to leave on a trip that was to see the completion of a contract. He liked it always to be the same, the two of them together in bed way beyond the usual time when everyone else in the city had risen. It amounted to a superstition with him. Since marrying he had never set out on a job without everything taking place exactly as he thought it should. He didn't want to leave any rows behind him, no unfinished arguments. When he left her and his daughters he wanted to be at peace with the world. If something happened to interrupt the pattern, he doubted very much if he would go ahead. But there had never been an interruption. Now there were less than two hours before the flight to London.

Demionscuk lay back on the pillows with his hands behind his head and watched Barbel get dressed in the darkened bedroom beside the window. The closed shutters striped her body with horizontal lines of bright daylight. As she moved, she looked like a computer-generated drawing. She pulled a pair of pants on over her wide buttocks and covered her large breasts with a bra that cut deeply into the flesh of her shoulders and back. She put on tights and a thick woollen dress that went over her head and bundled at her hips till she wriggled and smoothed it out with her hands to its full length. She sat at his side on the edge of the bed to put on her shoes. She leaned back and kissed him gently on the eyelids.

'No idea how long you will be this time?' she asked tentatively.

He shook his head. They hardly ever discussed his work, though Barbel was well aware of what it involved. Her own father and brother were also involved in the same business, but to a lesser degree. That was how they met in the first place. She kept up the myth in their circle of friends that he was a widely travelled business consultant, and simply preferred not to know the details of individual jobs he undertook. She rarely mentioned his work, even when they were alone, but always brought up the subject at the last moment when his departure was imminent. It was her way of showing her concern without continually pestering him; her way of letting him know that she would be thinking about him when he was gone. He had promised he would retire in a few years' time and get a respectable job, maybe buy a little business somewhere. But he hadn't really decided one way or the other yet.

'Is it a difficult one?' she asked with her lips against one eye so that he could not see.

'Not difficult,' he replied. 'Complicated. It is someone's idea of a clever trick, a joke almost, you might say.'

'You can handle it?'

'Yes. There is little danger for me.'

'For others there is danger?'

'They have provided me with a colleague. He is the one in danger.'

103

'He is a new man? To be trained?'

'No. He has crossed someone. He is dispensable.'

'Take care, my darling Cossack.'

'I will. Don't worry.'

'I must learn to drive; then I could drive you to the airport,' she said.

Barbel knew all she wanted to. She got off the bed and picked up the tray with the breakfast dishes from the floor. 'Maria will be back soon with the girls,' she said. 'You do not have much time.'

He rose the moment she was out of the room and wrapped a towel round his waist to go through to wash in the bathroom. He splashed plenty of cold water on his face to rinse the tiredness out of his eyes. He shaved and cleaned his teeth and looked at himself in the mirror, pulling down the loose skin beneath his eyes to see the dull red lining on the underside. He squirted anti-perspirant under his arms and dusted himself down with talcum powder. His clothes were laid out for him when he got back to the bedroom. Two suitcases were already packed. It took him only a few minutes to dress and brush his hair. He pulled the shutter back and blinked in the avalanche of light.

Maria had returned. He had ten minutes to spare to play with his sleepy-eyed daughters while Barbel filled his toilet bag and squeezed it into one of the cases, checking that he had not forgotten anything. Then he kissed his wife and family-goodbye without another word and went down in the lift and out into the freezing winter morning. He shivered and walked quickly to Place Churchill to collect his car.

Murray Tarrant was waiting for him at the hotel, sitting in the Terrace Café watching the street through the huge plate-glass window. He drank his coffee too quickly when he saw Demionscuk get out of the car, scalding the roof of his mouth, and hurried round to meet him as he came in at the front door.

'*Moiën*, Renzo. That's Luxembourgish for G'day, Sport,' he said. 'Thought I'd show you I haven't been wasting my time here.'

Demionscuk did not say anything. His eyes passed over Tarrant, barely acknowledging his existence. He turned and walked out.

'G'day yourself, Murray my son,' Tarrant said quietly as he followed him out to the car. He threw his bags in the back and climbed into the passenger seat. Demionscuk drove towards the airport. Tarrant sat whistling softly. Snow was beginning to fall.

The big grey suitcase was heavy, and dragged awkwardly against his leg as Sandy McInnes made his way along the platform to the waiting train. It was full of old newspapers, carefully packed round the two Christmas-paper-wrapped bombs to hold them steady in the centre. The train was due to leave for Edinburgh on the half hour. The bombs were set to blow in thirty-five minutes.

McInnes felt strange. The initial surge of elation at the success of the operation earlier in the day had slowly faded, to be replaced by a curiously detached sense of disquiet. It had all gone so well, so absolutely according to plan. He had done exactly what he was supposed to do, exactly what he had been told to do. Yet, for the first time, he was experiencing doubts about his actions. He could not get out of his mind the image of the smiling, round-faced old woman who had wished him such a friendly good-morning. She had been sitting with her friends, sipping tea, enjoying herself in a simple fashion. And he had blown her apart, incinerated her flesh and bones, ended her long life in a single explosive instant. She would have died with the warm tea still in her throat and the smile still on her face. She had threatened no one, harmed no one. That had been the point of the exercise, of course. That was why McInnes had done it; hit the softest of targets to provoke the severest of reactions. That was the idea, and it had worked perfectly. Absolutely perfectly.

He chose the second of the four carriages that made up the train, standing back to allow two young girls to enter, then mounting the step and going in through the open door after them. The metal bars of the two luggage shelves beyond the interior sliding door were dented and scratched, and empty except for an orange rucksack and two small hold-alls. He placed the suitcase on the lower shelf and shoved it back against the wall. Somebody bumped into him as they tried to squeeze past. He ignored the apology that was offered, and began to walk down the carriage. Talk to no one, General George had said. Just plant the suitcase and walk away from it. Casual as you like.

It was a busy train. Most of the seats arranged in facing pairs were already taken. People looked up at him; old faces and young faces, male and female. At the first table he had to lean sideways to let a man pass in the narrow central corridor. His hand rested on a couple of glossy magazines. The top one slipped off, making him lose his balance and fall a little to the side. A woman was sitting in the corner seat with her back to the partition, facing the direction of travel. She was a middle-aged woman in a red coat and white-framed glasses. 'Sorry,' she said, smiling politely as she took both magazines off the table and put them on her lap.

'Sorry,' McInnes mumbled nervously as he straightened up and hurried along to the end of the carriage. His dismounted and began to walk back along the platform towards the main concourse. A last-minute rush of people was climbing aboard. A few, like him, were going in the opposite direction. He glanced in the window of the carriage. The woman was reading her magazine unconcernedly. A younger woman had taken the seat next to her and was tugging at her hair with a brush. Railway staff were slamming the doors shut. The sounds made hollow echoes under the barn-like glass roof of the station. McInnes reached the front end of the platform and turned to watch the train leave. It sat there with steam rising between it and the edge of the platform, billowing up and into the high empty space above it. Ahead of it in the darkness there was a confusion of red and green lights apparently floating in mid-air. A final late passenger ran to the last carriage and climbed aboard. The train still did not move. McInnes looked at his watch. It was already three minutes late. He walked to the ticket office and back again. The train was still there, with the smudged faces of the passengers invisible behind the pale lighted windows. It didn't matter, he told himself. Just go away. It can blow up while it is sitting in the station, if it likes. It doesn't matter. The idea had been for this to happen while it was moving at speed. More spectacular that way, General George had said; more dramatic. But it didn't matter. It really didn't matter.

The arrival of another train was announced over the loud-speakers. It pulled into the parallel track, spilling its pas-sengers out onto the concrete of the platform before it finally stopped. McInnes stood with his arms folded over his chest, staring past them, watching his train, thinking that maybe the police had been tipped off and were preventing it from leaving. Perhaps they were on board at this moment search-ing it for the bomb ... No. That was stupid. They surely wouldn't keep all those people on board as well. Or maybe they had already disarmed it and were watching him, waiting him to lead them back to the mastermind.

He looked at his watch again. Twelve minutes beyond its normal departure time. What was causing the hold-up? When he looked up, the train was moving. Thank God for that, he thought, as he turned and walked out of the station.

The train nosed out from beneath the protection of the station roof into the freezing winter's afternoon. It entered the long tunnel, travelling at a slow speed, and then out and through Cowlairs junction, where it shook a little from side to side as it crossed the lines to get onto its proper track. From there it rapidly picked up speed.

'Good afternoon. This is your guard speaking.' The inter-com system made him sound like a friendly robot. 'Welcome aboard the four-thirty Glasgow-to-Edinburgh express, stop-ping at Falkirk High, Linlithgow, Haymarket and Edinburgh Waverley. We hope you have a pleasant journey. Light refreshments will be available on trolley service. Please have your tickets ready for inspection.'

The passengers could see only their own reflections in the windows, and the city lights speckled all round them. The heaters blew warm air round their legs, making most of them drowsy, as they raced east past Bishopbriggs and Lenzie and Croy and out into the countryside where the lights were much more thinly spaced.

After twenty minutes the train began to slacken speed. Some people stood up, preparing to get off. When the guard spoke again in his metallic voice the woman in the red coat looked up at the ceiling from the magazine she was reading, and took off her glasses to rest her eyes.

'We will shortly be arriving at Falkirk High. Falkirk High.'

The brakes began to take a firm hold and the train shuddered. The woman in the red coat saw the lights of the station. The long-haired girl beside her was alseep. The man opposite was engrossed in a crossword. She closed her eyes and leaned back against the head-rest of her seat, thinking how good it would be to get home. Behind her the suitcase on the luggage shelf slipped fractionally sideways as the train stopped with a slight bump. Then the bomb exploded.

McInnes was waiting at traffic-lights when the alarm on his wristwatch squealed. He slapped at it nervously to turn it off as the lights changed to green. His car jerked and stalled. He cursed and tried to start the engine quickly. The driver behind him sounded his horn loudly. On the third turn of the ignition key the engine burst into life. He put his foot down and accelerated away just as the lights changed back to red.

Antonia Edwards adjusted the round pedestal mirror on the dressing-table until she was satisfied it was no longer reflecting the glare of the lights in the room. She leaned closer and her eye, magnified by the glass, almost filled the circle. She pressed her tongue lightly against her top teeth. The make-up brush made a tiny plopping noise as it came out of its bottle. She carefully began to apply mascara to her right eyelash.

'What's the matter with you tonight?' she said.

On the bed Christopher Edwards was lying on his side, propped up on one elbow, flicking rapidly through one of his wife's magazines. The coloured pages were a fast-moving blur he made no attempt to read or make sense of. He kept doing it again and again, running his thumb over the thick wedge of pages so that they blew a cold draught up into his face. The smell of the printed paper invaded his nostrils, inspiring vague memories of being at the back of a church while incense burners smoked on the altar in the distance. But all he could think of was how everything had happened that day exactly as Mortimer had told him it would. Twenty dead, they were saying now. Eight at the Glasgow tea-rooms and twelve on the train. At least twenty. The final total would probably be higher. Their blood was splashing onto Wallace's hands. He was already being blamed for both incidents. Mortimer had done well. There was just one more day to go as it had been planned. Wallace would be running round like a chicken with its head cut off. One more day, then it would be the end of the first phase and he could relax for a time.

'Are you listening to me, Chris?'

'What? Of course. What is it, darling?'

He stood up suddenly and brushed the creases from his dinner suit and checked that his bow-tie was on straight. He noticed a piece of broken nail on his thumb and began to nibble at it. Against his lips the loose bit felt huge, but when he tried to pick at it with the fingers of his other hand it was almost invisible.

'I said, what's the matter with you tonight?'

'The matter with me?' he repeated awkwardly. 'Nothing is the matter with me, darling. Should there be?'

The last thing he wanted was to make people think there was something the matter with him. What was happening, was happening hundreds of miles away, in Scotland. It did not really concern him. Why should it? Of course it interested him intellectually, as it would any other politician or follower of contemporary events. He had predicted that the National-ist code of non-violence was only a thin veneer, had he not? And, of course, the loss of life saddened him, but he would lose no sleep over it. This type of thing was all too common. He had always suspected that the Jocks would start fighting amongst themselves if they were ever allowed to run their own affairs. Now they were fighting before they even got that chance.

He finally got a proper hold of the piece of rag nail with his teeth and pulled it away with a jerk. It split off cleanly, run-ning round the curve of the edge and right down into the flesh of his thumb before separating. A tiny speck of scarlet blood appeared and quickly transformed itself into a round, bloated drop that shivered like a jelly and then began to run back round the edge of the nail. Edwards put the thumb in his mouth and sucked it dry. The blood of twenty people, he thought, and when he swallowed the saliva at the back of his throat he almost choked. When he removed his thumb the blood gathered again just as quickly, and he had to suck it again to stop it dripping.

'It's just that you're usually nagging me to hurry up around this time,' Antonia said, moving on to the left eyelash. 'You know how you hate to be late for things.'

'Plenty of time, darling,' Edwards said, looking at his watch without registering the time. 'We'll get there in the end.'

'It's not like you, Chris. Besides, you always said that Wagner gave you a headache. So how come you're so desperate to go to Covent Garden tonight?'

Her hands were working busily as she spoke, finishing with the mascara and then dusting some powder on her cheeks, applying some light-pink lipstick and then dabbing perfume on her neck and behind her ears. She was wearing a dark blue evening dress with narrow straps, like prominent veins, running over her shoulder. Her newly-washed hair shone. Each strand seemed to stand out individually. Edwards stood behind her looking down on the performance, assuming that her question was rhetorical and required no answer. He just did not want to sit at home in Kent. He needed to get out, to be seen among people, even if it was long after the event. He thought it was perhaps a primitive urge to provide himself with an alibi so that he could say, if anyone asked, that it couldn't have been him ... I wasn't there that night. We were in London at our Kensington apartment. We went out to Covent Garden, actually. It couldn't have been me. Just ask several hundred people. They all saw me ... All he could think of was getting to the opera. Even if he did hate Wagner he could surely stand it for one night. The headache was already there, anyway. He took his thumb out of his mouth and looked at it. The blood welled up round the side of the fingernail more slowly this time. The small patch of skin was stained the colour of his wife's lipstick. Her fingernails were painted the same shade.

Antonia got up and almost bumped into him. He stepped back hurriedly and went to fetch their coats.

'Well?' she said. 'Why the sudden passion for Wagner?'

'No particular reason,' he mumbled. 'Wagner's not all bad.'

'Go on. Why don't you admit the truth?'

Edwards felt a shock of surprise and anxiety spread outwards from his chest as if he had been punched in the heart. She couldn't possibly know or guess. He had been so careful. He had covered his tracks. He had calculated and minimised every risk. Antonia did not know. She could not know.

'Go on. Admit it.'

If she had somehow found out, he thought, she must approve of his actions. She was smiling at him. He might have misjudged her. Her eyes were twinkling. She slipped on her full-length fur coat and the surface rippled as if the minks themselves were still alive and swarming all over her body.

'What?' he said.

'Admit that you just want to go out on the town with your wife, you conventional old devil, you.'

The second shock he felt was one of relief. Antonia took his arm and kissed him on his hair so as not to leave a lipstick mark.

'I admit it,' he said quickly, tucking his white scarf inside the lapels of his coat. 'Let's go.'

He licked the last of the blood from his thumb. The bleeding had stopped.

CHAPTER ELEVEN

A terrorist group supposedly supporting the cause of the Scottish Nationalist Party has been blamed for two explosions which resulted in the deaths of twenty-two people today. Fifty other people are in hospital, many with serious injuries.

The We're With Wallace campaign is a shadowy organisation whose previous activities have been confined to anonymous threatening letters to various newspapers and the defacing of road signs.

Strathclyde Police tonight confirmed that the group's symbol, three interlinked letter Ws, had been found at the scene of the first explosion in Glasgow.

BBC Radio

Robert Shand thumped his fist down hard on the table, making the carafe of water in the centre jump on the polished surface. The glass tumbler upturned over its top rang like a cracked bell.

'For Christ's sake, Andrew,' Shand shouted, red-faced. 'If I knew who these bastards were, do you think I'd be sitting here? I'd be breaking heads for the stupidity of it.'

'I know, Bobby. I know. I'm not accusing you of hiding anything from me, but we've got to go through all the possibilities ourselves. You can rest assured we won't be the only ones doing it.'

Shand subsided a little, leaning against the back of his seat and breathing through tightly-closed teeth. Wallace had already gone through the angry phase, and had done his shouting at Hamish Henryson when he had arrived at the Party headquarters. Now he had regained his self-control and was trying to analyse the situation as objectively as he could.

They were in his room, with the blinds pulled down over both windows. The antique furnishing and ornately-framed oil paintings were a legacy from the company that had occupied these premises in Edinburgh's George Street before the Party had taken them over.

Shand thumped the table again and Wallace reached out to remove the glass from the top of the carafe. In the outer offices the level of noise was gradually increasing as more and more people arrived for the Press conference that had been called.

'It's so fucking stupid,' Shand said, emphasising the words with sharp nods of his head. 'Fucking stupid.'

'We know nobody that is capable of this, do we?'

Shand did not look up from his hands, which were poised with only their fingertips on the table. 'Not a soul,' he replied. 'All our lunatics are stuck at the claymore stage. This is light years ahead of them.'

'Is it even remotely conceivable that one of ours could be involved in some way?'

'Nothing is impossible, I suppose. We should have done more to find out about this We're With Wallace campaign before now. I thought it was just harmless stuff, just kids spray-painting graffiti.'

'We all thought that, Bobby. Maybe that is the way it started out. Maybe one kid got a little too clever for his own good.'   .

'He couldn't do this on his own. *No one* has done this on his own. The bombs are too sophisticated and there is a plan to it all. It's not just one and run. There were two. Who knows how many more?'

'Four altogether. That means another two.'

Shand was startled. His whole body jerked as though hit by an elecric shock. 'How do you know that?'

'The note that was sent to all the newspapers earlier this week. It said four blows for freedom. I think we may have had two, with another two to come.'

'My God,' Shand said. 'I thought it was a bloody joke. Is it as definite as that?'

'Hamish is getting a copy for us to look over just now.'

'Some bloody joke. I don't hear anybody laughing.'

113

Wallace sighed and massaged his forehead. He got up from the table and went to the window. He pushed the edge of the blind aside and looked down on the frozen street. He imagined he could feel the coldness of the air beyond the thin pane of glass, in contrast to the warmth that surrounded him. People outside were staring up at the building, pointing and talking. A large estate car drew up at the door. The occupants got out and hurriedly began to lug their camera equipment across the pavement and up the entrance steps.

'The tragedy is that it is all so unnecessary.' Shand was still sitting at the table, still staring at his hands. 'We were going along so well. Now this will encourage the faint-hearts to spread their gospel of despair. This could finish us.'

Wallace walked away from the window as Henryson came into the room holding a blue plastic folder in one hand and a single sheet of paper in the other. He held the paper up in front of him and began to read.

'"It will begin in Glasgow and there will be four blows for freedom."' He handed the photocopied sheet to Wallace. 'I knew it was something like that. They've all got copies of it out there, and they are ready for you now, Andrew. It would be best to get it over with so we can get our view across on the television news programmes tonight. The BBC want you in the Queen Street studio for Newsnight at ten-thirty.'

Shand came over and stood beside Wallace, and they both looked at the piece of paper. The three Ws at the top were much darker than the typed message underneath. They read it over in silence together, then Shand took it to read it again by himself.

'This is no prank by some clever kids,' he said finally. 'There is more to it than that. It has been too well planned.'

'I agree,' Wallace said. 'The only problem is that they're not with us at all. They're acting against us.'

'God knows what the next two blows are going to be,' Shand said. 'Are you sure this Press conference is a good idea, Andrew? Why don't we just issue a denial of any involvement and leave it at that? I hate playing the media's games.'

'The day we start running away from the Press is the day we can all give up hope. Besides, if I can make a direct appeal to these idiots, maybe we can pacify them, stop them before

114

wider Nationalist movement which has over the years proved itself to be committed to constitutional change by democratic means alone.

'The use of violence of this sort, indiscriminate violence against innocent people, must be repugnant to any thinking person, and can only hinder the true Nationalist cause.

'If the group responsible for today's bombings believe themselves to be Nationalists, then they are sadly misguided and mistaken.'

Wallace remained standing, watching as the faces which had been lowered to follow his words on the hand-outs moved in a single wave to look up at him. The heat from the lights was making him sweat. There was a burst of activity as some reporters left the room to meet early deadlines. Everybody suddenly spoke at once, and it took a few moments for one voice to establish itself over the others and ask the first comprehensible question.

'Mr Wallace, you say you had no knowledge of this group, and yet you must be aware of the letters received by many newspapers earlier this week detailing its aims and objectives?'

'Of course. I regret that because we had no knowledge we did not take the letters seriously at that time.'

'But is it not the case,' said the same questioner, 'that the symbol of the three Ws has been appearing on walls and posters and road signs all over Scotland in the last few months?'

'It is. However, I'm sure you'll agree that the cold-blooded murder of innocent bystanders is more likely to merit the concentrated attention of the police than is the defacing of a few road signs.'

Another questioner jumped in. 'The letter talks of four blows for freedom, Mr Wallace. Does that mean we have still to suffer another two blows?'

Wallace closed his eyes for a few seconds. 'You are as capable of drawing conclusions from the message as the next man,' he said. 'I can only hope the obvious conclusion is the wrong one.'

There was confusion for a few seconds, then a strident female voice imposed itself. 'Do you have absolutely no idea who these people might be, Mr Wallace? They have named their group after you, and they do claim to support the same objective.'

Wallace stared into the lights and waited until there was complete silence. 'These people may use my name,' he said quietly, so that his audience strained to hear the words. 'That does not mean they are with me, as they put it, or with any other member of the Party. They do not share the same objective, because our objective is to achieve independence by peaceful means. We have a political problem in Scotland, not a military one. There can be absolutely no justification for the killing of any human beings in any attempt to solve that problem.'

'Does that mean your country is not worth fighting for?' somebody shouted from the rear.

'That is the kind of vacuous and asinine remark that shows a breathtaking ignorance of the political situation here.' Wallace was aware of the anger in his voice, like the serrated edge of a very sharp knife. The Press cameras started clicking again to capture his changed mood. 'Twenty-two people have died today, and I am finding it increasingly difficult to keep my temper under control when faced with such a display of insensitivity and crass stupidity.'

You haven't answered my question,' the anxious voice insisted, breaking a little as it rose in pitch. The other reporters turned to see who it was. Wallace glimpsed a mop of untidy hair, fat squirrel cheeks, and a protruding stomach. 'Does what you are saying mean Scotland is not worth fighting for?'

'What I am saying is that the fight in Scotland is a political fight, not a military one. Violent opposition to the existing government is pointless, because we already hold the keys to success. Our weapons do not draw blood. Our weapons are the arguments we advance and the votes we win. The people are to be persuaded — not intimidated, not frightened, not forced, not threatened, not bullied. The people are to be persuaded that the best hope for their future is the Nationalist Party. There is nothing to stop us doing that, and there is no way in a democratic society we can be stopped. We believe we are winning the struggle to persuade the people. To start

118

blowing up innocent people and somehow try to make out that it is in the interests of the SNP is ludicrous, weak-minded and illogical.'

Shand was on his feet beside him, aggressively jabbing the air with a forefinger. 'I resent the implication that the Party is involved in or somehow approves of what has happened today,' he shouted. 'Our opponents have not been slow to make political capital out of it, and that is almost as loathsome to me as the acts of terrorism themselves.'

Wallace patted him on the shoulder and they both sat down together. Shand has his hands balled into tight fists. Henryson gently kicked Wallace in the ankle, urging him to end the Press conference as soon as possible.

'But, Andrew, you can't be one hundred per cent certain that SNP members were not involved.'

'Of course I can't, Willie,' Wallace said, changing his tone in response to a familiar face in the front row. 'All I can say is that if you look at our track record you will be hard pushed to find any evidence of violent tendencies. This kind of thing is totally alien.'

'But they call themselves "We're With Wallace" and they claim to be on your side.'

'They can call themselves what they like. They are neither with me nor on my side. If they are somehow linked to the Party, I disown them here and now. I wash my hands of them but, having done that, I do plead with them not to repeat the outrages that have already sickened the public so much. For God's sake, enough is enough.'

'Are you making a direct plea to the bombers?'

'I'll make a direct plea to Auld Nick himself if it saves just one innocent life.'

A new questioner stood up to speak. 'If these bombs are so blatantly against the interests of the Nationalists, would it be fair to speculate that they might have been planted by opponents keen to have the blame put on the SNP so as to detract from any political successes that have been made recently?'

'That is a possibility but it is not for me to speculate one way or the other. All I know is that these bombs have exploded, and twenty-two people have died. Whoever is responsible, whatever the motive, they must be hunted down and punished. That is a job for the police.'

There was another barrage of competing questions before a single one emerged from the pack. 'The very success of the Nationalists in recent years could be held responsible for today's bombings, could it not?'

Wallace stood up once more, holding Bobby Shand down as he did so. He waited for silence, establishing his authority over the crowd. Ten seconds passed. The sweat was trickling down the small of his back. The reporters began to fidget uncomfortably under his steady gaze.

'No,' he said finally. 'What blame can there be in adhering to principles you believe in? You can't just stop believing in those principles because of the irresponsible actions of unknown people.'

'But does not your campaign for independence encourage the men of violence to think they are helping you?'

'It most certainly does not,' Wallace said, feeling Henryson's warning nudge against his leg. 'Since becoming leader of this Party I have made it entirely clear that independence can and will be achieved by purely democratic means. That is the raison d'être of the Party — its sole aim. We have never been, and never will be, a front for any organisation or grouping that seeks to flout the democratic process.'

'That all sounds very reasonable, but the wild men do not often listen to reason, and is it not you who have let them out of their cage?'

'I repeat that acts of violence can only harm the Nationalist cause,' Wallace said slowly. 'I cannot make it any clearer than that.'

'But your opinion may . . .'

'Ladies and gentlemen,' Wallace interrupted, keenly aware that he was very close to losing his temper, 'if you will excuse me, I am afraid I must bring this meeting to a close. Thank you for your attendance.'

The crowd closed in on the three of them as they made for the door. Cameras flashed. Microphones were shoved in front of Wallace's face. More questions were shouted. He ignored them, clutching Henryson's arm to protect the old man from the worst of the crush, and following Shand as he barged his way unceremoniously out of the room. They escaped into the relative quiet of the office, where Sandra had laid out coffee and sandwiches.

'What did I tell you?' Shand said. 'Crows. Bloody hoodie crows pecking at our vitals.'

Henryson stood tapping the hearing-aid behind his ear. 'This thing isn't working properly,' he said. 'I couldn't make out all the questions, but I think Andrew gave as good as he got.'

'He gave them a few withering looks,' Shand admitted. 'You should have made more of that guy asking if it might all be a con trick by our opponents to discredit us.'

Wallace was at the window, holding back the edge of the blind to watch the exodus from the front door. 'And suppose it turns out to be some of our own wild men?' he said without looking round.

'Do you think it might be?'

'I hope not, but I think it's better to wait until we have a surer idea before making any accusations.'

'Two more, remember,' Henryson said. 'Two more to come.'

'God, yes.' Wallace turned back into the room. 'They are either very stupid or very clever. Two more blows for freedom and each one will put it that little bit further out of our reach.'

A couple of bottles of fine wine with a big Chinese meal bought from the local carry-out shop was the way Major George Mortimer decided to celebrate the successful first day of his carefully-prepared campaign. McInnes was sent out for the food just before midnight, and on returning he sat in sullen silence on the opposite side of the table in the living-room, stuffing himself with fried rice. The Scots did have their uses, Mortimer thought, but he never would really understand them as a race. He watched McInnes curiously, feeling the mixture of pity and contempt that all good soldiers reserve for collaborators. It was no great pleasure to be forced to kill innocent people, but when it was necessary, such things had to be done. In the situation that existed there was no alternative. Hands had to be got dirty. Blood had to be spilled. Soldiers should always know the score, even when they didn't wear a uniform.

'Cheer up, Sandy,' he coaxed. 'We are on the same side, you know. You did a damn good job today. You will find that we will not prove ungrateful. You have served your country well.'

McInnes twirled his fork in his fingers and did not look across at his companion. When he had got back from Queen Street station he had gone through General George's luggage while he was splashing about in the bathroom. There had been nothing to give away his real identity, apart from a set of car keys with the registration number written faintly in ball-point pen on the fob. Strange that: he had arrived by taxi, saying he had taken the train up from England. He might have parked the car close by but wanted to keep it a secret. Of course, he might just have left it at home. McInnes memorised the number and decided to get young Jimmy Menzies from the bottom flat to follow General George the next time he ventured outside, just to discover where he went. He had to go out some time.

The only other item of interest was a tiny wooden crucifix with the wounds on its Christ figure coloured with specks of bright red paint. A bloody Pape, McInnes thought. That explained a lot. He was puzzled by an old brown leather case with Major Magic written on the lid, but he did not get a chance to open it because the bathroom lock snapped over just at that point.

'The more dead bodies we make, the fewer people there will be to vote for Wallace,' McInnes said.

'So you have got a sense of humour, after all,' Mortimer said, reaching over to touch him on the shoulder. 'I knew there had to be a real person behind that dour exterior.'

McInnes smiled and started to pick food from some of the silver-foil containers spread over the table. Mortimer's hand dropped from his shoulder and lay lightly arched on the cloth like a fat pink crab stretching out from his shell. McInnes considered the strong desire he felt to stab at it with his fork, and he smiled again. Instead, he lifted some meat to his mouth. He was ravenously hungry, but no matter how much he ate he still felt hollow inside.

The entire front page of the evening paper was taken up by

a photograph of the blackened hole in the wall in Sauchiehall Street, with the headline OUTRAGE across the top. The railway disaster had happened too late for the newspapers, but the teatime radio and television news bulletins were full of it. Passengers told of a huge blast knocking the train from the rails and upending the carriages. A bomb seemed the only explanation. It was universally assumed that both explosions were linked, once the first one had been attributed to a bomb. When the fact emerged around six o'clock that the three Ws of the We're With Wallace organisation had been freshly painted in the toilet of the Willow Rooms, the culprit seemed to have been identified. Special programmes were hurriedly compiled and talking heads were produced to blame it all on the upsurge of nationalism in Scotland. An inevitable consequence of unleashing forces that nobody could control, they said. Andrew Wallace paraded in front of a rowdy Press conference he had called to try and dissociate himself and his Party from the tragic events. Later he appeared in the more sober environment of a television studio. Mortimer sat watching and listening intently, shouting out loud and thumping his fist into the palm of his hand at regular intervals. McInnes sat silently, chain-smoking and drinking whisky, watching his guest, and thinking that he agreed with most of the things Wallace was saying. The alcohol was having little effect on him. All it did was stop his hands trembling. The tobacco was like a cushion for his brain to rest on.

The wine Mortimer had brought was smooth and good. McInnes had drunk most of it, constantly topping up his own glass while the other man's remained virtually untouched. So it was not any excess of drink that had altered Mortimer's taciturn and reserved character so dramatically. He had become garrulous and animated. His eyes shone with a religious zeal. The Adam's apple in his throat bounced energetically against the wrinkled skin of his neck, like someone behind it frantically trying to punch their way out. He had completely lost his aura of authority and power. He had become a brittle shell which looked as if it would crumble to dust if poked with a finger. McInnes recognised a guilty conscience. It gradually dawned on him that the Englishman was having some difficulty in coming to terms with his part in

123

the deaths of all those people. True, he had made sure he kept himself well out of the way. He had led from the rear: issued his orders then kept his head down with his fingers in his ears. Now he seemed almost embarrassed by the outcome, although it was exactly what he had asked for.

McInnes himself was experiencing no particular feelings of guilt. He was sad that innocent people had to die, especially those two women — one in the tearoom and the other on the train. Their last smiles were forever frozen on the images he kept inside his head. But they were dead now, smiling away in Heaven or Hell. He had never killed anyone before. Now he had done so, and it was no big deal. Everybody had to die. McInnes made little distinction between the fleeting sadness that kept conjuring up the trusting faces of those two women and the weariness that made his shoulderblades ache with the effort of sitting upright. He imagined taping one of the Christmas paper bombs under the seat of Mortimer's chair and blowing the hypocritical bastard right through the roof.

'You don't know how lucky you are, getting this chance,' Mortimer said, blinking rapidly. 'You've picked the right side and you won't regret it. I'll see to that. I've got contacts, you know. Top people — high-level contacts. You can't get much higher. Oh no. Stick with me, Sandy. You'll be all right with me.'

McInnes did not say anything, but concentrated his full attention on selecting tiny morsels of food from the foil containers, alternately scooping up forkfuls of rice grown cold. Mortimer could not stop himself talking. He leaned closer over the table, lowering his voice.

'A future Prime Minister is one of our backers,' he confided. 'A man with a good pedigree, you could say. Ha, ha — an excellent pedigree. We are not cowboys or extremists, Sandy. We are securing the future. We have to be proud of what we are doing.'

He hesitated, running the tip of his finger round the rim of his wine glass. Glancing over to McInnes he saw him chewing slowly and rythmically like a docile bull. McInnes was not a big man, but at that moment he somehow gave the impression of tremendous strength and latent violence. That was what he was, Mortimer thought: a domesticated animal, content to be led by the nose, unaware of the tremendous power he possessed. Equally unaware of the powerlessness he could impose on those who sought to control him, by simply refusing to submit.

'Before I came up here to Scotland he wrote me a letter,' Mortimer said, anxious to share his little secret. It would not do any harm to tell McInnes — he probably would not recognise the significance of it. 'It wasn't really much of a letter, just a note offering encouragement, but it was there and it was signed by him, by our backer. He didn't have to do that. It was a dangerous thing to do, to put his signature down on paper. If it ever got out it could ruin him totally. Yet he had every confidence in me. He took the risk because he knew he could trust me. I appreciate that trust. So should you, Sandy. So should you.'

McInnes looked back at him for the first time in five minutes, his eyes large and sleepy, glazed over with too much alcohol. Mortimer waited for him to say something, but the man just stared dumbly. An animal, a docile animal, Mortimer thought again. He reached out and patted him on the arm.

'Are you going to be all right for tomorrow?' he asked. 'It's another big day tomorrow, remember.'

McInnes started to speak but had to swallow food and clear his throat before he could get the words out. 'I'll be just fine,' he said.

'I'd better get some tea made. Clear our heads, settle our stomachs. I don't know about you, but that meal is weighing me down.'

McInnes rubbed his stomach. It still felt empty. He put back his head to drain his glass of wine and it lined the inside of his mouth and throat, tasting vaguely like washing-up liquid. The room had grown very dark. The television flickered silently in a corner. Mortimer had been talking to himself rather than to an audience, making no attempt to ensure that he was properly heard or understood. McInnes was able to make out individual words, focusing on them as he would focus on a thread about to be passed through the eye of a needle.

Mortimer went away for a while, and came back with two

mugs of tea. It was strong and sweet and boiling hot.

'They told me to destroy the letter, the one from our backer, but I didn't. Do you know what I did with it?'

McInnes feigned indifference. Who was this important man, this future Prime Minister? Not the kind of person he would envy or admire or look up to. A clone of General George he would be, all mouth and no balls. Someone who would be your pal while it suited him, and then disown you the moment the going got tough. All his life McInnes had hated people in authority, any kind of authority. School-teachers, policemen, traffic wardens, park attendants. What the hell was he doing running errands for a future Prime Minister? Why was he doing the dirty work for some fat-arsed swine in a pinstripe suit shouting the odds from the safety of London? Fuck the bastard.

'Let me show you a trick,' Mortimer said.

He took a pen from the breast pocket of his jacket, and a paper napkin from the pile on the table. He put both things in front of McInnes and told him to write down his name. McInnes complied.

'Now watch carefully,' he said, picking up the napkin and folding it into a tight square which he held between finger and thumb. 'Now you see it . . .' He flicked his fingers and the paper disappeared inside his clenched fist. 'Now you don't.'

Mortimer grinned artificially and opened his hand again to reveal the slightly crushed square of paper lying on his palm. 'Is it the same one?' he asked, raising his eyebrows.

McInnes nodded, watching carefully to make sure that it was not switched at the last moment.

'Go on,' he said. 'Take it. See for yourself.'

McInnes took the napkin and unfolded it. He turned it over and over in surprise. There was no writing on it at all. 'How did you do that?' he demanded.

'Magic,' Mortimer replied smugly. 'It's one of my hobbies. What's this?'

He reached forward and seemed to take something from behind McInnes's ear, presenting in his palm another sheet of paper folded in an identical manner. McInnes snatched it and opened it out to find his name where he had written it a few minutes earlier.

'Ye must hae picked up two at wance,' McInnes said. 'Ye slipped wan up yir sleeve while ah wis writing.'

'It's easy to be wise after the event. If I hadn't shown you it, you would have been convinced the first one was the correct piece of paper, wouldn't you?'

'Ah suppose so,' McInnes admitted, trying hard not to be impressed.

'That was how I kept my letter,' Mortimer explained. 'They made me burn it in front of them but they didn't realise I was burning a blank piece of paper.'

'Whit does it say, this letter that is so important to you?'

'England expects me to do my duty.' Mortimer sat up suddenly as if he was going to salute. 'No more than I expect of myself.'

'Whit about me?' McInnes swallowed a rising belch that left an unpleasant taste on the back of his tongue.

'You too, Sandy. You too.'

'Whit's so special about this letter that ye hae tae keep it?'

'Don't you see?' Mortimer's eyes shone wetly with pride. 'It will be a priceless document when history comes to be written. It would have been sacrilege to destroy it. Remember, it is the winners who get to write the history.'

'I hope ye've got it in a safe place, then.'

'Oh yes. It's invisible. Would you like to see it?'

'What? Now? Go on then. Show me.'

Mortimer clamped his lips shut, thinking that maybe he had gone too far. He sucked in his upper lip, looked dramatically from side to side, then bowed his head forward. 'All right. Wait a minute. I'll go and get it.'

He left the room and returned a few moments later with the battered old suitcase McInnes had failed to open earlier. He thumbed open the catches and lifted the lid, pointing to the name written there. 'Major Magic,' he said proudly. 'That's me. Veteran of a thousand children's parties, and I've got the scars to prove it. I wear one of my old uniforms and they think it's great.'

'Ah thought ye were a general?'

'That's in a different world, Sandy. I'm a major in the world of make-believe. Watch carefully now.'

He took a black tube and a white tube out of the case,

displaying them so that McInnes could see that both were empty and open-ended He waved them about a bit, then placed the black one inside the white one, and when he pulled them apart it had changed to red. He did the same thing again and it came out blue.

'There is no need to applaud,' he said. 'This is all straight-forward stuff.'

Mortimer inserted the blue tube inside the white one again and showed it to McInnes, turning it over and over without letting him touch it.

'Empty?' he asked.

'Aye,' McInnes replied, fascinated in spite of himself.

'But, Sandy,' Mortimer said, 'the letter I was talking about is there. Can't you see it? Something wrong with your eyesight, is there?'

He held the white cardboard tube high up in front of his face and slowly drew out a rolled-up sheet of paper from the inside, pulling it free with an ostentatious flourish.

'How the fuck did ye dae that?' McInnes demanded.

'Magic, Sandy. I told you. Watch and I'll make it disappear again.'

He tapped the top of the piece of paper so that it gradually went back inside the tube, then handed it to McInnes. Once again all he could see was the smooth interior. There was so sign of the paper, no matter from what angle he went at the thing.

'Whaur is it?' he asked, shaking his head.

'In a safe place,' Mortimer replied.

'Ye're not going to show me yir bloody letter, then?'

'Sandy. Sandy. You know I can't do that.' Mortimer's tone was one of infinite patience. 'It is signed, and you know the no-names rule. No names. No names. No one but me in the Forum knows your name, Sandy. Not a soul, I assure you. And you don't need to know anybody else's name. It is best that way for all of us. It would be far too dangerous any other way.'

'Wouldn't it just,' McInnes murmured under his breath.

'Let me show you another trick,' Mortimer said quickly, pulling back his sleeves, producing a pack of cards from the case, and fanning them out. 'Take a card, any card.'

McInnes chose one of the red-backed card from the centre and laid it face-down on the table without looking at it.

'Bet I can tell you what it is,' Mortimer said.

'So tell me.'

'The nine of diamonds.'

McInnes raised a corner of the card with his thumb and tilted his head to one side. 'How the fuck did ye ken that?' he said, flipping it over.

'Magic, I told you, Sandy. Magic.' Mortimer winked and laughed. 'Care to try again?'

McInnes took another card, sliding it out of the pack and raising the corner. 'Hey, it's the bloody nine of diamonds again,' he protested.

Mortimer turned over the cards to show that they were all different. He took the card back from McInnes and pushed it into the centre of the pack, shuffling them rapidly and pouring them in a long stream from hand to hand before offering McInnes another choice. He could hardly believe it when he pulled out the nine of diamonds for the third time.

'It's magic, Sandy,' Mortimer said, gloating. 'I have you in my power.'

CHAPTER TWELVE

The mask slipped from the respectable face of Scottish nationalism yesterday to reveal a face of barbaric savagery.

Twenty-three people have died horrifically as a result of two cowardly bombings. Fifty-eight lie maimed and crippled in hospitals in the North.

Mr Wallace almost had us convinced that his Party was a civilised one, untainted by the violent psychopaths, so familiar elsewhere, whose aim is to achieve power at any cost.

Mr Wallace said his people would abide by the democratic process. Mr Wallace said he was in control. Mr Wallace said his Party was an example to every other nationalist movement in the world.

Yesterday's evil deeds tell a different story and Mr Wallace, though innocent of any physical involvement, must bear full responsibility for the carnage which springs from his fine words.

Daily Mail

Behind the high railings and the mature trees, the gardens in the centre of Charlotte Square in Edinburgh had a deep and even covering of virgin snow. White caterpillars of frozen snow lay the full length of bare branches swaying gently in the wind. The façades of the high Georgian buildings looked down on every side. Everything was grey and black and white apart from the multicoloured cars, like a gaudy fringe to a blanket, nosed up against the raised pavement surrounding the central island. Traffic constantly circulated on the wide road, exhaust fumes ballooning out into the cold air. Pedestrians were numerous on the south side of the square, mostly standing in shuffling bus queues, and on the west around its junction with George Street and where it led down to Princes Street. The other two sides were relatively empty.

Sandy McInnes had driven through from Glasgow that morning and gone round and round the square for more than twenty minutes before he finally managed to get a parking space when somebody reversed out in front of him just as he was passing. It was on the north side, just where he wanted to be. General George had been adamant he had to choose a target on that side. He had repeated his instructions that morning while McInnes was nursing a terrible hangover. It must have been the wine, he decided. He wasn't used to good wine. Nonetheless, he was now sitting in the ideal spot. If he wanted to, he could set the timing device and sit with the bomb in his lap until it blew. That would have the desired effect and solve all his problems. He would never have to listen to the Englishman's grating accent again. He would never have another headache, never have to worry where his next drink or his next meal was coming from. That would certainly be one way of annoying General George.

McInnes remained inside his car fiddling idly with the Christmas-paper-wrapped package he held in his hands. The windows quickly misted up. He was aware of the car beside him pulling out of its space and being immediately replaced by another one. He slid a finger under the fold at the end of one of the packages and prised the piece of sellotape loose. The red paper sprang up and he peeled it apart, being careful not to tear it, to reveal the column of push buttons under the thick layer of polythene. How long should he give himself, he wondered? General George had said ninety minutes, so perhaps he should make it two hours. But then one hour would be more than enough time to get over the Forth Bridge and be well out of the way. He pressed two buttons and two yellow lights appeared. He pressed the larger button at the foot and a red light glowed. He pressed it again and all the lights went out.

A tap on the car window startled him. He saw an indistinct profile through the condensation as he hurriedly shoved the bomb out of sight below the newspapers on the passenger seat where he had been reading about his exploits. There was nothing he could do but open the window and see what was wanted. It was probably a traffic warden. He had to brazen it out.

She was a young woman, probably younger than him but he was hopeless at guessing women's ages. She had short, curly dark hair and strawberry red patches of colour on her cheeks. The bottom half of her face was hidden behind a dark-coloured scarf, emphasising the size and roundness of her eyes. Green eyes. Like a cat. He thought she was looking at him as a cat watches a trapped bird. The car behind her was green too. She couldn't be a warden, though. She was wearing a long dark coat. No uniform.

'Excuse me,' she said and the skin around her eyes wrinkled a little as she smiled behind the scarf. 'I wonder if you could change a five-pound note? I have very little change on me and I need to get tickets for the full two hours. Can you help, by any chance?'

McInnes was glad to help. He searched through his pockets and produced large amounts of small change. General George had given him plenty of money to see him through the day and he had broken one of the fivers when he had stopped at Harthill on the motorway, for the newspapers and a cup of coffee to take the edge off his hangover. The woman thanked him. He wound up the window and wiped the windscreen clear, and watched her clamber over the mound of frozen snow to go to the ticket machine against the railings and come back to her car. She leaned inside for a few moments and then stood up straight. She climbed back onto the pavement and turned to pull down her scarf and mouthed something to McInnes where he sat in his car. He thought she might be blowing him a kiss. She turned on her heel and walked away. Three women now, he thought. One at each place. He frowned and rubbed the cold spot on his cheek where he imagined the kiss would have landed. Did it mean something?

When she was out of sight, he acted quickly. Two hours, she had said, so he set the timer on the bomb for one hour and sealed the Christmas paper again. He had a roll of insulating tape and intended to fasten the package under the rear wheel arch, but when he opened his door he noticed that the back window of her car had been left slightly open, just

132

enough to take it. One step outside was enough to enable him to reach the window. He pushed the package through the slot and saw it fall onto the back seat among a scattered array of children's books and toys. Merry Christmas, he whispered to himself.

His headache was worse than ever when he started up the engine and reversed out of the space to join the flow of traffic. At once another car filled it behind him.

Andrew Wallace sat with his feet on the desk, staring up at the dirty white sky with his eyes focused in the middle distance. His mind was wandering, alternately creating good and bad scenarios of how the latest turn of events might eventually work out. Logic pushed him towards the bad outcome, optimism urged him towards the good. It was hot in the room. The central heating had been turned up full, amd he had taken off his tie and rolled up his shirtsleeves. He had given himself two hours to clear all the routine paperwork, but had finished it in one. Life went on. He should really have called Sandra in, because he knew she would not interrupt him unnecessarily until the deadline was up, and there was still plenty of other work to be done on the preparations for the New York trip on Saturday. And Graham Turnbull wanted to discuss how the Press should be handled in the changed circumstances. Wallace was tired, and finding it immensely difficult to concentrate on anything for more than a few minutes at a time. He had refused to give any more interviews until he was clear in his own mind about exactly what was going on. He had spent all night at the Party offices, unwilling to go over to the flat by himself since Helen was not there, desperately wishing it was Friday night so that he could go and join her at the cottage. She had offered to come back from Argyll but he had talked her out of it. There was nothing she could do. He would join her tomorrow, he told her. It might actually be quite useful to take himself out of circulation, anyway.

He had slept fitfully, unable to control his thoughts and shake off the feelings of guilt that would not leave him alone. The morning newspapers had not been kind. Now, as he daydreamed lethargically, he was virtually sleeping with his eyes open. The frame of the window merged with the featureless whiteness of the sky, so that he was seeing nothing. When a dark line suddenly sliced across his field of vision he thought it was just a temporary hallucination. Only when it remained there, as annoying as a piece of grit on his eyeball, did he begin to take notice of it.

The explosion ripped the rear of the green car apart. The main force shot upwards through the thin metal of the roof, and outwards through the back of the seat and the boot. The front of the car lurched and then sagged forward with the bumper touching the ground, largely unmarked except for the shattered windscreen and the doors flapping open at the sides like elephant's ears. The shock-wave of the blast broke every window in the overlooking buildings on the north side of the square. There were no pedestrians in the immediate vicinity and only a single passing car, which was knocked onto its side so that it skidded into the high kerb and bounced off to end up back on its wheels again with the driver looking round in astonishment, blood streaming down his face. The debris rained down, dislodging showers of frozen snow from overhanging branches, and pockmarking an area of the untouched blanket of snow in the central gardens. In front of the Roxburghe Hotel a woman fell to the ground clutching her leg. On the other side of the George Street junction a man carefully put his briefcase down on the pavement and then collapsed, holding his head.

The rear axle had been torn loose from the green car. Rolling on its shredded tyres as if it was following a predetermined route, it left a trail of burning petrol along the road and round the corner onto North Charlotte Street, where it quickly gathered speed and careered away down the hill.

Wallace became aware of the crack appearing in the glass in the same instant he heard the sound of the explosion. He sat still, too stunned to move, for a few seconds, then jumped to his feet and went to the window. He could see nothing from there except people standing and staring or running along the street. He ran out of the room. Sandra was standing in the lobby unaccountably looking up at the ceiling.

'What was it?' she asked.

He shook his head and went past her and down the stairs and out into the street, running with the crowds. It was less than one hundred yards to Charlotte Square. When he got there he saw all the smashed windows, and the jagged edges of metal pointing up at the sky along the row of parked cars, and the small pale flames flickering on the roadway, and a woman with frightened eyes on his left lying on the pavement as someone covered her with a coat, and to his right a red-faced man being helped from his battered car. When he looked more closely, he saw that the redness was blood. A group of people were crouching over another casualty right in front of him. A traffic jam was already building up: the square was blocked on three sides and cars were backed all the way along George Street. Horns blared in the distance, sounded by people who did not know what was happening.

Wallace stood where he was, dimly conscious of the cold pricking at the surface of his skin under the thin material of his shirt. Four blows for freedom, he thought grimly. This must be number three. Was he really guilty of encouraging things like this, however unintentionally? He had rebutted the question last night. Would it be the same answer now?

Policemen began to appear on the scene. The ear-splitting wail of an ambulance siren came up behind him. He hugged his arms round his body and his teeth chattered. He found Turnbull standing beside him, also without a jacket, tugging at his arm.

'You don't want to be seen here, Andrew,' he said.

They turned together to hurry back to the offices, moving against the flow of people. Wallace kept his head down, not wanting to be recognised. Four blows for freedom, he kept thinking. Still one more to go.

The green and yellow doubledecker bus — advertising chocolate on one side, fresh fish on the other, and a local car-rental firm on the back — accelerated hard just as the traffic lights were changing from green on the junction where Aberdeen's

King Street joined Union Street at right-angles. It went through on the red, sweeping round to the right and halting with a harsh grinding of brakes at the stop opposite the sparkling granite walls of the Town House. That was where the bomb should have gone off, Sandy McInnes thought, but the run through the changing lights had put the bus slightly ahead of schedule.

It had a seating capacity of seventy-five and was three-quarters full. Fifteen people got off and about the same number boarded. The entrance and exit doors sighed shut and the driver pulled out into the road again. The new passengers were still finding seats when McInnes, seated upstairs, killed the alarm on his wristwatch at the first peep of sound. He had it running as a stopwatch and had counted down the seconds. Now he looked out of the window with his hand resting on the bulky object in the pocket of his blue and red anorak.

The bomb would have ripped a jagged hole in the side of the bus and shattered windows on both sides of the street. The bus would have tottered drunkenly but stayed upright as it veered across the oncoming traffic in the half dark of the winter's afternoon. Screaming pedestrians would have scattered as it mounted the pavement and scraped along the wall of a bank, metal screeching on stone, to finally come to rest lying at a crazy angle. Half a mile away to the north McInnes, sitting in his car, would have heard the sound of the blast and would have seen people in the street turn to stare in its direction. A boarded-up window beside where he had parked would be covered with the piecemeal scraps of hundreds of ancient fly-posters flapping in the wind — and with three letter Ws in faded black paint sprayed across its breadth, partly hidden by newer posters. Sitting there, he would have turned off the alarm on his digital watch. Within minutes the sirens of the emergency services would have been converging on the scene. Fire engines would have raced past him in a deafening cacophony of noise. Ambulances would have chased them, blue lights flashing dramatically in the late afternoon gloom.

On the bus, McInnes sat looking down dispassionately at the crowded pavements. There had been no woman this time.

No words spoken by female lips before the deed could be done. It didn't fit the pattern. There had been that old woman in the tea-rooms in Glasgow, the middle-aged woman on the train at Queen Street Station, the younger woman in Charlotte Square in Edinburgh. But there had been nobody this time. He had looked carefully around — but nothing. He had travelled the route twice during the afternoon. The idea was to plant the bomb in a simple plastic bag in the luggage space below the stairs of the bus, tucking it away in a far corner. Each time he had searched among the faces for some sign but, although there were always plenty of women, young and old, nobody caught his attention the way it had happened before. A couple of times he thought he had found the right person, but it wasn't the case. He couldn't go through with it, he decided. It didn't *feel* right.

The long drive north from Edinburgh had inspired an uncomfortable feeling of self-loathing that nagged away at him. Why was he doing all this for General George? Why was he putting himself at the beck and call of a man he despised with a lucid and ever-increasing ferocity? Why was he running all around the country like this? Why was he jumping when told to jump? Why was he rolling over to have his belly tickled as a reward for services rendered? The questions bothered him. He shooed them away, but they kept coming back like persistent flies. He had no real answers. There was the money, of course, and the tremendous kick he got out of wielding such power. But in the final analysis he was just doing what he was told to do — following orders. When he thought about it like that, it made him ashamed of his actions. Why did he always have to be *told* to do things? Why couldn't he think for himself?

The failure to plant the bomb was not the first instruction McInnes had ignored. General George had told him to book into a hotel in the city as soon as he arrived. The police would set up roadblocks, he said. It would be better if he stayed the night in the city and left in the morning. Choose an upmarket hotel, he had instructed. They are likely to check out the cheap ones and the boarding-houses, but not the four-star hotels. McInnes didn't want that: he was intimidated by posh places. He would feel like a fish out of water. Besides, there would be no roadblocks now. He decided he would head back to Glasgow immediately.

A long night stretched out before him. He got off the bus and joined the anonymous crowds thronging the pavements of Union Street. As he began to walk in the general direction of his car, he started to worry about what he would tell General George, then slowed down, giving himself time to think. Maybe he should stay the night in the city after all. He could sleep in the car. But first he needed a drink.

CHAPTER THIRTEEN

An elderly man was killed and several other people badly
injured when a car bomb exploded today in Charlotte
Square in Edinburgh city centre.

The bomb had been planted outside Bute House, the
official residence of the Secretary of State for Scotland,
and only a few hundred yards away from the headquarters
of the Scottish National Party.

Police refused to speculate on whether it was the work
of the self-styled We're With Wallace terrorist group
which has been blamed for the two bombings yesterday
which have cost twenty-four lives in Glasgow and
Falkirk.

Mr Andrew Wallace, SNP chairman, said he was
greatly saddened by the latest incident. The terrorists
have threatened 'four blows for freedom', and it is
thought the Edinburgh bomb is the third in a carefully
planned series.

Edinburgh Evening News

Mrs MacPherson was travelling far too fast when she turned
off the road and onto the rough driveway leading up to the
house in Glen Halkston. The sudden jolt as the car hit the
rut where the two surfaces joined made her huge bulk quiver
like jelly. Her head bumped the roof and her teeth closed
painfully on her tongue. The beams of the headlights bounced
over the white walls of the cottage, sweeping the darkness
aside. She stopped the car at the front and struggled to free
herself from its interior.

Helen Wallace was kneeling by the fireside dressed in jeans
and sweatshirt, surrounded on all sides by papers as if she was
a stone thrown into the centre of a pond and they were the

ripples spreading outwards. She was trying to immerse herself in her work and was completely unaware of Mrs McPherson's approach until Breck gave a warning bark and the car's lights illuminated the room. She heard the sound of it drawing up outside and looked out to see it parked in the driveway. She scribbled a last annotation in the margin of the document she was working on, and got to her feet. The fire was burning fiercely, crackling and hissing in the grate, and the room got progressively cooler the further she moved away from it. When she opened the outside door the biting wind plucked at her clothes and she stood back to wait in the doorway, dazzled by the headlights. Sleet was falling thinly, flashing diagonally down. Then the lights were switched off, and a giant figure loomed towards her out of the darkness. Breck wagged his tail furiously in welcome.

'Mrs MacPherson,' Helen said. 'It's good to see you. Come away in.'

The fat woman was panting for breath. She had one hand over her mouth and when she took it away blood was smeared over the palm.

'I bit my tongue,' she gasped, holding out her hand to show the evidence.

'So you have, Mrs MacPherson. Come into the warm here. What on earth happened? Did you fall just now?'

'No, no. I was driving too fast, when I hit a pothole there just now. I was bringing you some of my scones and jam for when Mr Wallace arrives tomorrow night. He is still planning to come, isn't he? You will have heard about this terrible business of the bombs, of course.'

'Yes. There isn't much of anything else on the radio.'

'A terrible business. A terrible business.'

Helen ushered Mrs MacPherson into the house, took from her the bag of food and her coat, and sat her down in a chair by the fire. She found some paper tissues to stem the bleeding in her mouth. Mrs MacPherson curled her injured tongue inside her mouth and dabbed at it tentatively. Breck laid his jaw on her knee.

'Hello there, boy. Are you looking after Mrs Wallace well, then?'

'I wouldn't like to be out here by myself without him,'

Helen said. 'It's good of you to let him stay with me.'

Mrs MacPherson nodded. 'You'll be safe with him here, just in case. I saw Mr Wallace was on the television last night as well, trying to disown these bombing folk. He looked right angry at it all. I've never seen him with such a face on.'

'He is very angry, and rightly so. He can't understand what is happening. It's almost as if these bombs are being set off to deliberately undermine him. Surely nobody could stoop as low as that?'

'There's a lot of funny folk in the world, you know,' Mrs MacPherson said. 'They do a lot of funny things.'

'I wanted to go back to Edinburgh straight away last night, after the first two bombs, but Andrew insisted it would be better for me to stay here. Then this morning there was the third bomb, just along at the end of the street from the Party offices, and he phoned up before I had even heard about it on the radio news and told me it had cracked the windows in his own room. You don't think I should go back, do you, Mrs MacPherson?'

The fat woman held up a hand like a witness taking an oath. 'Not at all, dearie. If Mr Wallace says you should wait for him here, that will be the best way to do things, I'm sure.'

'What could I do in Edinburgh, anyway?' Helen said. 'No. He's still intending to come out here tomorrow. Better get out of the way, he says.'

'He will be right,' Mrs MacPherson nodded, crushing the pink-stained tissues in her fist. 'The news is saying there's likely to be a fourth bomb. There is nothing they can do to stop it because they don't know where to start looking.'

'God, it's like a nightmare. I've been trying to take my mind off things by working, but it's really difficult to concentrate.'

'It will be. It will be. And these people are claiming that they support Mr Wallace — that they are Nationalists just like him.'

'But they can't be. They must be insane if they are. Why should we need their kind of help, for goodness' sake? Can't they see what they are doing to us? They are ruining the Party.'

141

'It disnae really matter what folk say, Mrs Wallace. What really matters is what the folk hearing it believe. Am I no' right now?'

'Actions speak louder than words?'

'Aye. I'll tell ye what, lassie. I'll make us a nice cup of tea, will I? I'll just use your toilet first.'

Mrs MacPherson hauled herself out of the chair and started panting again with the effort involved as she shuffled over to the corner of the room. Helen stood by the fire, feeling strangely light-headed. Andrew had constantly warned that something might happen to disrupt the smooth flow of events. He had told her not to become too complacent or too confident. But even he had not anticipated anything like this — to be compromised by people who were supposedly on the same side. If they really were on the same side.

Her own father had warned her about nationalism as a philosophy — before he had actually met Andrew and been converted to its legitimacy. He had said it was flawed because it did not attempt to address any social or economic problems. It merely stated that a country should be run by whoever happened to be in power. It did not say how that country should be run. Communist or fascist, as long as they were born in the appropriate place, were equally welcome in nationalist parties. He used to say that as a creed it attracted supporters who viewed the world in simplistic terms of black and white, good and bad. The kind of people who would readily believe that a couple of well-placed bombs were the most effective form of argument against faceless, inertia-bound institutions. He had actually used that phrase about the well-placed bombs. She could remember the occasion vividly. She could remember the words. They echoed in her ears as she stared into the flames.

In the toilet Mrs MacPherson clutched her arms tightly around her body and shivered in the cold. Looking up, she could see the sky through the hole in the ceiling, which was covered by the sheets of thick polythene. A pool of water or ice lay in the centre of the hole like a lens, and the thin plywood walls visibly moved in and out with the pressure of the wind. It would probably be well into March before the builders would be able to get back to finish the job. If the

142

weather got much worse, she thought, the whole place might blow away and they would find themselves starting again from scratch.

She stood up and began to rearrange her clothing. Her tongue still throbbed uncomfortably where it had been bitten. She pressed it against her finger to gain some relief. It had stopped bleeding, at least. She would not tell Mrs Wallace, of course, but she had always known that this Nationalist thing would end in disaster. Mr Wallace was a very nice man, but there must be others around him who were not so nice, and they were only now showing their real colours. Some people would use any excuse for violence and blood-letting. It was a dreadful business, all right. She shook her head in despair — she had always known it would end in tears.

'You're getting a new neighbour for a little while,' she said, as she re-entered the main room. Breck followed her as she went over to the sink to fill the kettle. 'An Australian man, a Mr Tarrant. He's taken the Fowler house for a couple of weeks. I'll have to get it all prepared for him. He'll be arriving sometime next week, so it has to be ready from Monday.'

There was a ten-second delay between switching on the tap and the first thin stream of water appearing. Helen came over and began to butter the scones Mrs MacPherson had brought with her, glad to be part of this illusion of normality.

The bar was hidden behind a solid wall of people, all pressing forward together to try and attract the barmaid's attention. Sandy McInnes liked to be in the thick of it, glad to be lost in the crowd, reassured by the pressure of all the bodies around him, stimulated by the contact, entranced by the collective warmth. He was drinking fast, beer and whisky at the same time, paying for his order and retreating to a corner beyond the old sealed-off fireplace where he could lounge on his elbows on the narrow, waist-high shelf that ran round three sides of the room. From there he could watch everybody coming and going and pretend he was waiting for somebody to meet him. That way he didn't look too out of place. He would finish each fresh drink every fifteen minutes or so, and

143

then returned to the scrum — taking at least another ten minutes, sometimes longer, to collect more.

After wandering the Aberdeen streets for a while, he had picked the pub at random. It was a noisy, smoky place, divided into two levels. The lower room contained the bar itself, and was joined to the larger, upper room by a shallow flight of five steps. It had been relatively empty when he first found it, but now both levels were packed with young people. There were only a few in his age group, and a handful that were any older. Everybody appeared to be biting everybody else's ear because they had to lean so close together to make themselves heard above the permanent blare of the juke-box. The lighting was poor, apart from the blaze of white tungsten that framed the bar like a stage, with the heads and shoulders of customers seething in front of it like a frantic audience. McInnes stood in his dark corner watching without really taking any of it in. He had not eaten at all that day, and the combination of alcohol and endless cigarettes was making him dizzy and sleepy. The only thought he could properly focus on was the image of General George's bewildered face when he realised nothing was going to happen in Aberdeen. No outrage, no explosion, no dead bodies, no fuel for his sick propaganda war. Poor General George. He would be imagining all sorts of things and fearing the worst. Well, it might do him some good to sweat a bit. Maybe he would scuttle off back to the safety of the South without waiting for an explanation. If he didn't, McInnes had his story ready. He wouldn't mention the fact that he had not gone ahead simply because there was no woman around to say good-afternoon to him. No. His story was perfectly simple. The detonating mechanism had failed. The bomb had not gone off. You should never put your faith in foreign-made technology. That was what he would tell him if he was still there tomorrow morning when McInnes got back to Glasgow. It was a shame to lose the 100 per cent success rate of the operation, but it just couldn't be helped.

The bomb was still in the pocket of his anorak and that was bundled untidily with a host of others into a space between the edge of a bench and the fireplace. He could see the blue and red colours at the bottom of the pile. One arm of his

144

anorak jutted out onto the floor, to be kicked and trampled on as people squeezed by to reach their tables. McInnes stared down at it, then jerked his head up in case he aroused the curiosity of anybody nearby. It wouldn't be too difficult to set the timer now. Give them half an hour, have another drink, and then stroll out into the night while the pub was blown to kingdom come. Maybe that would satisfy General George. It would certainly create plenty of dead bodies for him. A change of plan, McInnes would say when he got back. The bus was empty, he would claim. There was no point in blowing it up. The bus was empty, but the pub was full to overflowing. Bodies everywhere. You couldn't move for swarming bodies.

McInnes swallowed his whisky, and poured the last drops into his beer glass before finishing that as well. He lit himself another cigarette and took a couple of pound notes from his back pocket before walking over to the crowd milling in front of the bar. All live bodies here, he thought, sniggering at his own private joke. Not a dead body in sight. He inserted himself between two people and eased further into the gap, pushing up against those ahead. Heads turned, feet shuffled, shoulders nudged. McInnes smiled at no one in particular, and swayed his head from side to side. If anyone complains, he thought, I'll send them a little present. A nice present all wrapped up in red Christmas paper with robins and snowmen all over it.

Someone shoved him from the side. He braced himself to resist and felt a head boring under his armpit. A rounded mass of dark curls forced its way under so that his arm was left draped over her shoulders as she looked up at him. She had a pleasant, chubby face with dark eyes made darker by heavy make-up. Her eyelashes were like the fronds of sea anemones. She wore wide, plain gold hoops as earrings. Her nose was long and straight and its glossy skin reflected the lights behind the bar. So did her painted lips, which had left a slight pinkish stain on her teeth. Her whole face was flushed with drink and when she spoke there was a hint of a slur on each word.

'Excuse me,' she said, straightening up under McInnes's arm. She was about six inches shorter than he was. 'I've been

145

trying to get to the bar for ages and all I've succeeded in doing is having my toes trod on so far. Drastic action is called for.'

McInnes made no attempt to remove his arm. He felt an emptiness grow in his stomach as if a plug had been pulled and the contents were draining out. This was the woman he had been expecting to find. She was younger still than the woman in Edinburgh. It would have fitted the pattern so well if she had been on the bus, earlier. She would have spoken to him then in her BBC newsreader accent, and he would have carried out his orders as planned. He would not have hesitated. But she had only just turned up now, appearing beside him as if she had risen straight out of the ground. He felt confused. He did not know what was expected of him. What did it mean this time? What was he supposed to do?

'Would you mind terribly if I attached myself to you for the journey to the front line? Men are so much better at these things, don't you agree?'

He nodded. They were still two rows of people away from the bar itself. Somebody was backing out with a tray of glasses. The crowd behind him was unwilling to move but was eventually forced to give way to let him pass. McInnes fell forward into the gap that was created. The woman went with him so that they were squashed together face to face, front to front. He could feel the mounds of her breasts pushing against him, and her legs down below. She had her hands on his shoulders. Their noses were almost touching.

'Would you like tae dance?' McInnes said.

'How about a quickstep?' she replied.

It took another five minutes to reach the bar and a few more minutes after that for one of the team of harassed barmaids to single McInnes out for attention. In that time the girl explained that she had been waiting for a friend in the pub next-door but he was late and it would teach him a lesson if he turned up now and found her gone. Mind you, they were supposed to go to a birthday party that night and she didn't really blame him for not wanting to go, because all the guys at it would probably be as bent as five-bob notes. She was a student, she said. Politics and philosophy. Second year. An English spy sent to watch what the Scots were up to. McInnes tried to tell her he was a Loyalist, but the juke-box was blasting out a particularly loud record and he couldn't make himself understood.

He ordered his own drinks and bought her a gin and tonic because she could not extricate her purse from her handbag in the crush. She then followed him back to his corner, unbuttoning her coat. She wasn't exactly fat, but dumpy, a little overweight. She was no great beauty either, but attractive enough in her way.

'Cheers,' she said, holding up her glass. 'My name is Phyllis.'

'Sandy.'

'And what do you do, Sandy?'

'I'm a scaffolder.'

'Really? I so admire men who work with their hands. You can come and erect scaffolding for me any time.'

McInnes laughed, unsure if she was trying to make fun of him or if it was just a harmless joke. He swallowed some beer so that he didn't have to think of a reply. He was always nervous around women, becoming tongue-tied and awkward. This one didn't seem to notice his shyness. She chattered on, beginning a long, complicated story about how she had once rolled herself up in a carpet like Cleopatra to hide from someone and ended up nearly suffocating. He heard some of it but it was too much of an effort to take it all in. As soon as she finished one story, she started off on another one. Individual words popped like bubbles bursting inside his brain, making no sense. Her voice came and went over the background music like an echo bouncing off the walls of the room. His head felt like a balloon floating somewhere up near the ceiling, as if connected to his body by a long string. He looked down on her moving lips and beyond them to the arm of his anorak sticking out from the pile of coats like the arm of a dead body — a corpse squashed flat at the bottom of the heap.

'Well? Do you fancy it or not?'

The insistent tone of the direct question somehow got through to him, bringing him back to reality. He hadn't paid much attention to what had gone before. His pint glass was almost empty now, so she must have been talking for quite a while. He noticed, too, that she had taken off her coat to show that she was wearing a white dress with black buttons down the front. She was like a snowman, he thought. Black coals for eyes. A magic snowman fashioned out of the latest snow-fall and come to seek him out. He stared at her, grinning inanely. A snowman that had stepped out from its place on the Christmas wrapping-paper round the bomb.

'Well?' she repeated, leaning so far towards him he could feel her hot breath against his ear. 'Are you coming or not?'

'Where to?' he managed to say.

'This party I'm supposed to be going to. I hate going to parties alone. It probably won't be much fun for you, though. Not being a student you won't know anyone, and I suspect that all they will talk about is politics and that most of the men there will be raving homos, knowing Adrian whose party it is. But there will be plenty of free drink and you'll be all right with me. Stick close and keep your bum to the wall. We'll be all right. I've got a bottle already in my bag, so what do you say? How about the twosome then?'

'You and me?'

'Me and you.'

'Fine. Let's go.'

They had some trouble extricating McInnes's anorak from the tight pile of coats, before wrapping up well to keep out the weather. It was snowing outside and the cold air sobered him up a little after the dry warmth of the pub. In the shelter of the narrow street the snow was descending vertically around them, like a never-ending curtain endlessly falling. Phyllis slithered on the icy cobbles in her high-heeled boots, and almost fell. She grabbed his arm to steady herself and kept a tight grip of it. In the anorak pocket the bulky package containing the bomb bumped against his thigh as they walked. They turned the corner and the wind hit them head-on, driving the snow into their faces and making them shield their eyes. At the taxi rank they took the lead vehicle in a queue of three. She spoke to the driver.

'Is it far?' McInnes asked as they bundled into the back seat.

'No distance at all,' she replied, holding his arm with both hands and leaning against him.

148

As the turbulent snow whirled about the streets, lights flickered and dimmed and then brightened again. From the back of the taxi McInnes watched it moving in many different directions at the same time, as though falling in separate layers and sliding apart on nearing the ground. On each side, the flakes marched downwards like ranks of soldiers crossing and interweaving on the drill square. At the front, however, it was as if the car was driving into the centre of an explosion — the snow flying straight at the windscreen and veering off at the very last moment before contact. It disappeared into the wet, shining pavements and walls, and converged on the bodies of people walking the streets. The whole city was being drowned in snow. There was not a square inch around them that was free of white flakes — pouring into every space, filling every gap. The taxi was safe, though, running like a submarine along the floor of the heaving white ocean, the sound of its engine muffled by the snow all around them.

The journey wasn't very far. The taxi took about five minutes to reach a street lined on both sides with old-style terraced houses, and then it slowed to a crawl as Phyllis leaned over the seats to point out to the driver the number they wanted. McInnes paid the fare and stood beside her on the pavement — they huddled together with the wind trying its best to knock them over. He wondered why they were not making some move for shelter, but when he looked down at her he saw that her face was turned up towards him. Her eyes were closed tight and her lips pouted. He sobered up a little more. They would all have wanted to kiss him, he thought. And *he* would have kissed them, if they had met under different circumstances at different times. The old woman in the tea-rooms, the woman on the train, the young woman who had parked her car beside his in Edinburgh.

A hand touched his cheek — it was as smooth and cold as a piece of metal — and guided his mouth down onto hers. They kissed as the snow fell into their hair and built up on their shoulders. Her tongue was like a warm animal burrowing between his teeth to reach its mate beyond. She pressed against him but he could hardly feel her through the padding of his anorak. Suddenly, she broke away and led him by the hand to the door of one of the houses. She rang the bell and waited with her head nestling against his chest. There was light spilling round the edges of the curtains at the window. There was music too, soft and faint, and barely audible above the howl of the wind — and another sound in the background, a distant roaring sound, that he could not identify. The door opened and the snow was sucked inwards like water into a drain. Phyllis and McInnes rushed in with it, and stood in the hallway stamping their feet and brushing the melting snow off themselves. The door was closed behind them.

'Phyllis and friend,' said the person standing beside it. 'Welcome to my humble abode.'

He was a tall thin man with short fair hair, a wispy beard, and a single dangling earring made from a tiny feather. His eyes were small and round and unhealthily pink in a pale face. He had bare feet and was wearing a long smock and tight jeans. When he took their coats and threw them carelessly into a side room McInnes noticed that his fingernails were painted silver.

'The gang's all here, Phyl,' he said, looking at McInnes. 'It's always good to have new blood, though.'

'Adrian, meet Sandy.'

'How do you do, Sandy,' Adrian said.

'I'm a'right,' McInnes replied gruffly.

'I'm sure you are, Sandy. I'm sure you are. We're through here. Follow me.'

'Remember,' Phyllis whispered to him. 'Bum to the wall. If they get a sniff of it they will be down on you like a pack of dogs.'

There were about twenty people crammed into the small room, equally divided between males and females. Most of them were sitting crosslegged on the floor, some others were leaning against the walls. One couple was rolling on the carpet beside the record-player, locked in a passionate embrace. McInnes's eyes immediately began to stream because of the cigarette smoke. A few people nodded and smiled at Phyllis. At the window there was a table laden with cans of beer, and bottles and boxes of wine, and plates of cheese and hunks of bread. Beside it, rising from the floor, was a pyramid of empty cans that was already three feet high. McInnes took a plastic pint tumbler and filled it more than

150

half full of wine. Phyllis giggled and got herself a normal-sized wine glass to fill. They stepped over the bodies in the centre of the room in order to reach a sofa that had been pushed back against the wall and was already occupied by a pair who moved across to let them squeeze into one corner. Almost as soon as they sat down, Phyllis set their drinks down on the floor and twisted round to climb on him and start kissing him again. He responded as best he could, letting his hands roam all over her ample body, moulding her flesh as if he wanted to form her into a different shape. But he was sitting in an uncomfortable position, getting a stiff neck and feeling the circulation to his legs cut off by her weight. There was not enough space to change their position, and he didn't like to complain. Every few minutes she would pause to let them each have a sip of wine, then she would take his glass away and start again. His jaw began to get cramp with all the kissing. He was aware that the music kept stopping and starting, as the couple on the carpet rolled on the flex and pulled the plug out of the wall socket.

McInnes must have eventually fallen asleep, because when he next opened his eyes he was alone on the sofa. He stretched out on his back and fumbled blindly over the side for his drink. All he could find was a can of beer which he could not remember opening. He found a packet of cigarettes, too, and lit himself one. The room had become darker; the music had become softer. There were still people sitting in a group in the middle. He could see their black shapes when he glanced sideways and could hear them talking. Two voices dominated the conversation. One had an accent very much like his own; the other was posh — an English accent not dissimilar to General George's. They spoke quite distinctly, and might have been talking to him directly, but McInnes didn't pay much attention to what was being said. Beyond them he glimpsed a white shape floating ghost-like at the other end of the room. He thought it must be Phyllis in her snowman dress. Then he heard the name of Andrew Wallace mentioned, and curiosity made him concentrate on what was being said.

'These bombs are crucifying Wallace,' said the voice with the strong Scots accent. 'All his arguments rely on non-violence and the use of the democratic process. Now the wild men are shitting in their own nest, acting like this. It's plain daft.'

'It's not daft,' responded the posh English voice. 'It's a deliberate but probably unconscious reaction to try and undermine the success of the independence campaign Wallace has been running.'

'A deliberate policy? Why, for fuck's sake?'

'Because a lot of Scots don't want to take on the responsibility of controlling their own lives. They want to shout about the mess other people make in doing it; and they don't want to be left with nobody else but themselves to blame.'

'I cannae believe that.'

'You Scots don't want to believe it, but it's true.'

'Whit? Nationalists that dinnae really believe in nationalism? It's all a game they would prefer tae lose? If they get close tae winning, then they're going tae have to score a few own goals to even things up?'

'Exactly. You Scots make a great noise on the football terraces singing about being a nation again, but then you go home at night and forget about it. When a man like Wallace comes along with the guts to take the song literally, you have no choice but to follow him to keep your self-respect, but you know it's not what you want to do. So you go along with him for a while, and then decide to fuck things up for him before they go too far.'

'So naebody really wants independence?'

'Of course not. You Scots are quite happy to have your decisions taken for you. My God, life could be a lot worse up here, couldn't it? London does all right by you. Why take a risk with all that? You Scots are a servile race. You need a master in charge of you. Why fend for yourself in the wolf-pack outside, when you can be fed and watered by nice keepers in the zoo?'

'You're an arrogant bastard. Answer me this. How come the Nationalists have got this far?'

'This far and no further. A talking shop in Edinburgh to make you think you're in charge, and to keep the dumb natives from getting too restless — that's about the extent of it.'

'Meanwhile, England calls the shots?'

'That is the way God meant it to be. It's no use fighting against it. I admit that Wallace came close to upsetting the natural order of things, but now that he is seen to be unable to control his own supporters, his power base will crumble. Just you watch. He's had his chance and he's blown it. You Scots know your station in life. You're used to doing what you're told.'

Anger built up slowly inside McInnes as he listened to the disembodied conversation. He began to think it was almost as if they were talking about him personally — and nobody got away with telling him to do anything he didn't want to do. He rolled onto his side to see if he could make out who was talking, but it was too dark to see any faces. He took another drink of beer and swung his feet round to sit up on the sofa, suddenly aware that someone was close by the arm where his head had been resting. He saw the white face of the party host, Adrian, kneeling there with his fingers spread out over the rough material, the nails like stubby icicles.

'She was never going to let you sleep with her, you know,' he said, smiling just enough to show a bottom row of even white teeth,

'Who wisnae?'

'My old friend Phyllis. Oh, she has told me all about you. A scaffolder, isn't it? Very working-class. That's how she gets her kicks: picking up blokes like you and letting them have a quick grope. She likes workers, you see. They're so much more ideologically sound than intellectual students.'

'Fuck off,' McInnes hissed, spitting out his anger with the words.

'I apologise,' Adrian said, holding his face in his hands. 'You too are an intellectual, a master of the reasoned argument and the merry quip. I did not realise.'

'Fuck off,' McInnes repeated. 'Where is she?'

'Phyllis? She's long gone. Don't look like that. By obligingly falling asleep you saved her the trouble of thinking up some exotic excuse to get away from you. There are only us boys left now. We're all boys together here.'

'Fuck off,' McInnes said for the third time.

'You should stay,' Adrian pleaded, touching McInne's wrist before it was snatched out of his reach. 'It will be fun. Go on.

The real party is just about to begin. So stay.'

'No one tells me what to do. Let me out of here.'

He stood up and swayed a little until he got his bearings. He stumbled over shapes who laughed and grabbed at his legs as he made for the door in the corner. There were only about six men left in the room. He stopped at the door and looked round, but could not see Phyllis anywhere. Realising he still held the beer can in his hand, he flung it at he pyramid of empties, sending the whole thing crashing to the floor.

He found his anorak in the bedroom, lying on the floor where it had been thrown. The bomb was still in the pocket, and he momentarily considered priming it and hiding it under the bed. That would round off their party with a bang, he thought. Blow their arses out the top of their heads. Phyllis was too fat for him anyway. He didn't like them fat. He wouldn't have slept with her even if she had begged him. Now she was gone — disappeared as suddenly and mysteriously as she had appeared. Perhaps she had been a snowman, after all. Perhaps she had melted away to nothing because it was too hot for her inside the house. He took the bomb out of his pocket and held it in front of his face. Perhaps she had gone back to her position on the wrapping paper.

He went out, leaving the front door wipe open. The snow was still falling, but more sparsely. The wind was as savage as ever, threatening to blow him off his feet. He turned so that it was gusting directly into his face, tearing at the roots of his hair, and he began to walk away.

The streets of houses did not continue long, and then he was walking on wet grass with a thin covering of snow. He walked on blindly. He could not see where he was going, but somehow made out that he had reached a golf course. He started to run across the undulating land. That roaring sound he had first heard when they got out of the taxi seemed to grow louder all the time. He missed his footing and fell, winding himself as he thumped into soft ground. He thought it was mud at first, but when he looked closer he recognised it as snow-covered sand and realised that he was lying in one of the bunkers. He lay where he was, regaining his breath, hoping the bitter cold would neutralise the alcohol in his blood.

154

'Naebody tells me whit tae do,' he shouted at the top of his voice, looking up at the ragged clouds flying fast overhead. 'Naebody,' he said quietly. 'Naebody tells me what to do.'

He scrambled out of the bunker and started running again. The horizon was an artificially straight line. In the moonlight he caught sight of a tunnel and headed towards it. The roaring sound rose to a crescendo inside it, echoing off the damp walls, then he was through and onto the beach and the North Sea stretched out ahead of him with the white-capped waves dipping and diving like targets in a shooting gallery. He stumbled over the soft sand and onto a firmer surface and right down to within a few yards of the water's edge. He listened to the constant roar and thought how it was like the sound of a never-ending, powerful explosion. He picked up a piece of wood and drew three overlapping Ws in the sand. 'Naebody tells me whit to do,' he repeated calmly. There he stood, trapped in the middle of the explosion, with the shock waves of the wind clawing at his face and eyes and tugging at his clothes. He had no idea how long he stood like that, but when he finally moved his face was soaked with the spray and his own tears, his legs were stiff with the cold and his teeth were chattering freely. The sea was lapping round his shoes. The three Ws had been wiped out by the incoming tide. He patted the bulge in his anorak pocket and smiled. He had made up his mind, and knew what he should do next.

CHAPTER FOURTEEN

The three brutal atrocities perpetrated by terrorists in Scotland over the last few days are a salutary reminder about the inherent dangers of any break-up of the UK.

Mr Andrew Wallace and his fellow Nationalists may be sincere in their devotion to non-violence, but the pedigree of some elements of their supporters cannot be guaranteed.

Any appeal to Nationalism arouses strong emotions, and Mr Wallace appears to have summoned up a frightening monster from the depths, whether he likes it or not.

Scotland is not Ireland, you may argue. These are isolated instances. Tell that to the families of the victims who lie dead today because of ill-advised attempts to challenge the constitutional integrity of the UK.

London Times

Cecilia had a beautiful backside, and she wasn't shy about showing it off. The picture of her reversing out from under the bed was a classic, even if it was fairly dark and slightly out of focus. It looked like the moon or the winter sun shining out from a background of misty clouds. They couldn't use it, though, because Demionscuk pointed out, quite rightly, that it could have been anyone, male or female. Tarrant couldn't see how it could be anything but a female backside, but he didn't argue too much about it. It was a nice picture and he was happy to have it in his wallet as a keepsake of a most pleasant afternoon.

Tarrant had assumed they would be going to a hotel when they arrived in London. Instead he was taken to a third-floor flat in a Holland Park block hidden away behind a row of

156

trees. It was a big place, and Tarrant was given a room to himself with a portable television, a couple of old armchairs, a double bed and a rickety wardrobe. He was told it had been set up to resemble his own bedroom back in Adelaide, and he made approving noises although it didn't really look anything like it. The window and the bed, it was true, could have been interchangeable, but the other furniture was all wrong, and the wallpaper was the wrong pattern and the carpet the wrong design. Back home above his bed he had a big moody poster of an Australian sunset over the outback, so he spent two days raking round the London shops until he found one almost the same. It just added that touch of authenticity, he said. In fact he found what he wanted on the first day, but he didn't buy it straight away because he liked acting the tourist and having the time to himself. The first things he bought were a personal stereo and some classical music tapes to entertain him as he walked round. He also bought plenty of magazines and newspapers to read all about Mrs Helen Wallace and her husband. There was no shortage of material because of the sudden spate of bombings. He watched Wallace appear on television to condemn the outrages, and felt an instinctive sympathy for him. He would rather drink a night away with a bloke like Wallace, he thought, than have the Demon dogging his steps all the time.

There were half a dozen bedrooms in the flat, but only three were occupied. Tarrant had one. Demionscuk had the room next to it, and there was a caretaker-type guy in the room beside the front door. When he was introduced as Bruce, Tarrant thought it was supposed to be a joke. But no, that was his name. His face was big and round and the features on it seemed to be almost rubbed away by the passage of time to create a perfectly smooth ball. He had wide shoulders and massive hands, and obviously his job was as much to keep out unwelcome visitors as it was to dish up particularly unappetising food for breakfast and lunch. At night, an old woman in a black dress came in and prepared much better stuff.

Cecilia did not look much like Helen Wallace when she turned up for the photo session. Bruce answered her knock and leered behind her as she was shown into Tarrant's room.

She was the right height and shape and she was certainly attractive enough in her own way, but she looked nothing like the pictures in the papers. Her hair was far too short for a start, Tarrant tried to tell Demionscuk, and it was bleached almost white. Twenty minutes of rearrangement in the bathroom to put on her make-up and an auburn wig produced an amazing transformation. Cecilia had become a different person, the person they wanted her to be. Demioscuk waved the Polaroid camera about and his strange laugh gurgled behind the incongruous, expressionless mask of his face. Trust me, Murray, he said. Trust me.

The story was that Tarrant had been part of a crowd which had picked up Helen Wallace, not knowing who she was, in a bar in Adelaide last summer and taken her back to his flat for a prearranged party. He had then monopolised her attention and the two of them had spent a sleepless night drinking beer, taking pictures of each other, smoking dope, and shagging, not necessarily in that order. When the police arrived in answer to neighbours' complaints about noise, she hid under the bed until they left. In the morning she was gone and it was only much later that Tarrant chanced to find out who she was by seeing her photograph in a magazine. Then, he latched onto the idea of making a little profit out of the one-night stand, and had followed her back to Britain to cash in on his unintentional investment.

Cecilia was told that they wanted the pictures as evidence in a divorce case and she was posing as the unfaithful wife. She clearly didn't believe it, but she was a professional and ready to play any game they wanted. Tarrant was Bob. Demionscuk was Jim. The curtains were drawn to make the room dark. Cans of Australian beer and bottles of Scotch whisky were strategically placed around the room. Cecilia had bare legs and open-toe sandals. She was wearing a simple, white summer dress with red underwear as instructed, because Demionscuk had read somewhere that Helen Wallace had a fetish for that colour.

The first few pictures were straightforward enough. He had Cecilia stretch out on the bed with her dress riding up provocatively over her thighs and her face obscured behind her hair. Then she was on the edge of the bed with her legs crossed, smoking a cigarette and blowing smoke at the camera. Then she was at the side of the bed with one foot on a chair and a glass of whisky balanced on her knee, always showing as much leg as possible. Each time, Demionscuk would take the picture and then wait patiently for it to develop before studying the result and making up his mind what he wanted next. He really wasn't much of a photographer. The pictures looked exactly what they were meant to be; happy snaps taken by an amateur. He used a whole film on fully-clothed shots and then had her strip down to her bra and pants to fire off another two films. Then it was another two films worth of full frontal poses all over the bed as well as peeking out from under it. She had small breasts and narrow hips but her backside was big and beautiful, like a ship in full sail.

All the time Tarrant stood in the background, whistling silently while he watched the performance and got more and more aroused. When it came to his turn to join her he took off her clothes and dived under the covers beside her, embarrassed at being naked in Demionscuk's presence. It had been decided to take just a few of the two of them together because Tarrant was supposed to be the photographer. The table was placed at the foot of the bed and the camera was put on it and set to automatic. He kissed her and had to hold their lips for several seconds before the flash went off. The wig smelled of plastic. Then they were toasting each other with whisky and she was smiling quite genuinely while their thighs were touching and he was thinking that he had not slept with a woman since leaving Australia. He reckoned it had to be the cold that had taken his mind off it. Demionscuk had Cecilia sit astride him and lean forward so that her hair poured all over his face. 'Three falls or a submission decides the winner,' she whispered in his ear. Demionscuk seemed to like that pose because he took three shots of it. Then he had Tarrant lie on top of her with the sheets pulled right down to expose his backside. 'I submit,' she said as the flash went off.

After that the session was over. Demionscuk gathered up his stack of photographs. 'Don't get up on my behalf,' he said, closing the door and leaving them lying together in the bed.

'Doesn't your friend ever smile?' Cecilia asked.

'Never if he can help it,' Tarrant replied.

'Do you think we've done enough to get you a divorce then, Bob?' she said, reaching for her cigarette packet.

'It's not me that wants the divorce. It's a business acquaintance we are helping out. He wants to get rid of his wife, and you're the spitting image of her done up like that. Once she sees these pictures she'll give him his divorce.'

'Won't she wonder when she did it?'

'She's got a drink problem. That's why he wants rid of her. She'll assume she did it and can't remember.'

'I see. Do you fancy her yourself, this drunken wife?'

Tarrant wrinkled his nose. 'Not particularly.'

'That's not the impression I got when we were having our pictures taken. But then maybe you've just got the knack of rising to the occasion.'

He felt her hand rest on the top of his leg and slid his own hand up over her flat stomach to fondle her breasts. She stubbed out her cigarette without having smoked any of it.

'You could be right,' he said.

'If you don't fancy the wife, how about me, then?' She pulled off the wig and tossed it onto the floor.

'From the moment you came in the door.' He kissed her neck and ran his hand over her blonde spiky hair. 'Tell me, is Cecilia your real name?'

'Does it make a difference?'

'No. Just that there is an old song. You know, it goes: "Making love in the afternoon with Cecilia up in my bedroom".'

'The afternoon has hardly started.'

'Well? Is Cecilia your real name?'

'It is while I'm working.'

'And when are you working until?'

'I'm booked for the whole afternoon. I'm not going anywhere for a while.'

Tarrant swung his legs down off the bed and went across to lock the door. He looked back at where Cecilia was stretched out on the bed under the colourful poster of the Australian sunset, and licked his lips. Renzo, you Demon you, he thought, you're not such a bad sort after all. In fact you're a real sport.

The sky over Edinburgh was the colour of dull steel. The snow-dusted city had the appearance of an ancient, blurred black-and-white photograph. The wind scoured the streets, forcing what few pedestrians there were to shelter close in against the walls as they scurried to and fro. The traffic moved relentlessly on the shining dark ribbons of the roads, bright rectangles belching trails of vapour that seemed to solidify in the freezing air and make it more opaque by the minute. On top of the dome of the university's Old College the statue of the Golden Boy was gradually fading into the gathering gloom.

It had been a long time since Andrew Wallace had drunk whisky at lunchtime. Now he and Hamish Henryson had finished half a bottle between them, after abandoning the claustrophic atmosphere of the George Street offices for the peace and quiet of the flat and an extended lunch-hour. The others would probably be looking for them by now, but neither of them was in any mood to go back. The day could not pass quickly enough for Wallace. He was desperate to get away and join Helen at the cottage in Argyll. The phone was ringing constantly but the volume had been turned down as low as possible so that it could hardly be heard, just a faint cheeping like a sleepy caged bird.

Wallace stood looking out over the city with his elbow supported by the palm of one hand and a whisky tumbler almost hidden in the fist he held against his neck. He took a drink, washing the whisky round his teeth so that his gums tingled. He remembered when the streets below had been thronged with people enjoying themselves as they looked forward to the New Year. And while that had been going on, somebody somewhere had been plotting the murderous campaign of bombings. Perhaps the very person, knowing exactly what was to come, had been in the crowd round the Tron Church, singing along with everybody else and staring up into the falling snow when Wallace had leaned out only a week ago to acknowledge the cheers. Four blows for freedom. Three down and one still to come. Wallace's shoulder-blades itched as if he expected a knife to slice into the flesh as he stood there. For the first time he noticed a cluster of pigeons huddled together on a high ledge on the church opposite, grey balls of fluffed-out feathers cowering away from the blood-chilling cold, but with nowhere to go to escape it. The phone stopped ringing.

'Well, Hamish, the man asked the question. Is our country worth fighting for or not?'

There was no reply but Wallace did not turn round. He kept watching the pigeons and the blasts of wind that ruffled their feathers like invisible fingers poking at them, checking to see if they were fat enough yet to eat.

'He hit it squarely on the head, you know, that wee fat bloke on Wednesday night. He came out with the one question I have never been able to answer for myself. Do you fight for what you believe in? If things were different and it was a case of an armed struggle, what would I do? Oh, I know the pat answer: the fight in Scotland is a political one, not a military one. But supposing it was just that? Suppose for a minute they tried to ban the Party, tried to outlaw national-ism? Would it be justified to take up arms, then? I keep harp-ing on this idea that democracy is our greatest weapon. Supposing they take a vote to abolish democracy. Where does that leave us? What other weapons can we use if that happens? If these We're With Wallace maniacs are really on our side, do we adopt their tactics, then?'

Wallace rubbed the rim of his glass against his top lip. There had been many previous drinking sessions in the flat when he and Henryson and a group of friends had thrashed out the problems of the world in general, and Scotland in particular, and finally drawn up the strategy that had advanced the Nationalist cause so far in such a comparatively short space of time. The trick was to drink just enough to loosen your inhibitions and let your ideas roam free, without losing control. The large amount of alcohol that did get into your blood was quickly burned up by the mental energy of the debates. Those long-winded, open-ended sessions had helped him to sort out his own thoughts and ideas, to sift the fan-tasies and the impossible dreams and concentrate on the realities. The reality to be faced now was twenty-four people dead and perhaps more yet to suffer the same fate.

'So when does it become justified, Hamish?' he asked. 'When do the ends justify the means? When is right on our side? Is it worth fighting for at all? If the price tag on independence is only one hundred dead people, is that a bargain for the other five million?'

A strong gust of wind rattled the window frame and buffeted the pigeons on the ledge of the church wall so violently that one fell off. The bird tumbled downwards before opening out its wings and gliding back up. It fluttered frantically at the edge for a few moments till it was able to regain its perch, crowding in amongst the group that reluctantly shuffled sideways to make space for it.

'Come on, Hamish, help me out here. Suppose for a minute we get a majority of seats here, suppose we get all the bloody seats, and the bastards in Westminster just outvote us and tell us to toe the unionist line. Like it or lump it, Edwards and his Government threaten, but we stay in control. What do we do then, Hamish? Do we say: "That's okay, gentlemen. We just thought we'd ask nicely. If that is your answer we'll just away home and forget about it." Is that what we say, Hamish? Do we take no for an answer after playing the game by the rules? Or do we go all out to win, whatever the consequences?'

He turned from the window. Henryson had fallen asleep. He was sitting in an armchair with his bony knees sticking out, his hands loosely curled in his lap, and his head drooping down onto his chest. He was snoring quietly as Wallace gently released the empty whisky tumbler from his grasp and placed it on the table beside the half-full bottle. He remembered promising Henryson at one session not so long ago that independence would be achieved within his lifetime. He had believed it was possible even though Henryson was an old man and there could not be all that much time left for him. How swiftly and dramatically things had changed. Would there be enough time now? Wallace closed his eyes and shook his head slowly.

'It's a dangerous game we are playing,' he said softly. 'Maybe we should just ignore the difficult questions for as long as we possibly can.'

The phone started ringing again, quiet as a whisper. This time Wallace went to answer it.

163

* * *

Young Jimmy Nairn confronted Sandy McInnes the moment
he entered the tenement close in Pollockshaws, stepping out
from his doorway so that the two of them almost collided at
the foot of the stairs. The teenager was wearing a scruffy
brown duffle-coat, fastened tightly under his chin, and a
woolly Rangers hat pulled down over one ear but exposing the
other with its full-length curve of gold studs and rings.

'You owe me a tenner, Mr McInnes,' he said, holding out a
hand. 'Ah followed him like ye said ah should.'

McInnes nodded, recovering from his surprise. 'Good boy,
Jimmy. Did ye find the car then?'

'Aye. It wis in a big car park on the ither side o' the Clyde
wi' yon number you said it wis. He went an' got it late last
night and brought it back and parked it roond the corner. Ah
followed him a' the way on ma bike.'

McInnes dug into his pocket and handed over a crisp ten-
pound note. 'Good boy. Is he up the stairs jist now?'

'Naw, he's never come back inside since last night. The
car's still roond the corner and he's been wanderin' up and
doon the street a' day starin' at the close. He must be a bit o'
a weirdo, is he no', Mr McInnes?'

'He's English, Jimmy. Whit dae ye expect? Whit kind o' car
is it?'

The boy was opening and closing the ten-pound note as if it
was a book. 'A Vauxhall.'

'You still got thon set o' keys for doin' the cars?'

'Aye. Ah can nick it fur ye if ye like.'

'Ah dinnae want ye tae steal it, but ah'll probably hae a
wee job for ye tomorrow morning if ye're aboot. It'll be worth
double.'

'Twenty quid?' Jimmy's eyes grew larger. 'Ah'll be here if
ye want tae knock me up. You goin' tae the match against the
Hibs the morren, Mr McInnes?'

McInnes mounted the stairs. 'Ah'll be there, Jimmy,' he
said over his shoulder. 'Ah never miss a home game if ah can
help it.'

The flat was empty. The beds were made, the dishes were
washed and stacked away, the furniture had been dusted and

there was a smell of polish hanging in the air. He had never seen the place looking so clean. General George had left no trace of himself at all, apart from the typewriter lying forgotten on the carpet, partly concealed behind one of the curtains. McInnes sat down in a chair by the fire and wiped his nose. It was streaming with the cold after his extempore trip to the freezing beach in the middle of the night. It had taken him three hours, walking around in his soaking-wet clothes, to find his way back to his car. He had got changed there, but it was too cold to sleep in the car so he started heading south immediately. He had stopped at a back-street bakery to buy some freshly-made rolls, and the baker was a friendly, talkative chap. McInnes saw his chance and spun a story about wanting to travel back to Glasgow but being worried he was over the limit and not having the cash for a hotel. The baker took the hint and let him bed down on a stack of flour bags in a small room beside the ovens, which was as hot as a sauna. McInnes slept like a baby and the baker obviously forgot he was there, because it was after eleven before he shook him awake and sent him on his way.

General George must have slept out as well. He did not take any chances and, when nothing had happened in Aberdeen, he must have feared the worst and quickly decided to abandon the flat in case the police came looking for him. Three out of four wasn't that bad a success rate for the first phase of his operation, and he wouldn't have much difficulty finding plenty of other mugs to carry out his orders when he was ready to launch the second phase. McInnes had always been expendable, like the wrapping paper round the bombs — just a means of getting them delivered to the appropriate places. At the first hint of potential trouble he had been abandoned without a second thought and left to his own devices. The typewriter had not been forgotten, McInnes suddenly realised, but deliberately left behind to link him with the notes sent to the newspapers at the outset. He had been set up perfectly. His claims of working under the direction of the mysterious General George would be dismissed as fantasy, and he had no real evidence to back them up. If the police had been on to him, it was an open and shut case. He could almost admire the professionalism of it all.

The living-room door burst open and McInnes got a shock, even though he had been waiting for it to happen. He sprang to his feet and spun round to face the intruder.

'Where the deuce have you been?' Mortimer shouted.

'Ah could ask you the same thing, General,' McInnes replied, feeling the words come easily. 'Ah thought ye might hae done anither wan o' yir vanishing tricks.'

'What happened in Aberdeen? Why wasn't the fourth bomb laid?'

'It was laid a'right. The fucking thing wouldnae go off, though. It wis a dud. Ye were lucky ah got the chance to go back and rescue it afore somebody found it.'

'What went wrong?'

'Dinnae ask me. Ask the man that made it. All ah ken is that it didnae blow when it was supposed to.'

'You've brought it back with you then?'

'Naw. Ah got rid o' it. Ah wisnae going to cairry something like that round wi' me when ah didnae have tae. Ah flung it in the sea.'

Mortimer sat down and rubbed a hand over his chin. McInnes resumed his seat, bending down to switch on the electric fire. He was in control now. He had the upper hand. The confidence that had filled him as he stood looking out over the North Sea, with the wind and the sleet pile-driving into his face, had not deserted him. Nobody was going to tell him what to do any longer. He regarded Mortimer with cold detachment, almost feeling sorry for him. You should have run away in your little car, he thought. None of your magic tricks can help you now.

'You threw it away?' Mortimer repeated.

'Course ah did. Ye're lucky I didnae jist dae a runner wance ah'd planted it on the bus like we planned. But ah didnae. Ah caught it the next time round and there was ma wee bag lying jist whaur ah'd left it, sittin up and begging like a dug wi' naebody tae tak it on. So ah took it back and poked it a bit and shook it. Then ah found a nice, busy pub and I set it up again wi'a the lights burning as they should, and ah went round the corner and stuck ma fingers in ma ears.' He shrugged his shoulders symbolically. 'Nothin' again. Half an hour beyond the mark, ah goes back in and there it is sittin'

166

unloved and unwanted in the corner wi' a'body pretendin' it's no there. So ah retrieves it for a second time and goes down tae the sea and hurls the fuckin' thing as far out towards Norway as ah can. Foreign-made stuff it wis, General. Ye jist cannae rely on it at all.'

'Why didn't you come straight back and tell me all this?'

'Ah'd had a bucket by then. I couldnae walk straight, never mind steer that heavy bastard o' a car o' mine. Ah couldnae run the risk o' being stopped by the polis.'

'You should not have chucked it away, Sandy. Perhaps we might have been able to salvage something from it.'

'Too late, General. The only place for defective equipment is on the scrapheap or at the bottom o' the sea. The wan in Edinburgh worked a treat, though. The other wan must jist hae been a dud. Whit could ah dae, ah ask ye?'

Mortimer looked at him curiously through narrowed eyes. McInnes wiped his nose on his sleeve and thought that maybe he was being too outgoing, too eager to provide the explanation. He was acting out of character. He should have been more restrained, less inclined to haver on. But he couldn't help it. He wanted to get the story told, to have it on the outside and not just as an idea inside his head. Once it was out it would have a life of its own. Even he himself might begin to believe that it had happened, then.

'It was nae fuckin' joke rescuing your bomb, ye ken, General. Twice ah had tae dae it, as well, and a' the time the bloody swine could hae blawn up under ma nose. Ah wis shittin' masel, ah'll tell ye that for nothin'. Ah could have left it, but naw, ah thought, ah'll be a hero. Ah'll risk ma scrawny neck fir General George so as nobody knows we've been droppin' bombs around the place like a hen droppin' eggs.'

'Perhaps you should have left it on the bus,' Mortimer said. 'An unexploded bomb would have got us just as much publicity, the way things are going.'

'Thanks very fuckin' much, ye bastard. Now ye're tellin' me ah shouldnae hae bothered riskin' ma life. That's nice tae know.'

'I'm not blaming you, Sandy,' Mortimer said, patting the air in front of him as if it was the top of a wall. 'God knows it's easy enough to come up with the best solution with the

167

benefit of hindsight. I'm not blaming you at all. You did what you thought was best at the time.'

'That's a'right then.'

'Maybe it's better what you did, anyway. They are all expecting a fourth blow for freedom, so they will keep sweating, thinking it is going to hit them at any moment.'

'That's what ah reckoned on when ah slung the box intae the sea.'

Mortimer nodded, smiling. 'It's just a pity we can't put down a hundred per cent record for the first phase. Still, it can't be helped now, I suppose. We'll just have to wait for the next phase to start up before we get a chance to redeem ourselves. You game?'

'As long as the money is right, ah'm game.'

'Good answer, Sandy.' Mortimer got up and began to walk restlessly about the room. 'You had me worried, you know. I was convinced something had gone wrong and you had been arrested.'

'And they were comin' fir you next, eh, General? Is that how you've scrubbed this place so squeaky clean?'

'I've been walking along this same street every twenty minutes since early this morning waiting to see what was going to happen.'

'It wis either me or a police car. Glad ah didnae disappoint ye. Ah slept the night in ma car. Whit about you?'

'Me? I booked into a little hotel just along the road.'

'The Shaftesbury?'

'I don't recall the name now.'

McInnes wiped his nose again. Still trying to hide the fact that he has got his car up here with him, he thought, feeling much more assured about his intentions than he had expected to. The lying bastard must have been frozen solid sitting all night in his car.

'Next time jist gie me decent equipment and ah'll see tae it that the job gets done properly,' he said.

'It was supposed to be highly reliable. I can't understand how it can have failed to explode.'

'It wis duff. Ask fur yir money back. When does the second phase begin anyway?'

Mortimer stood at the window, looking down. 'We'll have

to evaluate the reaction to our efforts so far, and assess what else needs to be done to ensure our goals are achieved.'

'Are ye coming back, or no?'

'I'll be back, Sandy. You can count on it.'

McInnes sat staring at the back of Mortimer's head for a while, trying to think of something clever to say, wondering what his real name was and what the grandchildren he had mentioned so frequently were like. If things had run to plan, he had said he was going to stay over in Glasgow until Saturday afternoon, because that was when his grandchildren were supposed to be going back home after a week with their other set of grandparents and he wanted to catch them on the way down. McInnes didn't want him to change his plans.

'Are ye staying the night or not, then?' he said.

Mortimer turned round, grinning. 'Since you asked so nicely, Sandy, how can I refuse your kind invitation.'

'Whit about your bags, then? Where are they?'

'My bags?' he said, glancing down at his feet as if he expected to see them there. 'I must have left them.'

'At the hotel,' McInnes prompted.

'Yes. The hotel. I'll go and get them just now.' He walked across the room to the door.

'Need a haund?'

'I can manage, thank you.'

'See and bring yir box o' magic tricks back, will ye? Put on a show for us again tonight.'

'Sure thing, Sandy. I'll do that. There is nothing I like better than an appreciative audience.'

CHAPTER FIFTEEN

Scottish Nationalist leader Andrew Wallace was last night besieged in his luxury flat in Edinburgh, refusing to speak to Press reporters anxious to talk to him about the deteriorating situation in the north.

Mr Wallace (48) went to ground as police worked desperately to try and discover where the 'fourth blow' promised by the Nationalist terrorists is intended to fall.

At SNP headquarters, Mr Graham Turnbull said that the speech to the United Nations General Assembly would go ahead as scheduled on Monday.

Meanwhile, another two women have died as a result of the bomb explosion at the Willow Rooms in Glasgow on Wednesday, bringing the death toll to ten so far. A total of twenty-six people have died in the three bombings believed to have been the work of the mysterious We're With Wallace terrorist organisation.

Daily Express

The wind had died away completely during the night. A slight thaw had set in and then the frost had returned. A sudden downpour of heavy rain had eaten away at the covering of snow on the hillsides of Glen Halkston, leaving bare patches like holes in a ragged white blanket. Stretches of the road shone black in the pale sunlight. The burn at the side of the house was swollen with rain and meltwater. It had increased dramatically in size overnight, transformed from a meandering trickle at the bottom of the stony channel to a twisting torrent as thick as a man's thigh.

Andrew Wallace brought the hand-axe down on the log in front of him and jumped out of the way as one half flew over his shoulder. He worked quickly, splitting another dozen logs and throwing them on top of the dry peats in the big wicker basket. It had been a good night, a long night, and he wished it could have gone on longer. It had been so warm in the small bedroom that they had lain under a single sheet with the door open, listening to the storm thrashing furiously above and around them. The fire was banked up with peats that smouldered throughout the night. The air was suffused with their earthy odour and with a reddish glow that made the place look like a photographer's darkroom.

He had finally arrived after a three-hour journey from Edinburgh. The snow was still deep then, although it was shrinking rapidly under the pouring rain. The roads had been mostly clear except for the last few miles, when he had to drive the big, wide-wheeled Jaguar very carefully in the glen itself, following the electricity poles which marked the edge of the all-but-invisible road. He had seen the lights of the cottage from a great distance but was unable to hurry because of the conditions. At one point he had skidded into a drift and the wheels spun frantically as he cursed and swore and tried to reverse out. He had thought he was stuck but they suddenly gripped the surface and the car lurched backwards onto the road again.

Helen was waiting for him at the door, anxiously concerned to hear from him what had been going on and keen to add her own theory to the list of interpretations of what it all meant. They had eaten supper and then gone to bed, taking the hi-fi system through with them so that they could listen to music. They had slept when the storm was at its height, and woke to make love again when the wind had faded to a whispering whine and the rain was a muted drum-roll on the roof. Dawn broke and the morning light was harsh and uncompromising. He got up and closed the door, pulled the curtains more tightly together over the window. But it didn't work. The spell was broken.

Wallace buried the sharp blade of the axe in the tree-trunk chopping block. Tucking the golden lion and its chain back inside his shirt, he picked up the basket and squeezed between the car and the wall, with it under his arm, to reach the front door. A drop of water from the gutter struck him on the side of the face, stinging him with its coldness. Inside, bacon was sizzling and spitting loudly in the frying-pan.

'Chopping wood is excellent therapy for us brain workers who seldom get to use our muscles.' he said.

'It is also good for keeping the fire going,' she replied.

'It sure is, Hanson. I hadn't thought of that.' He slipped the basket into its space between the oven and the wall and warmed his hands at the fire. 'How are we doing?'

'One egg or two?'

'Two, please. I need all the sustenance I can get.'

'You haven't seen that wooden-handled carving knife around, have you, Andrew? I can't find it anywhere.'

'Not guilty.'

'It was the sharpest knife in the house. I just can't find it.'

She was wearing a sweat-shirt and jeans and had her hair tied back in a thick pony-tail. He went up behind her and slipped his hands into her back pockets. She leaned back to kiss him on the neck and broke the eggs one-handed to drop them into the pan.

'Anything on the news?' he asked, knowing that if there had been anything serious she would have already called him in to listen.

'Nothing new.'

'Thank heaven for small mercies. How do you fancy a spot of hill-walking this morning? Want to make the trek up to the top with me?'

'Let's have breakfast first. It's ready now.'

'The radio didn't mention anything new happening?'

'Nothing.'

They ate breakfast, chatting brightly, playing footsie under the table, deliberately avoiding any serious subject, trying not to think about the bombings and their implications. It was a fragile atmosphere they created but even the frequent lapses into long meditative silences were not enough to destroy it. Immediately after breakfast they got dressed in heavy walking boots and fur-lined parkas and mitts and set off up the slope at the rear of the cottage. The temperature was below freezing and the snow crunched crisply under their footsteps. The ground was iron-hard beneath. It was a comparatively calm day and the going was fairly easy. The snow was about four inches deep on the hillside except where it lay in drifts, piled up behind some barrier. The wind was no more than a gentle breeze. The sun was a cold, white-gold ball in a grey patchy sky. Before they had gone one hundred yards Wallace decided to go back for their sunglasses to protect their eyes from the reflected glare of the snow. He checked the shanty-built toilet for signs of leakage as he passed, and took the portable phone from the Jaguar as well, just in case there were any urgent calls.

The entire glen was empty apart from the two of them. He and Helen followed the burn's channel upwards, sending small avalanches of snow and dirt down into the roaring water. Then they turned at right-angles to use the flat surface of a horizontal sheep-track for a few hundred yards before turning again to climb the slope. The snow got deeper at that point, reaching up to their knees in places. The soles of their boots slipped on the shifting mass of small scree stones underneath. They held hands and laughed as they struggled and stumbled. Once he fell over and pulled her with him, so that they rolled several yards backwards in a flurry of snow. They stayed on their backs for a while staring up at the sky, and then jumped up again before the mood grew too sombre.

Finally they made it to the shelter of the vertical face of the rocky outcrop. No snow lay within ten yards of it, although it was crowned with an overhanging fringe of white and every few minutes a miniature snowfall drifted down to instantly disappear, swallowed by the damp ground. There was a jumble of large, man-sized rocks against one part of the face of the outcrop. Wallace climbed onto them and sat down on a flat slab that was like the seat of a chair, with the other rocks around forming the back and arms. He helped Helen up and she squeezed in beside him, sitting with her hands between her knees. They were both breathing hard from their exertions, and sweating freely under the layers of warm clothing. Ahead of them they could see the mountainous countryside stretch away into the misty distance. Below, the glen was like a giant animal about to rouse itself and shake off the covering of snow that was clinging to its fur. The river was a snail's silvery trail. The red Jaguar and yellow Citroën were the only specks of colour in a sea of white and browny-grey. A thin line of smoke drifted sideways from the chimney of the cottage.

The horizon was foreshortened by low cloud hanging over the tops of the hills. The sun was gradually being obscured by the clouds. The wind was freshening. Their sweat dried on their skin and they shivered and huddled closer together. It was getting colder. The temperature was dropping rapidly.

'More snow soon,' Helen murmured. 'Perhaps we'll be stranded here for the whole winter.'

'We can't escape it all as easily as that. They would come and get us. Remember, Hanson, civilisation is just over that hill.'

'I don't want to remember that.'

Wallace was becoming more and more preoccupied. His mind was no longer solely concerned with her, now that the afterglow of their love-making had dwindled and they were sitting quietly with too much time to think. To the public he always seemed so calm and assured, self-confident in the extreme, but with her he was able to relax and acknowledge the doubts and uncertainties that existed just below the unruffled surface. She had often seen him nervous like this before some big occasion that was likely to have great bearing on his future career. She was not selfish enough to demand his undivided attention, because she knew how important his other life was to him. She had known of his love, his obssession, for Scotland when she married him. To deny it would be like a new wife demanding that her husband stop loving his mother. All night and all morning she had had him to herself. She would have to settle for that for the time being.

'It's terrible, those bombs. Who could do a thing like that?' she asked, grabbing his arm and squirming in as close as she could get.

'It's terrible, all right. Three so far and probably another tragedy to come, and all I can do is sit here and wait for it to happen. What else can I do?'

'Nothing, darling,' she said soothingly.

'I never wanted to be a politician, you know. I used to hate them, always telling people how to run their lives — pompous fools that they are. Why not let people get on with running their own lives? I thought.'

'I know, darling.'

'But then I began to see things differently. Politicians are

174

necessary. So are sewage farms. It was a case of practicalities. You need people to take decisions and order priorities. Somebody had to run the show, and I reckoned my qualifications were as good as anybody's, if not a damn sight better than most.'

'Of course, darling.'

'Having identified the problem, I had to make the effort to solve it, because the no-hopers doing the job were so pathetically inadequate. Does that sound terribly arrogant?'

'Not at all. When you put it that way you've got no real choice. It would be more arrogant not to try.'

He put his head back against the rock. 'God, sometimes I hate it all. It's so bloody slow. I wish there was some way of simplifying things so that a single act brought positive results straight away, instead of all this cumulative pressure and gradual progression stuff. And I don't mean random bombing of old women.'

'What do you mean?'

'Well, I wish it was more like the old days when you fought a battle and decided the winners and the losers by the end of the afternoon. If we are going to achieve independence, I wish it could be as clear-cut as that.'

'Remember Bannockburn and all that, like it says on the flags.' She pulled off a mitt and scratched her nose. 'It's still a battle when you think about it, though, isn't it, Andrew? Words are the weapons these days. It lasts a lot longer than one afternoon, but it's still a battle and you are the leader of the Scottish troops. Stick in there.'

'Do you know the story about Bannockburn? How the two armies lined up facing each other and this English knight rode forward challenging opponents to fight? It was Robert Bruce himself who went out from the lines to meet him, cutting him down with his battle-axe, and inspiring his own side to ultimate victory.'

'Is that a true story?'

'It's a true legend. The Englishman was heavily armoured, and when he charged with his lance he came straight on like a bull. It was a relatively simple matter for the lightly-armed Bruce to sidestep him and kill him with the axe.'

'As easy as splitting a log on the chopping block?'

'Maybe a wee bit more hazardous than that. Anyway, the point is that Bruce showed his own men, who were out-numbered three to one, the way to defeat the cumbersome English army by out-manoeuvring it. That's what I would like to do, ride out from the lines and show the way to the boys behind me.'

'A national hero, eh? Like George taking on the dragon?'

'Almost the same thing, but a different context.'

'Anyway, Andrew, you are showing the way. You *are* out-manoeuvring them. Every time you open your mouth in public you are setting the example.'

'Yes, I know, but there was a beauty, a terrible beauty, in the simplicity of the old days. It is so much more complicated today. I can't be sure that everybody understands my message. Words don't draw blood. Words don't get rid of the opposition.'

'You're persuading them, darling. Chop down a few Englishmen next time you are down in London, and they'll soon come round.'

Wallace sighed. 'Forgive me my little romantic fantasies. We're living almost in the twenty-first century, not the four-teenth. I suppose I would be condemned as a bloodthirsty warmonger or something if they could hear me havering like this, especially with these idiots running about blowing people up all over the place. The Party has got this far without spill-ing any blood. Independence might not take that much longer if we have patience.'

'Shame,' Helen said teasingly. 'I could fancy you in chain-mail mounted on a white charger.'

He turned and kissed her, their cold lips taking several seconds to warm under the mutual contact. She reached up and held his face in her mitts till he could hardly breathe and had to break away. The wind was getting stronger by the minute, sweeping over the glen with a keening howl.

'You see what I mean, though,' he insisted. 'A one-to-one confrontation. A winner and a loser, and that would be it — settled.'

'What happens if you turn out to be the loser?'

He shrugged. 'Winner takes all, Hanson. That's the rules.'

'Unfortunately, as you say, this is nearly the twenty-first

century. Things don't work like that any more. But you can be my champion if you like. You can fight my battles, protect my honour against all comers.'

'I'll take the job.'

They kissed again and sat with their heads resting against each other. The clouds swirled above them, sending wide shadows racing over the ground. The sun appeared and disappeared behind the patchwork canopy like an eye blinking open and shut.

The muffled noise of the phone beeping caused an abrupt change of mood. Wallace reached inside his parka and brought it out, extending the aerial as he did so. 'I told you civilisation was just over that hill,' he said casually. 'Hello? Graham, is that you? Not bad news, I hope?'

He looked at Helen and smiled to indicate that the answer had been a reassuring one. She got to her feet and jumped down from the rocks. The bare ground rang like a bell as the heavy soles of her boots landed on it, jarring her legs slightly. She paced back and forward to keep warm as she waited for him to finish the call. She hated being interrupted in their special place, and wished it was already time for him to return from America so that they could once again shut themselves off from the world for a few more hours in their own private glen. After some minutes he jumped down beside her.

'Don't tell me,' she said 'You've told them you can't go to New York because your wife needs you at home.'

'Sorry, Hanson. My country needs me over there.'

'The flight hasn't been delayed or anything like that?'

'I'm afraid not. Everything is still right on schedule.'

'What did Graham want?'

'The vultures are on their way here. Our little subterfuge to keep the Press in Edinburgh has finally collapsed. Somebody let the cat out of the bag. Graham says they set off in convoy and that there will be two dozen smelly reporters on our doorstep within the next few hours.'

'I don't feel much like playing the good hostess today.'

'Neither do I, so I think we'll hold court in the shed outside. They won't hang around very long if it's too cold for their delicate pencils.'

'We'll put a brave face on it, you and I. Come on then, we

177

had better get back, I suppose.'

They started off down the hill, hand in hand, feeling the freezing air slide smoothly over their cheeks as they headed towards the tiny cottage far below them.

CHAPTER SIXTEEN

The repudiation of the recent spate of terrorist acts by the Scottish National Party has a more than usually authentic ring about it.

Being as objective as one can when twenty-six innocent people lie dead, it simply makes no sense for true Nationalists to begin a campaign of terror at this particular time.

The SNP always has and always will operate within the law of the land. Its great achievement in recent years has been to exploit the democratic process to grow from sincere pressure group, to influential power-broker. In the near future it could well become a Party of government.

What then can be the motives of people who suddenly seem to think that change can be brought about by violent means? It is illogical and nonsensical, and because of that it is all the more frightening.

Scotsman

The first reporter to be seen by Murray Tarrant was from the *Sunday Mirror*. He was a middle-aged bloke in a blazer and scuffed black shoes. His teeth were bad and his skin was blotched and oily. The bags under his eyes were like water-filled blisters. There was a spiral notebook sticking out of his side pocket and two silver pens clipped onto his breast pocket. Two fingers of his right hand were stained almost brown by nicotine and he had a cigarette permanently stuck between them, which he seldom seemed to bother raising to his mouth.

Big Bruce had been sent to collect him from the rendez-vous point, to frisk him for recording devices and then bring him up to the flat. He remained standing guard at the door with his arms folded over his chest, watching disinterestedly as the well-scripted little drama was played out in front of him.

Tarrant showed the reporter the pictures, now contained inside plastic jackets to keep them clean. He and Demionscuk, who had disappeared early in the morning, had chosen just three from the Cecilia selection, as Tarrant called it. One was of her sitting on the edge of the bed, another was of her all alone on her back with the covers only up to her waist, and the last was of Tarrant and her grinning self-consciously at the camera from the bed. That should get them suitably excited, Demionscuk said, curling his lip. Tarrant agreed. The interview was taking place in the Demon's bedroom in the flat so that there would be no similarities could be drawn between Tarrant's room and the background in the photographs.

'All very well, Mr Tarrant,' the reporter said gruffly. 'But how do we know this is the real Helen Wallace?' He held each picture close to his face in turn, peering at it like a jeweller examining a diamond. The ash from his cigarette dripped down his sleeve.

'Because it is, sport. Plain as the nose on your face. Look, compare them with this newspaper one.'

'They're not exactly pinpoint sharp, are they? Any of them?'

'They weren't taken in a bloody studio, you know. We were just playing around. I didn't even know who I was playing around with at the time. As far as I was concerned she was just a pommy sheila out for a wild night.'

'When did you find out who she was?'

'A few months later. I saw her photograph in a magazine and it brought all the sweet memories flowing back. I checked up then.'

'Can you be absolutely certain it was Helen Wallace?'

'Absolutely. You have the evidence in your hands. She was passing through Adelaide that night. That is documented history. Up till now the bit about her passing through my bedroom has been missed out.'

'Hmm.' The reporter sat down with one of the pictures balanced on his knee. 'Tell me about her, then.'

'I'll tell you anything you want to know, if you bid high

enough to get to hear the full story.'

'It's up to you to convince me you've got a good enough story to sell before we start talking folding stuff.' He looked around for an ashtray and Tarrant gave him an old saucer to use. He immediately lit another cigarette and held it between the two badly stained fingers.

'How much convincing do you need? You know that even if she denies everything it is my word against hers. And I've got the pictures.'

'Out-of-focus pictures don't count for a whole lot. Tell me what she was like in bed.'

'Keen and ambitious.'

'She ever mention her famous husband? You know, in the heat of passion?'

'More than once. Of course, you realise I didn't appreciate the significance of it at the time. As far as I was concerned he was just some poor bum who couldn't keep the pot boiling to feed a hungry wife so she had to eat out, if you get my drift.'

'So what did she say about him?'

'Lots of things. She was quite a talker. I couldn't shut her up once she got going. Things that would make your hair stand on end.'

The reporter leaned forward blowing bad breath. The bags beneath his eyes wobbled. 'Kinky things?' he asked breathlessly, spilling ash onto his trousers.

Tarrant closed one eye in an exaggerated wink. 'All sorts of things you wouldn't expect a respectable person to indulge in,' he said. 'But it will cost you to find out. Make me an offer.'

'I'll have to speak to my desk.'

'You've got till Monday. Then you can contact my representative.'

'Mr Smith?'

'Yeah. Mr Smith. He likes to stay in the background until the real negotiations start. We are looking for at least two hundred thousand pounds, by the way.'

The reporter stuck out his jaw and showed his teeth in an artificial grimace. 'That's big bucks in anybody's language.'

'Big bucks buy big stories.' He took back the pictures. 'Time's up. Bruce will show you out. It's been nice meeting

181

you. Be sure and call us, now.'

Tarrant listened to the two of them leaving the flat. He put out his arms and spun round in a circle in the middle of the room. The bloke had swallowed the bait whole, and the hook was firmly in his mouth. According to Demionscuk, some freelance journalist was already poking around back in Adelaide. He would find what he was supposed to find there, and that would confirm what was on offer over here. It was a pretty smooth operation that was being laid on, and so far he was enjoying his part in it. It was just a pity he had to bugger up the Wallaces to complete the job. He felt he almost knew them from what he had read about them, and he had a particularly soft spot for Helen Wallace. She seemed a really nice person. He liked to think that they would have hit it off if they had met in Adelaide last year. Maybe the pictures would have been real enough, if him and her had got together. Who could say?

He had about an hour to kill before Bruce returned with the next reporter, from the *News of the World*. They were sending a lady. That was something to look forward to. Then there was to be a man from the *Mail on Sunday* as well and one from the *Sunday People*. He lay down on the bed and put on the headphones of his personal stereo. He switched the tape on and heard the first movement of Dvořák's Seventh Symphony begin. *Allegro maestoso*, it said on the box. Back home in Australia that music would help him travel at least fifty miles, closer to sixty with his foot hard down. He closed his eyes and whistled along to the music, imagining himself to be in the cab of his lorry again with the image of Cecilia's big, beautiful backside looming up on the horizon ahead of him like the rising sun.

The blue-shirted Glasgow Rangers winger swerved in from the touch-line, leaving the Hibernian full-back for dead. He pushed the ball ahead, hurdled a wild, lunging tackle from another defender that made a brown slash in the lush turf, and then crossed it on the run before losing his balance and falling over the advertising hoarding onto the perimeter track. The ball curved in towards a ragged line of three teammates advancing on the goal. The keeper started to come to meet the cross, changed his mind, stumbled, and was left stranded in no-man's land. The onrushing striker was just inside the six-yard line when he met the ball flush with his forehead, knocking it straight and hard against the bar which sent it spinning up and over the top into the closely-packed crowd behind.

The moment before the ball hit the bar, every person in the Copland Road stand at Ibrox Stadium had risen from their seats, like iron filings bristling above a strong magnet, to acclaim the goal. But the deep-throated cheer changed abruptly to a disappointed groan, followed by a fierce burst of approving applause to encourage the home players to greater efforts.

Sandy McInnes sat down again, loosening the tight knot of his scarf round his neck. His throat was already sore and all the shouting he was doing was only aggravating it. His nose was running constantly and he was sweating freely, convinced that he must be coming down with the flu as a result of his paddle in the ocean on Thursday night. The biting cold of the wind in his face at that moment would not be helping either. Not that it mattered. His cousin Liam and the family would look after him once he got to Londonderry. He had booked his car on the late-night ferry from Stranraer.

The man beside McInnes stood for a little longer, dramatically posed with his head back and his hands covering his eyes. He was wearing an armless, badge-covered denim jacket and had a scarf tied round each wrist. His bare arms were wreathed in blue and red tattoos. When he finally sat down he was red-faced, with flecks of white spittle at the corners of his mouth.

'Did ye see that, pal?' he demanded of McInnes. 'That big fuckin' fairy couldnae score if he wis the only prick at a whore's weddin'. The manager should get him aff the park now.'

'He should tell the laddie tae open his fuckin' een when he heids the fuckin' ba',' McInnes agreed. 'Then he might see whaur he's puttin' it.'

The fans were singing. On the field, a Hibs player clumsily took the legs from an opponent in the centre circle with a cynical late tackle. The entire stand again rose as one to protest and hurl insults in his direction, as other players converged on the scene and began to push and shove each other.

'Ya Fenian bastard. Come up here an' try that,' roared McInnes's neighbour.

'Fuckin' animal shouldnae be allowed on the park if he cannae play fitba' properly,' yelled McInnes himself, feeling the strength of his voice fade away with the words. 'Fuckin' animal!'

The referee broke up the mêlée and waved a yellow card in the face of the original offender who was trying to plead his innocence. That pacified the furious crowd a little. A trainer ran on to give treatment to the injured player. McInnes sat down again, briefly protected from the wind in the midst of the forest of bodies, his head aching. There were patches of snow on the track and on the roofs of the other tiered stands enclosing the pitch, which was kept free of frost and snow by its undersoil heating. The roads outside were clear enough, though, according to the radio. General George should have had no problems on his journey south. He should have had a free run. He should have reached the border by now.

It was almost half time. McInnes had missed the first ten minutes of the match because General George had taken so long to make up his mind to leave. It was after two o'clock before the bastard lifted his bags and headed for the door, still insisting he was heading for the station to catch a train south. Let the train take the strain, McInnes thought, as he was finally left on his own. Young Jimmy Nairn was waiting at his door to be paid for his morning's work. 'Nae bother, the job's done,' he had said, grabbing his money and running out of the close.

McInnes looked at his watch, and then looked up, grinning stupidly at all the people round about him. One minute to go, he thought. It had been simple to steal the cardboard tubes from the Major Magic case that morning, when General George was shaving off his beard in the bathroom. There were only two of them, each with a flexible, detachable skin in white, blue, green, and red and a raised lip at top and bottom so that when they were neatly slotted together it looked as if there was only one. He had to wait until General George was gone before he could examine them more closely.

184

He found the letter in a slim, curved pouch on the inside of the white cylinder, along with two sheets of similar paper that were blank. It did not look like much, only a single paragraph and a signature that McInnes did not recognise at first. 'England expects you to do your duty.' So this was the priceless document. He began to think that maybe General George had been talking rubbish about his influential friends. It was only when he was on his way to Ibrox that it suddenly came to him that it must be a letter from the Prime Minister. Edwards, the Prime Minister. No. Not the Prime Minister, but the Prime Minister's son: Christopher Edwards. A future prime minister, General George had called him. A top person. A high-level contact. A man with a good pedigree. He had not been kidding after all.

The Rangers goalkeeper collected a pass-back, bounced the ball twice, and kicked it high into the air. The wind carried it deep into the Hibs half. A defender tried to trap it and only succeeded in passing it directly to the Rangers striker. The young boy steadied himself before shooting for goal. The ball was blocked and rebounded to give him a second chance. This time he feinted to shoot again and instead chipped it delicately over the advancing line of defenders and ran through into the penalty area. The 'keeper rushed out and spread himself at his feet, but the big striker calmly took the ball round him and tapped it into the empty net.

The crowd roared with delight and the blue scarfs waved wildly. McInnes and his neighbour embraced enthusiastically, bouncing up and down with the swaying mass of bodies.

'Ya little beauty,' McInnes shouted as they broke apart, punching the air. 'See whit ye can dae wi' yir een open.'

It was only when the crowd were settling down and the ball had been returned to the centre circle for the kick-off that McInnes realised his watch alarm was squealing. 'Ya little beauty,' he murmured hoarsely to himself, grinning hugely as he turned it off.

One hundred miles to the south Major George Mortimer had just passed Gretna, and the WELCOME TO ENGLAND sign at the side of the road was in sight. He was thinking how good it was to be clean-shaven again and how glad he was that he had stayed in Glasgow the extra night to give him the chance to go in to see his grandchildren on the way home. Then he died instantly as his car was ripped apart by the powerful explosion. The debris was scattered on both sides of the border.

The big Boeing 747 standing in the snowstorm on the darkened runway at Prestwick Airport was just visible from the window of the VIP suite. The plane had been thoroughly searched. Andrew Wallace thought the suggestion that he might be the target for the fourth blow for freedom was ridiculous, but no chances were being taken. Then there was the report in the last hour of the car-bomb explosion down near Carlisle. That could have been the fourth blow, or it could have been the bombers' luck running out. The occupants of the car had not yet been identified and, by all accounts, there was not much left of them to identify. There was no certainty that the incident was linked to the We're With Wallace people anyway. The size of the explosion made it a possibility, but it was too early to be sure.

Wallace was standing beside the pilot, who had come in to shake hands and introduce himself for the benefit of the television cameras and the Press photographers who were there to record the departure and wanted some action. Wallace had done all the interviews, answered all the questions, smiled and frowned at the appropriate moments. He was tired and edgy and looking forward to sleeping during the long flight across the Atlantic. The speech for the self-determination debate was finally written, changed repeatedly since its original draft form until he was happy with it. It was good stuff, stirring stuff, oldfashioned rabble-rousing stuff. It was guaranteed to go down well with his audience, even though the big boys at the United Nations were not so keen on it.

The pilot had a clipboard under his arm. 'Don't worry about the weather, sir,' he said. 'It may be a bumpy take-off but we will soon get through this little storm, and it's much clearer further out, according to the Met office.'

'Thank goodness for that, captain. Keep it as smooth as possible. I hope to catch up on my beauty sleep.'

'I'll do my best.'

Wallace almost said something about everybody trying to do their best, but decided it sounded too patronising, so he just shook hands again instead. The pilot followed the crowd of media folk being shepherded out of the room by Graham Turnbull, one of only two companions accompanying Wallace on the New York trip. The other was his personal assistant, Laura Thomson. There were also six reporters and two television crews with them on the flight. Laura appeared in the doorway, fighting against the tide of people moving out. She came straight across to him.

'I've just heard that the office in Edinburgh received a telex this afternoon from Dave Sheahan,' she said.

'Dave Sheahan? What does he want? He only left us last week.'

Laura looked at her notebook. 'He says he accepts the invitation to the celebration dinner planned after your speech on Monday.'

'What? Are we having a celebration dinner?'

'Well, we're having a small reception in the hotel.'

'Did you invite him?'

'No.'

'Did you, Graham?' Wallace asked, turning to Turnbull now that the room was empty.

'Not me. The first I heard about it was when Laura told me two minutes ago.'

'Well, somebody must have invited him. Maybe it was me at the New Year party in the flat. I don't remember, but never mind, it will be good to see him again. I'm sure he owes me a drink, anyway.'

'The telex asks where we are having the dinner.'

'Tell him to contact our hotel. Have you got time to send a telex in reply before we leave?'

'I think I could just about manage that. The plane is just starting to load its passengers. We'll be following them in ten minutes or so.'

She hurried out of the room. Wallace turned to the window and stared out into the swirling snow. The saltire on the tall tail was momentarily isolated from the rest of the plane, and then connected again.

'I'll be glad when we get above all this,' Turnbull said.

'So will I, Graham,' Wallace replied. 'So will I.'

187

Sandy McInnes saw the huge, lumbering shape of the jumbo jet silently leave the ground as he drove past Prestwick. Its rising lights had blended smoothly with the flashing lines of falling snow and then suddenly disappeared as if the storm had sucked it up out of sight.

McInnes was sweating, and beginning to shiver as well. He had taken medicine which had dried up his runny nose, but his temperature was high and his forehead felt as if a blowtorch was being held against it. He had given himself plenty of time to reach Stranraer because of the weather and because of his condition. There was little traffic on the road and there were no hold-ups. He travelled at a steady forty miles per hour. He stopped in a lay-by at Ballantrae Bay and wrapped his scarf tightly around his neck and fastened his anorak before opening the door and stepping out in the cold of the night. He took the typewriter in its case from the boot of the car and climbed over the low fence and down the slippery, rocky slope to the shingle beach. The wind clawed at him and the snow stung his eyes, making him blink. He swung his arm back and forward a few times and then tossed the typewriter out into the sea. It splashed down on the choppy surface, floated for a few seconds, and then sank. At once, he hurried back to his car and continued his journey south to the ferry port.

McInnes had typed the letter wearing an old pair of leather gloves to avoid leaving any fingerprints. He had spent a lot of time wiping and rewiping the letter itself to ensure it was clean. He wasn't planning on staying in Northern Ireland permanently. He was the home-loving sort, and he wanted to come back to his own country once all the fuss had died down. Then he would make a fresh start.

He had addressed the letter to the Detective Superintendent Bryan Leslie at Pitt Street who had been named as the leader of the inquiry into the explosion at the Willow Rooms in the first *Evening Times* story. He had used the typewriter so that it could be linked with the sending of the original notes on the WWW campaign to all the newspapers. Presumably the forensic boys could establish such a link. The

lower-case d had a distinctive tilt, and the capital P had the
bottom half of its stalk missing. It was obvious enough to
convince the police this was no hoax. General George was not
so smart after all, McInnes thought smugly. He should have
stuck to selling carpets. There had been a fourth blow for freedom, but not the kind he would have approved of.

CHAPTER SEVENTEEN

Scottish Nationalist leader Andrew Wallace left for New York last night as the whole of Britain braced itself for a new terrorist onslaught.

A massive car-bomb exploded in a vehicle travelling south to England yesterday afternoon, and it is believed that the bomb may have gone off prematurely as it was being moved into position.

The driver was killed instantly, but has not yet been identified. Police fear that the terrorists' failure to deliver the promised 'fourth blow' may provoke them to launch a renewed bombing campaign south of the border.

Mr Wallace again condemned the use of indiscriminate violence as he left the country to take part in a debate at the United Nations. His attractive young wife remained behind at their £100,000 luxury cottage in a remote glen north of Glasgow.

News of the World

It was too cold to be outside. Murray Tarrant went for a walk first thing on Sunday morning, but it only lasted ten minutes because the freezing air collected in his throat and lungs like bundles of sharp-edged icicles. In the Holland Park flat, Big Bruce sat all day watching the television beside the hissing gas fire in his room. He didn't say much, and when Tarrant wasn't sitting beside him, he was marching impatiently up and down the corridor listening to music, or he was lying on his bed reading magazines and books and newspapers. He watched the sky darken and the stars emerge and heated cans of beer in front of the fire to take the chill off them. By the time the old woman came in to make the evening meal just

190

after six he was pretty drunk. The grey wrinkled skin of her face looked as if it had been dabbed with pink paint.

Renzo Demionscuk arrived back an hour later.

'Well, have we got a sale?' Tarrant asked.

Demionscuk shrugged as he unwrapped himself from the layers of heavy clothes. 'Maybe.' he said finally.

'What do you mean, maybe? Didn't that set of mongrels believe me, then?'

'It's not a question of not believing you, Murray,' Demionscuk said soothingly. 'They believed you, all right. It's a question of us pushing the price up a little.'

'How do you mean? How much have they bid?'

'Not enough. We need some more pictures.'

'Good on you, mate. Get the girlie back and let's fill an album.'

'No, Murray. Real pictures of you and Helen Wallace together, that's what we need. Then we can mix them in with our sexy ones and make the story seem even more authentic.'

'Oh yes? Tell me how we're going to get the lady herself to drop her knickers for us. And why all the fun and games with Cecilia if we can.'

Demionscuk's mouth twitched in the way that Tarrant associated with a smile. 'You misunderstand, Murray. All we need is you standing next to her, maybe shaking hands or something like that. We don't need her on her back with her legs in the air. We've got that kind of picture already. A perfectly innocent pose will take on a whole new meaning when it is set alongside a compromising one. It's all to do with juxta-position.'

'My feelings exactly.'

'It just involves a little more work for us. We'll have to head north for a couple of days probably, till we get a chance to approach her.'

'When? Want a beer?'

'Soon. No thanks. Tomorrow, maybe the day after.'

'Good. I'm bored hanging around here. It's so bloody cold.'

'It will be even colder up north.'

'Yeah, I'll be glad when I can get back to my truck — and the sunshine of dear old Oz. How long do you think that will be?'

'Not long now, Murray. Getting homesick, are we?'

Demionscuk went into his bedroom and turned on the gas fire there. The flames appeared with a sudden whoosh. He bent down and held his hands close to the heat and rubbed each finger individually. Tarrant stood in the doorway, leaning casually against the frame. With one hand he carelessly flipped open and shut the cassette cover of the personal stereo attached to his belt.

'We just go and knock on her door and take her picture, do we?' Tarrant said.

'Simple as that, Murray. Tell her a joke to make her laugh and click, the whole world will think she is welcoming a long-lost lover.'

'I've been reading quite a lot about the Wallaces, Renzo. I feel as if I've got to know them, and I think I could even get to feel sorry for them. It almost seems a shame to have to bugger them up like this for the sake of a few dollars in the bank.'

'Turn on your cassette and let's hear the violins in the background, Murray. We've got a job to do, and we can't afford to let our emotions get in the way.'

'I mean, the bloke's only trying to have a say in running his own country, as far as I can make out. He is only doing what he thinks is best. What's wrong with that?'

'Nothing at all. Another bloke is having his say by trying to stop Wallace from having his say. What's wrong with that?'

'You mean the bloke that is paying for all this?'

'Yes. Remember him? You won't read about him in any of the magazines, but he's just as entitled to do what he thinks is best. Maybe if you knew his version of things you'd feel sorry for him.'

'That's always been my big problem, being a stupid sucker for a sob story. I always seem to agree with whoever is telling it at the time.'

Demionscuk came over and stood in front of Tarrant. His eyes were as cold as the freezing air. His face was a frozen mask. 'I'm telling you this time, Murray,' he said slowly. 'And I'm paying you. Don't start listening to anyone else. Just listen to me.'

'Sure thing, Renzo,' Tarrant said reasonably, not wanting to antagonise him too much. 'I'm with you all the way. Don't get the wrong idea. I was just thinking out loud. I know whose side I'm on.'

'Don't be taken in by Wallace. He's just another scheming politician out for himself, and no different from any of the rest.'

'I can see that,' Tarrant said. 'But you have to admit he's got a lot more flair than the others who are around at the moment.'

'And he has got an attractive young wife who is about to prove to be his downfall.' Demionscuk turned away, going back into the room. 'Just imagine the story we're selling has all been true, then maybe you won't feel so sorry for him.'

Tarrant realised that he was getting to Demionscuk by talking about having sympathy for Wallace. Normally, he would have backed off so as not to provoke him any further — but he was bored, so was acting like a boy taunting a vicious guard-dog in the knowledge that its master had given it strict instructions not to bite. He wondered how far he would have to push the Demon before he got a really violent reaction, because the man's impassive face betrayed hardly any emotion at all. He couldn't smile, he couldn't frown, but you could see what he was thinking reflected in his eyes. Maybe the Demon thought it was unprofessional to sympathise with a victim, or maybe he himself had some sympathy for Wallace. Maybe that was what was making him so angry.

'You're from Ukrainian stock, aren't you, Renzo?' Tarrant said. 'Don't you have some fellow-feeling for Wallace and his nationalist cause up there in Scotland? Your people have been under the heel of the Russians for a long time now. It's pretty much the same thing for the Scots, the way he tells it.'

Demionscuk pulled his jersey over his head and began unbuttoning his shirt. He kept his back to Tarrant as he spoke. 'Let me give you some good advice, Murray. Put your faith in yourself, not in any collection of dirt and rocks that calls itself a country or a nation or whatever. Borders are just lines drawn on a map. Loyalty begins and ends with yourself and those you choose to be part of your own family. Don't trust anybody who wants to tell you how to live your life.'

'But nationalism is about people, not countries. It's about

like-minded people banding together, forming their own family.'

'Crap! Nationalism is about power.' Demionscuk selected a clean shirt from his suitcase and unfolded it. 'For Wallace it's about getting people to do what he wants them to do. You've been reading too much of his propaganda. Why should an accident of birth dictate your politics?'

'You're not a nationalist then, Renzo?' Tarrant said thoughtfully. 'It was you who told me you were Ukrainian.'

'As accurate a description as any. I could have said I was a Cossack, but I was born in the United States and then brought up in Italy from the age of eight. My mother was Italian, my wife is Yugoslavian and I live in Luxembourg. What have I got to be nationalistic about?'

'But you told me you were Ukrainian,' Tarrant insisted. 'You didn't say American. You didn't say Italian. Surely that must mean you have some feeling for the place?'

Demionscuk tucked the new shirt into the waistband of his trousers and adjusted his collar. The smell of cooking had entered the room, indicating that the evening meal was almost ready. He looked across at Tarrant and there seemed to be a sadness in his eyes, a look that Tarrant had never seen before.

'Listen. My grandfather was a Ukrainian patriot. He was a founding member of the independent government that was established in Kiev and lasted for three years after the Russian Revolution, before Stalin decided he didn't like the idea. He finally got out in the 1930s, when my father was just a child. They ended up in Milan. It was either that or starve to death under Stalin's own particular brand of Russian nationalism that created the great famine in the Ukraine. There was plenty of food but it was simply taken away from the people and sent to Moscow. It was a lesson to teach the Ukrainians who was in charge. They had a choice between the Russian hand feeding them or the same hand throttling them. They learned the lesson.'

'Just like the Tsar used to teach his peasants.'

'The same thing under a different name, Murray. Big countries will always control small countries, one way or another. To his dying day my grandfather never stopped tell-

194

ing stories about his beloved homeland. He always spoke in Ukrainian, which is a bit like Italian, actually.'

'And you don't feel the same way?' Tarrant prompted.

'My father had a healthier attitude to life. He said: "Son, remember where you have come from, but that doesn't mean you should go back." And I never have been back. I've never seen the land of my ancestors and I doubt if I ever will. It's all in the past. I've moved on.'

'Where have you moved to?'

'Wherever I find myself, Murray. That's where I'll be. I've learned a lesson too. I've learned to draw a circle round myself and my family. That is my boundary. That is my nation. Beyond that the rest of the world can go fuck itself.'

Demionscuk decided to end the conversation. He came over to the door, obliging Tarrant to back into the corridor. 'It smells good,' he said. 'Let's eat.'

CHAPTER EIGHTEEN

When Mr Andrew Wallace, the President of the Scottish Assembly, addresses the United Nations today, he will be only the third representative of a non-member institution to do so.

The first was Pope Paul in 1965. The second was Mr Yasser Arafat, leader of the Palestine Liberation Organisation, in 1974 and again in 1988.

Mr Wallace (48), Chairman of the Nationalist Party in Scotland, has been invited to speak at the opening of the debate on self-determination despite active behind-the-scenes lobbying by the UK to prevent him obtaining such an influential platform.

Mr Wallace and his Party make no secret of the fact that their ultimate aim is complete independence, and therefore the dissolution of the UK. Many political observers believe such an outcome is increasingly likely.

New York Times

Andrew Wallace could feel the adrenalin surging through his veins as he stood in front of the General Assembly of the United Nations. His own voice was booming strangely in his ears. His hands rested lightly on the edges of the lectern, but not once did he have to look down at the text of his speech. The words and phrases flowed easily as he stared out over the orderly rows of serious faces ranged in front of him.

He had known it was going to be a good day as soon as he woke up early that morning. Seen from his hotel window, the shining metal towers of the New York skyline were bright and gleaming under an intense winter sun. Snow and ice sparkled playfully. He had been desperately eager to get on with it throughout the endless handshakes with grinning officials and the polite small-talk of the morning and the long lunch with the Assembly president and the Secretary-General and a horde of hangers-on. Then, at last, the formal opening of the debate, and his introduction and the walk to the podium, escorted by the UN Chief of Protocol, and the momentary silence as everybody waited for him to begin. And finally there was the outpouring of words. Yes, it was going to be a good day.

'Nationalism is a powerful emotion. I cannot deny it. But, like love and hate and fear and sadness and joy and anger, it is an emotion that cannot be purged from the human soul. It is a dangerous emotion, too, held responsible for countless wars and deaths down the centuries, but it is an emotion that is essential to our lives.

'Nationalism can be horribly destructive, or it can be gloriously creative. Take it in isolation, give it free rein unfettered by conscience or concern, and it will rapidly grow into a terrible, frightening, uncontrollable monster. But handle it properly, acknowledge its existence, balance it with the counterweight of civilised values, feed it with native culture, and you will banish the monster for ever and instead create a friendly beast that can harm no one, because to do so would be alien to its nature.'

Wallace waved a hand in the air, encompassing the whole auditorium in the sweeping gesture. 'We are all nationalists here. Each one of you represents your separate country. You are proud of that country, of its achievements, of its potential, of its position in the world and in the family of nations. You would not be here if that was not the case. But the majority of you would not *describe* yourself as nationalists, because for you the argument is over and you live safely within well-recognised borders. Your nationalism then is a beast under control. From some of you I can almost hear it emanate like the purring from a well-fed cat. You have no reason to be aggressive in defence of your nationhood. The beast is adequately fed and watered. Its claws are sheathed and blunted from long disuse. But they are there should it ever prove necessary to have recourse to them.

'I, too, as a citizen of the United Kingdom of Great Britain and Northern Ireland, am represented here. I see that Sir

197

David Goldman, my ambassador, is not with us at the moment.' All eyes turned briefly towards the empty seat of the UK delegate. 'Perhaps he is out there sharpening his claws in the hope of making an effective reply to my speech. It is no secret that Sir David tried exceedingly hard to prevent me from being given this opportunity to address the plenary session at the beginning of the debate on self-determination. You see, Sir David is a UK nationalist and he does not want to see an independent Scotland. He regards the UK as an inviolable unit and has been quoted as saying he will resist the break-up with all the resources at his command. I respect that point of view. I do not agree with it, but I respect it. But I am afraid I must further provoke him and test his strength by explaining why his UK nationalism has become a bogus political contrivance that should be made redundant.

'Scotland is a country now claiming its independence and its rightful place in the world. There have been wars of independence all over the world, but three hundred years ago our sovereign Parliament in Edinburgh voted to tear up its own constitution and join with the much larger English Parliament at Westminster. In effect it sold its birthright. Since then the voice of Scotland has been a frequently unheard whisper among the deaf ears of the our southern neighbours. There is every historical reason to believe that the union was tainted by corruption and selfish motives among the Scottish burgesses and aristocracy, but that has little or no bearing on the present-day situation. My claim for independence rests solely on the demonstrable belief that the Scottish people no longer want to be party to that union. They want to withdraw from it. They want to resume control of their own lives. They want to take on the responsibility for making their own decisions. They want their Parliament back. They want to be a nation again, in the real sense of the word.

'I said before that nationalism is a dangerous emotion. In its raw form it inspires many regrettable actions by those some call terrorists and others call freedom-fighters. Innocent people are killed, and the perpetrators' excuse is always that right is on their side and so are the people. I need offer no blood-soaked examples to show the nationalist beast at its worst. We have all seen them for ourselves, or read about them. Violence is among the most common expressions of nationalist feeling, but I and my Party repudiate all violence. The untimely death of a single man, woman, or child as a stepping-stone on the journey to independence would make the ultimate achievement a poisoned victory. In my opinion, the ends cannot be portrayed as justification for the means.

'Scotland has no need of violence, terrorism, or freedom-fighting. The will of the people does not have to resort to such methods. The will of the people does not have to be enforced by the barrel of a gun. It can be written down: a million crosses on a million ballot papers. The will of the people can give a clear and unmistakable message: *democracy is our means and our method.*'

Wallace paused. The sweat was beading on his forehead and he could feel it running down the side of his nose. The emotional high was causing tears to gather in his eyes. He took a sip of water. The faces out there were watching him — blurred ovals of pink and brown and black.

'It is rare, if not unique, for a country to quietly vote its sovereign parliament out of existence. The dubious political manoeuvrings of the ruling elite of the time may have been questionable but they were legitimate in their own way. All I am doing, three hundred years on, is asking that the vote be taken again, and this time the entire population should be asked to decide. I am confident it will be a vote that we should exist once more as an individual and separate nation.

'If the majority of the Scottish people vote in such a fashion, there can be absolutely no justification or authority for maintaining the union. No political system is sacrosanct. We are using the system's own rules to change the system. No blood needs to be spilled; no shots need to be fired. Democracy can and must decide the argument.

'What happens in Scotland over the next few years can set the fashion for the rest of the world. If we can win the hearts and minds of our people and demonstrate that democracy is a strong enough means to deliver nationalist ends, then perhaps the terrorists and freedom-fighters and guerillas in other places may, they just may, decide to lay down their guns and follow our example. Perhaps they may see that there is a way to fight for their beliefs without having to die — or have others die — to get their message across.

'Democracy is on trial in the United Kingdom and both sides have to agree to abide by the judgement. The advocates of union must be prepared to concede independence if the majority of the Scottish people vote for it, and we Nationalists must be prepared to concede defeat if the people vote against it. Either way, the system should be flexible enough to cope. The losers' only recourse can be to redouble their efforts to change hearts and minds. Another vote in three years or three hundred years can change things again, if it can be shown that that is what the people want. It is a very civilised way of doing things. But if the majority of Scots unhesitatingly vote for the only overtly anti-unionist political party in the UK, and the Westminster Parliament uses its in-built majority of English members, who make up what is supposed to be an equal union, to ignore that expression of intent, then democracy itself will be the loser. If that happens then the beast may become increasingly restless. I do not want to dwell on that eventuality.'

He changed the pace of his delivery, taking a deep breath and slowing down, deepening his voice. 'I am convinced the people of Scotland will vote for independence because I myself have been convinced that it is right and proper that a country with its own national and cultural identity should have the courage to take its own decisions on how life should be lived within its boundaries. That is not a negative attitude. That is not to say that we want to turn our backs on the rest of the world. Nationalism does not preclude internationalism. On the contrary, we want to take our true place in the world. He paused once more. A second. No longer.

'Self-determination is a precious commodity. Self-respect is even more precious. Scotland can have neither until we have both.'

There was silence for a few moments as the last words were translated in the ear-pieces of the delegates. Then the applause began and the delegates rose to their feet. Wallace stood back to graciously accept the ovation. A good day, he thought, feeling himself drained of all emotion. For a few seconds the applause seemed to sound like the snarling of a ferocious animal, then it became a pleasing sound, a soothing sound. He forced himself to smile even wider. A good day, he told himself. A very good day.

The phone-call was made just before nine in the evening. Christopher Edwards had the bedroom extension turned off, but he heard it ring in the living-room, and he heard his wife stir herself from in front of the raucous television soap opera to answer it. It was the personal line, known only to close friends and family. All other calls were diverted to an answering service. Edwards sat up in bed. His pyjamas were soaked with sweat and he was shivering despite the warmth in the room. Antonia spoke only a few words that he could not make out properly. Then there was a pause, and a few more mumbled words. He imagined — rather than heard — her lay down the receiver and begin to move towards the bedroom door, and then there was the loud crack of her heels on the wooden boards as she stepped off the carpet. The door handle turned.

Edwards had taken to his bed on Sunday, claiming incipient flu, after George Mortimer was named as the victim of the dramatic car-bomb explosion near Carlisle the previous afternoon. Arthur Fairchild was unable to offer an adequate explanation of what might be going on. His advice was sit back and play dumb. Mortimer was well and truly dead. There was nothing to link him with the Forum. The police would not have any clues to point them in their direction. Don't worry, Fairchild maintained; we've covered our tracks. Meanwhile the worry was making Edwards ill — a persistent headache refused to go away. Had the explosion been deliberate? Had it been an accident? It must have been an accident. A faulty detonator or unstable explosive probably. That would account for the failure in Aberdeen. But why was Mortimer bringing it back south? Why take the risk? Why not just dump it, for God's sake? Edwards gripped the bed covers tightly and the sweat oozed out of his hands as if he was squeezing water-filled sponges.

'It's your father, Chris,' Antonia said, entering the bedroom but stopping by the door when she realised he was awake. 'I told him you were poorly but he says it's rather urgent.'

'I'll take it here. Thanks, dear.'

'How are you feeling now?' She smiled solicitously.

'As well as can be expected, I suppose.'

She closed the door as he picked up the phone by the bed. It was slippery in the palm of his hand. He pulled a dressing-gown from a chair and draped it across his shoulders while he waited until she had set down the receiver in the living-room.

'Hello, Father,' he said. 'What's the problem?'

'What the fuck have you been up to, Chris?' the Prime Minister replied.

Edwards felt as if something was boring into his stomach. His father *never* used bad language. The pain behind his eyes vibrated like a newly-struck tuning-fork. 'What do you mean?' he said lamely.

'The police are on their way to question you about the bombings in Scotland. They think you may be associated with that man who died in a car explosion yesterday.'

Edwards caught his breath. Jesus, Jesus, Jesus, Jesus — the refrain pounded inside his head, taking on the rhythm of the blood pulsing in his temple. He closed his eyes and rubbed the spot with his thumb, massaging the skin in a circular motion. Jesus, Jesus, Jesus, Jesus ...

'Why is this happening, Chris? Tell me.'

'I don't know, Father. I can't imagine why.'

'Tell me the truth, son. It's all going to come out sooner or later. It's nothing to do with this British Unionist Forum, is it? I told you to keep away from those people.'

'I assure you, Father, I don't know anything about these bombings and even less about the Forum, if it still exists.' He covered the mouthpiece to hide his heavy breathing.

'The police seem to think they have evidence against you,' the Prime Minister said.

'Evidence? What evidence?'

'I'm not entirely clear. It could be some kind of a letter.'

'A letter? I haven't written any letters.'

Edwards swallowed a mouthful of saliva and licked his dry lips. There were no letters. He had been supremely careful. There was nothing written down that could link him with the Forum. It was all word of mouth and personal contact. All easily dismissed and denied, if necessary. A straightforward case of one person's word against another, if traitors were found. Finance was routed through the impenetrable money-maze of Liechtenstein. That single message he had been persuaded to write to encourage Mortimer on the first mission had been destroyed completely, burned to ashes. There could be no evidence against him. That side of things was absolutely foolproof. A sense of renewed confidence made him open his eyes and sit up straighter.

'Don't lie to me, son. Let me know what I'm up against.'

'I'm clean, Father,' Edwards said firmly. 'It could be somebody deliberately creating trouble for me, maybe even for you.'

'Are you telling me everything, Chris? This could turn into a nasty scandal if we don't get our response right. I don't want to be caught with my pants down.'

'Of course,' he lied easily. 'I've done nothing to be ashamed of.'

'Are you sure?'

'I've done nothing.'

'I hope not, son. I hope not.' He hung up.

For a long time Edwards continued sitting upright in the bed, staring into the middle distance with the phone gently buzzing in his ear. He seemed to be sweating even more profusely, with moisture cascading down his torso and over his legs. It ran into his eyes and into the corners of his mouth. Single large drops rolled over his scalp, each tracing an erratic course through the hairs like balls in some biological pinball machine. His mind would only work very slowly, the thoughts turning over like the pages of a book. When the police came, should he stay in bed and put them at a disadvantage, make them feel bad about interrogating a sick man? Or should he get up and get dressed, use the protection of his Parliamentary authority and the prestige of his family name to shrug off their questions? All people in public life suffered from false and malicious accusations from time to time. It was an occupational hazard that had to be borne. It was a free country, after all. People could say what they liked. The police were only doing their duty in checking it out. No hard feelings, officer. I quite understand your position.

He dialled Fairchild's private number, but there was no

answer. He let it ring for a long time. The continual breep-breep sound somehow translated itself into the two syllables of the word Jesus, Jesus, Jesus, Jesus; the refrain echoed in his head, fragmenting his lines of thought. There was no physical evidence against him. He was untouchable. How dare they accuse him of such actions? What did they have? A confession? His membership card of the BUF perhaps, produced like a rabbit out of a hat? Name, rank and serial number — that was all he would tell them. A lawyer? He should contact Randolph Mannering as soon as possible. Randolph would slap them down.

He turned on the radio on the bedside table and Andrew Wallace's voice leaped out at him. 'Democracy is our means and our method,' he was saying. Cut to applause. A standing ovation at the United Nations, according to the commentator, a well-received speech greatly enhancing Wallace's image as an international statesman.

The bastard is little better than a terrorist, Edwards thought savagely. Those ignorant swine fawn over him while he dismembers Great Britain like a callous schoolboy pulling the wings off a butterfly. The talk of democracy was a front, that was all. It suited Wallace to be a democrat. Later it might suit him to be a murderer, if that got him what he wanted. It was him the police should be questioning, should be arresting. In a properly ordered society he would be seen for the evil, self-interested manipulator he was. He was the real criminal.

Edwards threw back the covers and got out of the bed. The dressing-gown slipped from his shoulders. His legs were weak and would hardly support him as he crossed the room to the window. He looked down into the street and saw a police car double-parked on the road. Its orange light flashed slowly, casting pale shadows again and again over the row of parked vehicles. Other unmarked police cars drew up. Men got out. Only one seemed to be in uniform. They stood on the pavement talking to each other, hunched against the cold like the deformed villains in a child's adventure cartoon. They had no evidence. No evidence at all.

The moon was lighting the scene from behind a thin veil of clouds. Edwards looked out over the rooftops and had the ridiculous idea of making a run for it over the frost-shining tiles and between the chimney-pots. He would scamper away into the safety of the darkness, find somewhere to establish a base and send out a call for all true supporters to rally round. From there they would begin an irresistible campaign which would catch the popular imagination. The UK would be saved. Wallace would be finished, beaten at his own game.

Edwards laid his forehead on the ice-cold glass of the window and his whole body trembled. Even if he was convicted, surely the country would realise he had acted in its interests alone? The people would appreciate that he was only doing what any man of honour would have felt obliged to do in the same circumstances? No, he had done nothing to be ashamed of. On the contrary, he was proud of what had been done. Besides, they couldn't have any evidence against him.

He sank to his knees. His forehead slid down the glass and came to rest on the window ledge. Jesus, Jesus, Jesus, Jesus; the refrain reverberated even more loudly inside his head. The pain behind his eyes intensified. Blood rushed to his groin, warming the region as though he had just stepped into a hot bath. Whatever happened, he had done it all for his country, not for himself. That was his final justification. He would make an impassioned plea from the dock, if he was destined to be a martyr. The people would understand. The people would remember him.

The celebration party in New York grew quite boisterous after a while. The hotel even had to take a couple of waiters off the buffet table and put them behind the bar to cope with the demand for drinks. The room was a long, narrow one with strangely-shaped light fittings twining over the walls and ceiling like stainless steel creepers in a metal jungle. Only about fifty of New York's great and good were invited, but double that number had arrived. Wallace told the doormen not to turn anyone away. He wanted to share his sense of triumph with the whole world. The nervous energy that had compensated for his lack of sleep over the previous twenty-four hours was slowly fading. He could feel his eyelids getting heavier by the minute, but the last thing he wanted now was

205

to go to bed. A video tape of his speech was playing constantly on a television set in one corner. Everyone wanted to shake his hand, kiss his cheek and slap him on the back. Somebody started to sing 'Auld Lang Syne', and the talking stopped as everyone joined in. They all held hands, arms crossed, and formed a ring. The heady atmosphere was shot through with the aroma of women's perfume and men's aftershave.

'It's just like New Year all over again,' Graham Turnbull said. 'Better even.'

Dave Sheahan appeared quite late in the evening. His serious, harassed-looking face was in sharp contrast to the general mood in the packed room. Wallace seized his hand and embraced him as an old friend.

'Dave, my good pal. Good of you to come all this way. It's amazing the lengths some people will go to have a drink bought for them. What will you have?'

'Bourbon.'

'Get him a whisky, and get me another one as well,' Wallace said to the waiter specially delegated to stay close to him. 'Why the long face, Dave? Tonight is a celebration. Did you hear my speech?'

'It was very impressive.'

'I hope I've won a few more friends with it. That attractive lady over there in the red dress and the pearl choker looks like one of my new converts — she keeps eyeing me up. Pity I'm a respectable married man these days, isn't it?'

The waiter returned with two generous drinks, then drifted back into the background. Sheahan swallowed half of his in a single gulp.

'Can I speak with you privately, Andrew?'

'Now?'

'Yes, now. It's important. It won't take long.'

'Well, there is a small lounge next-door. I suppose we could go there.'

'That will do fine.'

Sheahan was twitching nervously and looking all around him as Wallace led the way out into the corridor. The empty lounge, a few doors along, was quiet and warm. From the window they could see a small artificial lake surrounded by bare young trees, far below, set in an expanse of mottled snow. A cleared pathway curved away from the frozen circle of water like the stalk of a figure nine. Wallace did not turn on the lights. He preferred the half-darkness and the pale glimmering reflections of the stars deep inside the sheet of glass. He was curious about Sheahan's strange behaviour, though not particularly concerned. His self-confidence had never seemed more unshakable. He had the feeling that nothing and nobody could harm him.

'Shoot, Dave,' he said. 'What's the beef?'

'Sorry about the cloak-and-dagger stuff, but I think I'm under surveillance. That's why I sent a telex accepting your invitation to this party. They would monitor it and know why I was coming here. No serious reason for them to suspect any other motive.'

'They?'

'We've been running an operation to ruin your career.' Sheahan finished the sentence with an exhalation of breath like the sigh of a man pleased to relieve himself of a heavy burden.

'We?'

'We — the people of the United States. Who else?'

Wallace smiled, surprised that he wasn't more surprised by the revelation. 'You were behind the bombings and the We're With Wallace campaign?'

'I guess so. That would fit. I haven't been able to get chapter and verse, but we definitely have something in motion, strictly undercover, of course. I'm told our man is over there now, with strict orders to ensure that the United Kingdom stays united.'

'And he tries to ruin me while pretending he is on my side?'

'That's the way I figure it, Andrew. The word is they don't want to chance losing the use of Holy Loch. There's a lot of paranoia in the Pentagon about you Scots turning your back on NATO if you do go it alone. That would leave a big gap in the northern flank, open the door to the Atlantic for the Russians. They won't allow that.'

'Didn't you tell them I'm pro-NATO and pro-American?'

'You might be, Andrew, but what about the people around you? The ones that hardly ever show their faces?'

'You reported that, did you?'

Sheahan shrugged in embarrassment and sat down in a low chair with the fingers of one hand tangled in his hair.

Wallace smiled again and sipped his whisky. Let them keep trying, he thought. Nothing and nobody ... I bear a charmed life.

'I never took you for a CIA agent, Dave,' he said.

'They recalled me because they thought I was getting a little too close to the subject.' Sheahan looked up suddenly. 'Maybe they were right. Otherwise I wouldn't be here, would I?'

'I appreciate it, Dave. I really do.'

'I'm sorry. What more can I say?'

'How much do you actually know?'

'Only that the operation is up and running. Not much more. Our man is said to have recruited people to do the job over there. He is supposed to be one of our best fixers, and will probably have put two or three layers between himself and the actual live operatives.'

'Light the blue touchpaper and then retire to a safe distance?'

'And watch the fireworks.'

'Did you know about this guy that blew himself up — Major whatever? He was an Englishman.'

'He would be a recruit over there. We've got contacts at high political levels in England. They might not get their own hands dirty, but they would point us in the right direction.'

'Can we get any evidence to prove CIA involvement?'

'I doubt it, Andrew. Not at this stage, anyway. It's a clandestine job, with the man on the ground run personally from the very top. I'm only going on hearsay myself, but I think it's pretty reliable stuff. Our chief, Barrett Coleman, is the instigator. He's a real redneck when it comes to defence matters. The bombings in Scotland were the clincher for me. It all fits neatly into the pattern. It must have been us.'

'I suppose I should be flattered that a superpower takes such an interest in a tiny backwater country like Scotland.' Wallace raised his eyebrows, then shook his head. 'Would you testify in court, Dave?'

Sheahan grimaced as if he had been hit in the stomach. 'It wouldn't do you any good, Andrew. They've got a dossier on me showing how I'm a sucker for a Scots sob story. I would be destroyed in any witness-box.'

'So where does that leave us?'

'At least you know what you're up against.'

'Well, that's something, I suppose.'

Wallace went to the window. The warmth of the air around him seemed heightened by the sight of the frozen townscape outside. The geometric switchback lines of the horizon glowed with the hidden energy of the city. In the distance a silent helicopter — made up of three dots of red light and a whirling black shadow — dropped out of sight. He was physically exhausted but his mind was working furiously. He had always expected something like this to happen. He was not so naive as to be shocked by what Sheahan had told him. It was inevitable really, and now all those people were dead, and many more would have to die before it was settled one way or another. That was real power: the capacity to order the deaths of ordinary people to further long-term political goals. It was nothing personal. It was all done in the name of defending your country's interests. It had to be done — there was no alternative. Besides, if you wanted a comparison, Mother Nature was far more profligate with human lives than a million wild-eyed generals sending the troops over the top.

He stared into the eyes of his reflection, an insubstantial figure floating in mid-air a few yards beyond the glass. He was indirectly responsible for those deaths by simply existing and trying to do what he was trying to do. It was his fault. Every action has an equal and opposite reaction, so he had been taught in the physics class at school. If he announced his retirement tomorrow there would be no more killings, no more deaths. But he knew he couldn't do that. He was defending his country's interests. What he was doing had to be done. He had no alternative and, deep down, he had the utterly unshakable conviction that he was going to succeed.

The door opened and Graham Turnbull rushed in. Wallace turned as the ceiling lights blinked into life.

'Andrew,' Turnbull almost shouted. 'Have you heard the latest?'

'Probably,' Wallace replied calmly.

'You can't have heard this. They've lifted Chris Edwards.

209

The police are questioning him about the bombings.'

Sheahan spoke first. 'Good God. The Prime Minister's son.'

'True-blue fascist that he is,' Turnbull said. 'It has just come through on the agency tapes in the basement.'

Wallace smiled in bewilderment. This time the element of surprise was overwhelming.

CHAPTER NINETEEN

The Prime Minister's son, Mr Christopher Edwards, was last night helping anti-terrorist police with their inquiries into the spate of bomb attacks in Scotland.

This sensational development has thrown the Government into turmoil, and the future of the Prime Minister must now be in serious doubt. A Downing Street spokeswoman refused to comment.

Mr Edwards (37), a backbench MP, was taken from his sickbed at his Kensington apartment by police after a request for assistance from detectives in Strathclyde, who are investigating the three incidents which have so far resulted in the deaths of twenty-six people.

No further information was released, but it is understood that police inquiries are focusing on an allegedly incriminating document that has been found. It could not be confirmed if the death of Mr George Mortimer, a former army major, in a car-bomb explosion on the England-Scotland border on Saturday is connected with the latest move.

Mr Randolph Mannering, the solicitor acting for Mr Edwards, said his client has not been arrested but is voluntarily assisting the police to hasten the resolution of the situation.

Daily Telegraph

The house appeared suddenly from the darkness, unnaturally white in the strong headlight beams, with the four brown shutters and recessed door like a child's painting and the sloping roof merging with the black mass of the swaying trees beyond and the clouds streaming across the sky in an unbroken line. Murray Tarrant stopped his car directly behind the vehicle in front and switched off the engine. When the lights were doused the house vanished, and then slowly reasserted its shape like a bruise colouring on the grey-black skin of the evening. An invisible wind rocked Tarrant's car from side to side as he watched the fat woman climb out of the leading vehicle. Her great bulk was illuminated by the interior light, and then suddenly swallowed by the darkness as the car door closed with a hollow thump. Tarrant opened his door and shivered as the warmth around him quickly dissipated. He reached out to switch off the tape of the Elgar symphony that was playing. God, he thought, if it was cold in London it must be ten times worse up here.

'Let's get inside before we freeze to death then, Mrs MacPherson,' he shouted over the sound of the screeching wind.

They walked to the door, struggling to retain their footing on the uneven ground. The wind whipped gritty pieces of snow against Tarrant's face and eyes. He crowded into the comparative shelter of the doorway, pushing up against Mrs MacPherson, who bent over the lock with a jangling bunch of keys. It took several attempts to find the correct key and then they tumbled inside to an even more intense darkness broken by a thin yellow line at floor level. She moved ahead and the thin line expanded up into a tall rectangle. Tarrant came behind him and felt the heat strike his cheeks at the same time as he saw the peat fire blazing fiercely in the room.

'Home, sweet home,' Mrs MacPherson said. 'Welcome to Glen Halkston. I came over earlier this evening to light the fire.'

'That was very thoughtful of you,' Tarrant said.

It had been a long day. He had phoned the number given to him and warned Mrs MacPherson he intended to take up residence in the rented house that night. Then he and Demionscuk had travelled all the way up from London in a hired car, the Demon driving and Tarrant dozing in the passenger seat as he marked off the distance on the motorway with music in his usual fashion. At one point he was listening to Beethoven's Seventh and as it approached the end of its final movement he snapped his eyes open, fully expecting to see the body of a buck kangaroo strung out across the wind-screen, teeth chattering against the glass. There was nothing there, of course, just the snow-covered banks at the side of the motorway and the traffic droning along on all sides. But the thought triggered his imagination. That was where it had all begun less than a month ago; in the outback with that crazy, kamikaze kangaroo deciding to collide with the same few square feet of vacant space in the same split second it was needed by his truck. In retrospect that had been an important moment. Soon afterwards Tarrant himself was to set off on his own collision course, sent flying to the other side of the world to occupy the space alongside a woman he had never met, in some crazy, convoluted attempt to convince the world the two of them had indulged in a one-night stand and so discredit a successful politician they couldn't get at in any other way.

The plans to come north had been advanced. Things were hotting up now that a separate plot against Wallace had been revealed. Mad bombers had been just a little too mad to do a decent job. There was talk of the Government's resignation, a general election in Britain, and a landslide victory for the Nationalists in Scotland — exactly what he had been brought over from Australia to prevent. Stony-faced Demionscuk had been told to pull the finger out. Struth, Tarrant thought, only last month he had been complaining that life was too boring. Never again. He wound the tape back to the beginning of the final movement, and settled back in the comfortable seat, wondering vaguely which role he was now destined to fill: that of the kangaroo or the truck.

In Glasgow, Tarrant was told to hire himself another car. They travelled further north in convoy, into bleak country-side and worsening weather, and off the main roads onto narrow, single-track roads with passing places blocked by piles of frozen snow. Demionscuk did not hesitate once. He knew exactly where he was going, right to a remote village in Argyll and straight to Mrs MacPherson's door. The Demon stayed out of sight round the corner outside while she welcomed Tarrant. She gave him a refreshing cup of tea and some excellent home-made scones and jam, chatting away for half an hour as if he was an old friend. His story implied that he was a rich Australian looking for a bit of peace and quiet in the Highlands.

If she found that unusual she didn't show it. 'I think we can just about guarantee you that,' she said. 'Not much happens up here.' Then she got out her car to lead the way to Glen Halkston.

Tarrant ventured out to his car to fetch his suitcases and a box of groceries from the boot. Mrs MacPherson showed him round the house and explained where everything was, but declined the offer of another cup of tea. She did not mention neighbours and he did not ask about them. After fussing around for a while, she finally went off and left him alone. He closed the door as the red tail-lights of her car disappeared into a dip in the road, and went back inside to open a bottle of whisky.

The storm grew ever more violent outside. The shutters creaked and rattled as if some force was trying to tear them off. Loose branches ripped from the nearby forest scrabbled across the roof like marauding animals. The fire in the grate roared as it was drawn up the chimney. The fat yellow flames were like a transparent bag containing the dark lumps of red-edged fuel. Tarrant felt foolish as he tiptoed round the upstairs bedrooms just to convince himself they were un-occupied. He made a boil-in-the-bag instant meal and ate it quickly. Mrs MacPherson had left a supply of fruitcake and more of her delicious home-made scones and a pot of straw-berry jam. He helped himself to large amounts and washed it all down with whisky as he sat by the fire. The heat made him drowsy. His head began to nod.

He opened his eyes to see Demionscuk looking down on him, his face darkened by the shadows and reddened by the firelight.

'You found it, then?' Tarrant said.

Demionscuk did not reply. He sat down on the seat on the opposite side of the fireplace and held out a glass. Tarrant filled it, noticing that almost half the bottle was gone. He wondered how long Demionscuk had been in the house. He was only wearing a shirt and there was an empty plate on the table. He must have made himself something to eat.

'When do I go visiting, Renzo?' Tarrant asked.

214

'Tomorrow,' Demionscuk said. 'The cottage is down near the other end of the valley. You can see it from here in daylight.'

'Is she there just now?'

'Yes. Looking forward to some action, are you?'

'I hope she gets a good night's sleep so that she is at her best for me in the morning.'

Demionscuk continued to stare across at Tarrant as he helped himself to more whisky, taking it neat. Tarrant was intimidated and looked away. He thought how they were sitting on either side of the fireplace like two nodding-head ornaments that used to be on their mantelpiece at home in Adelaide when he was a youngster. His mother had sold them one of the times they were short of money. He picked up the poker and shoved the point into the hollow mound of burning peats, raising a flock of flying sparks. He had never seen the Demon drink like that before. It must have been because things were rapidly coming to a climax.

'Still feeling sorry for Mr and Mrs Wallace?' Demionscuk said as the shadows washed over his unsmiling face and the flames were reflected as bright silver specks in his glittering eyes.

'Not really,' Tarrant replied. 'They'll survive, I suppose.'

'You shouldn't let it worry you, Murray. It's nothing personal. It's just a job we're doing. If it wasn't us it would be somebody else.'

'Sure.'

'Hear that wind, Murray?' Demionscuk paused as they both listened to the storm thrashing around the house. 'That's us. People like you and me are forces of nature, just like that wind. That's what we are, Murray, forces of nature.'

'Sure.'

Demionscuk turned his attention to the fire. 'When I was a young boy we lived on a trailer park near Kansas City,' he said and his voice seemed very loud in the small room. 'One night we were hit by a tornado. I was in bed when the twister carved itself a path through the park, ripping apart everything it touched. I woke up in my bed without a scratch. Our trailer had disintegrated around me. It just wasn't there any longer. I was staring up at the stars, still wondering what had

215

happened, when they came to tell me my parents had been killed.'

'I'm sorry,' Tarrant said, taking a drink to hide his embarrassment.

'Nothing to be sorry about, Murray. You wouldn't expect the tornado to be sorry, after all. You wouldn't blame it. It was a force of nature. An impersonal thing, not vindictive. We are part of the same nature, you and me. If it hadn't happened, or if we had moved out of the park the day before, I would never have gone back to my relatives in Italy. I would be a different person.'

'You wouldn't be here with me.'

'No. But somebody else would, no doubt. And if it wasn't you, Murray, there would be somebody else as well. So don't take it personally. Wallace and his wife have got to take their chances along with the rest.'

'Forces of nature, eh? I like that.' Tarrant hesitated, trying to decide if he was choosing the right moment. 'Can I ask you a question, Renzo?' he said finally.

'Of course. Ask away.'

'You remember you told me you organise things for anybody willing to pay you enough?'

'Yes.' Demionscuk refilled his whisky glass.

'Does that organisation include killing people?'

'Murray, Murray. Where do you get these ideas?' The reply came swiftly. Demionscuk's mouth twitched as he shook his head. 'I'm a happily married man. A doting father. Do I look like a killer?'

'No,' Tarrant said very quietly, meaning yes.

'What do you think I am? A Mafia hit-man? A hired assassin?' He laughed in his own peculiar way. 'I'm just a businessman, Murray. I'm no tornado. A stiff wind at the most.'

'We're not here to kill Wallace, then, or Helen Wallace?'

'That would be bad business. If we create martyrs we would only be helping their cause, wouldn't we? We're here to knock off the gloss finish, cut the hero down to size. That's all. You can put your mind at rest.'

Tarrant didn't know if he was relieved or not. That was what he had been thinking: that they would not want to

216

create martyrs. The plan was too elaborate to end in such a manner. The Demon might look like a killer, but he seemed to be pretty soft underneath the façade. He was too much of a thinker.

'Besides,' Demionscuk went on, 'if I am an assassin what is the point of having you along for the ride, Murray? I wouldn't need any help if the job description was so simple.'

'When you put it like that I can't argue.'

Demionscuk raised his glass. 'Long live Mr and Mrs Wallace.'

'Likewise,' said Tarrant.

CHAPTER TWENTY

The Government was in disarray last night as informed speculation mounted that the Prime Minister was about to announce his resignation.

Mr Peregrine Edwards has been considering his future since his 37-year-old son Christopher was charged with conspiracy in connection with terrorist outrages in Scotland last week. A warrant has now been issued for the arrest of a second man, millionaire insurance-broker Lord Arthur Fairchild.

Sources close to the Prime Minister believe that he will decide to stand down because of the embarrassment and humiliation of the incident. Candidates for the succession are already beginning to jockey for position within the Party.

Although this Government still has two years of its term to run, because of the circumstances of Mr Edwards's resignation an immediate general election will probably be called to give his successor a renewed mandate.

Independent

The first thing Wallace saw when he was gently shaken awake was the bright pattern of threads that made up the company symbol in the centre of the wine-coloured tie of one of the pilots. It coalesced in front of him rapidly, like the image in a camera's view-finder being brought into focus. Each thread was like an individual brush-stroke in a painting. Bob, his sleepy brain thought. Bob Dutch. Bob's company. Bob's company plane flying east. Any chance of hitching a lift, Bob? No problem, Andrew. It's flying empty anyway, going to London to pick up the chairman. Plenty of room for a little one. It's due to take off from Newark tomorrow evening. The latest model of Jetstream, extra fuel capacity means it can cross the Atlantic non-stop. I'll tell them to expect you, shall I? You see, Bob, I want to surprise the wife by arriving home a day early. She flew over unexpectedly for my birthday the last time I was in the States and I'm thinking it would be nice to return the compliment. I get your drift, Andrew. Leave it to me. Thanks a bunch, Bob. I really appreciate it. Don't mention it, Andrew. Great party, by the way. Give my regards to Helen when you see her. I'll do that, Bob.

'Excuse me, sir,' the pilot said softly and his starched white shirt crackled more loudly than the drone of the engines. 'You asked me to wake you when we were nearly there.'

Wallace straightened up to ease his cramped muscles and the chair turned smoothly and noiselessly towards the window as the back slowly raised him into a more vertical position. He reached out and released the stiff blind. It was grey outside, neither light nor dark. The edge of the wing was barely distinguishable from the background. The rumpled cloud base was far below. He could see the moon, white and cold, or it might have been the sun. There were a few scattered stars.

'We ran into some turbulence back there, sir. I hope it didn't bother you too much. It was a nasty little storm but we're through it now and will soon be leaving it well behind.'

'I didn't feel a thing,' Wallace assured him, moving the blanket from his legs. 'I must have slept like a baby.'

The pilot grinned. 'Well, it will be chasing us all the way into Scotland. They probably won't thank us for bringing in the bad weather. A nice strong tail-wind is adding to our speed so we should be on the ground at Prestwick in about an hour's time. You can have a wash and brush-up in the rear, and I've just made some hot coffee for me and Tom up front at the pointed end. Don't hesitate to give me a shout if there is anything you need. We're a bit short on food, I'm afraid, just some crispbread and jelly. Have a nice day.'

'What day is it?'

'We're flying into Wednesday.'

Graham Turnbull had thought it was a great idea to fly back early to surpise Helen. The travelling reporters might complain but they were easily distracted. Turnbull was all for calling the Press back home and have them queuing up at the airport to record the happy reunion. It would be wonderful publicity. It wouldn't be much of a surprise though, Wallace told him. It had been a spur of the moment thing at the celebration party when his mind was in a whirl with all those women in figure-hugging dresses and Dave Sheahan informing him the CIA was out to get him and the news from Britain that the police had found the bombers and one of them was the Prime Minister's son. The idea of having Helen at his side somehow became imperative. How good and how reassuring it would be for him. He wanted to sneak back anonymously and drive up to the cottage in Glen Halkston and knock on the door. That would be a real surprise, now. Helen would love it. Turnbull reluctantly agreed. He would spread the story afterwards. It was too good to waste completely.

Wallace took the blanket off his legs and stood up. The air-conditioning blew a warm draught into his face. He massaged his eyes with thumb and forefinger and yawned, making the bones in his jaw crack. He had slept most of the way, untroubled by dreams. If the CIA were behind the We're With Wallace bombings then they must have got their fingers badly burned and would think twice before trying anything again. Christopher Edwards was just the type of lunatic right-wing MP who would join forces with the Americans in a crazy scheme like that. The sun would never set on the old empire inside his head. And what about dear old Perry. What would he do now? What could he do now? His eldest son was hope-lessly tainted, whether he was eventually charged with anything or not. No smoke without fire, the public would conclude. Before, it had been all talk and bluster. An embarrassment, of course, but one that Perry could live with. You can choose your friends but not your family. It wasn't his fault his son had turned out bad. But now it had taken on a different dimension. There was blood on his boy's hands. The blood of innocent people. And Perry could rationalise and try to distance himself all he liked but in the end he was connected to it by his own blood-ties. He was in an untenable position. He would have to do the honourable thing and resign. That would mean a general election.

Wallace went to the wash-hand basin at the rear of the Jetstream and filled it with cold water. There was hardly a ripple on its surface as he splashed it into his face and rubbed his bleary eyes. Then he went to the central alcove and poured some coffee for himself. It was strong and burning hot. He could only find powered milk so he didn't bother with that. The white plastic cup had a company symbol painted on its side. The coffee shone through the plastic as if it was the finest bone china.

Wallace yawned again and the tiredness suddenly fell away from him. The gentle vibration of the plane's engines was a pleasing sensation coming up through the soles of his feet. There would soon be a battle to fight, the most important election of his life. He was ready for it. It would be make or break for the Party. It was coming sooner than he had expected, but it was coming and he was ready for it. He searched for the golden lion rampant on its chain inside the front of his shirt and squeezed it tightly in his fist like a talisman. Nothing and nobody could hurt him, he reminded himself. It was more than a feeling. It was a faith. Nothing and nobody. He was almost there.

The public phone in the empty rear lounge of the village pub was on a small shelf in the window alcove, hidden behind curtains that had a fading pattern of pheasants and gundogs. There were two directories, one fat and one thin, and a badly scratched coin-box with the actual number of the phone completely obliterated. When he lifted the receiver, Renzo Demionscuk had to shade the grey liquid crystal display from the strong daylight to be able to read it after thumbing one pound's worth of coins into the slot. He punched in the number he had memorised and waited patiently, listening to the unfamiliar British ringing tone. It would ring thirty times before it was answered. Any normal person would give up. That meant the person who answered it would know exactly who the caller was.

It was cold in the sparsely furnished lounge. The light coming through the window hardly managed to penetrate into the room beyond the flimsy curtains. Tables and chairs were shapeless lumps. The metal mesh pulled down over the bar looked like hanging cobwebs in the gloom. Behind the barrier a doorway was framed by three strips of white electric light, and voices were just audible from the front bar, like the sound of trickling water. Demionscuk turned his attention to the window and the street outside. The bottom half of the window was below ground. The pavement was almost level with his waist so that he was looking upwards, his view blocked by a parked car at the side of the road. He leaned closer to the window and his breath clouded the glass. He picked up a glove and wiped it clear. Now he was able to see almost the length of the main street in one direction, the two rows of low buildings coming together under the slate-grey clouds like railway lines running into the distance. There was only one person in sight, far away and approaching slowly.

Demionscuk had planned to use the phone-box in the village but had found it to be out of order that morning, flashing the message that it would take emergency calls only. He cursed his bad luck. He had no idea where the next public phone-box was and he did not want to make himself too conspicuous by asking to use somebody's private phone in their house. That left the village pub with its sign telling him: you may phone from here. He had no option. The call had to be made.

He was glad it was so cold. He did not look out of place with the hood of his anorak pulled up and the yellow lamb's-wool scarf round the lower part of his face. There were only a few people standing at the bar when he entered, all of them well wrapped up, because it was not much warmer inside than out. 'We've just got the heating switched on,' the bearded barman told him defensively. 'It will be a wee while before it takes the chill out of the place.' Demionscuk bought a whisky and asked to use the phone.

The ringing tone stopped as the call was answered. Nobody spoke. Demionscuk watched the lone pedestrian get closer and closer. It was a woman, a fat woman. She waddled on stiff legs, bowed into the wind, moving slowly and carefully on the slippery surface. The large knot of her headscarf was lying on one side of her neck like the knot of hangman's noose. He knew who it was.

'I'm ready to go,' he said. 'Everything is set up.'

'She is there just now?'

It was a different voice from the usual one of the soft-

222

spoken American. It spoke more precisely, more com-
mandingly, like a military officer used to being obeyed. It
sounded as if the real boss-man had come to take charge for
the final act in the drama. Demionscuk tried to put a face to
the voice but could only produce an image of his own likeness
talking back to him over the phone.

'We were watching her this morning,' he said. 'She's all on
her own.'

'And Tarrant?'

'He still thinks it's a harmless little game. He's actually
quite keen to make the lady's acquaintance.'

'You have the details all worked out?'

'Of course.'

'There is probably going to be an election.'

'So I hear on the radio.'

'You'll have to move fast, then, if it's going to be effective.
Wallace is not due back from the States until tomorrow. Do it
tonight.'

'No problem. The sooner the better, as far as I am
concerned.'

'Do it, then. Good luck.'

Demionscuk hung up. The face of the woman walking
along the pavement outside was very familiar. Angry red
patches stained her cheeks and the tip of her nose. Her eyes
seemed to be staring straight at him, the skin around them all
screwed up as if she was trying to get a better view. It was Mrs
MacPherson, the cleaning woman from the Wallaces' cottage
when he visited it last year, who had taken Tarrant out to the
Fowler place the previous night. He turned his shoulder to the
window so that she would not see him. She walked straight
past on her tree-trunk legs. An old pair of socks was pulled
over the soles of her zip-fronted boots to give her a better grip
on the icy pavement. Her little shopping trolley bounced and
skidded over the ruts carved in the hard-packed snow. She
cast a shadow that came down through the window and over
Demionscuk, making the air seem to grow even colder for a
brief moment. He hurried away across the darkened room.

Murray Tarrant watched the faraway cottage through the

pair of high-powered binoculars, with Beethoven's Seventh Symphony pounding loudly in his ears. He had become obssessed with this piece of music, returning to it over and over again. It had been playing when that poor dumb kangaroo had committed suicide by leaping in front of his truck on the Stuart Highway back in the Northern Territory just before old Luigi Fachetti had sent him to the other side of the world on this weird and wonderful expedition. He had seen the 'roo coming all the way, watching its every movement until it was flipped up and broke its neck against his windscreen and didn't move any more. Now he was watching another victim, he thought, but this time he wasn't waiting for her to come to him. He was deliberately steering the truck towards her, to knock her down. 'Sorry, sport,' he mumbled to himself. 'Can't stop.'

Tarrant was lying on his stomach at the crest of the small hill about one hundred yards from the house. He had been there since early in the morning, having spread a covering of old sacks over the wet ground to protect himself from the damp. The fur-lined hood of his anorak was pulled well down over his forehead and the heat of his breath lingered in the scarf wrapped round his mouth. The rubber eye-guards of the binoculars were brittle in the cold when they should have been soft, and uncomfortable against his skin for any length of time, so he balanced the pair on a tripod of his gloved hands and held them just in front of his face. He whistled softly through cold-numbed lips.

Helen Wallace was sitting at a table just inside a window. He could just make out her profile through the bars, her head leaning forward. He had an impression of a pretty face with hair falling all about it, of shoulders, of breasts, of arms. She was reading a book, or writing something, he thought. Occasionally she rose and disappeared from view, but she always returned to the same spot. Sometimes Tarrant got up and walked around a bit, stamping his feet to help the circulation in the intense cold, or returning briefly to the house to warm himself at the fire there. Then he would get back down on the sacks to resume his observation, fascinated by the figure at the window. Once, she came right up to the window and peered outside. Tarrant believed she was looking directly at him, although he knew he was too far away to be seen. He held the binoculars in one hand and waved with the other. She raised a hand and seemed to be waving back. He smiled behind his scarf and thought that she smiled too before she went back to her table.

The wind was blowing from behind him, raking down the glen along his line of sight, skimming the layers of snow into a powdery mist that hung a few inches above the surface, clinging to the rolling contours of the land. It had been dark all day. Full daylight had never managed to break through the overcast sky, although the clouds were beginning to break up slightly. Sometimes when his concentration was drifting he would follow the small, individual snow storms that raced over the hillsides like flocks of tiny white birds. Or he would focus on the river where it fattened at the centre of the glen, the grey water flowing sluggishly between two shelves of ice. There were no animals to be seen. Nothing moved unless it was stirred by the wind. The music in his ears moved towards its climax in the final movement. The only other warm-blooded creature around, apart from Tarrant, was inside that distant cottage.

He felt a kick against the sole of his foot and looked round to see Demionscuk standing over him, his face swathed in a scarf so that only his eyes were visible. Tarrant fumbled at the cassette player to turn off the music and be able to hear what was being said to him. He got to his knees. The binoculars hung down on his chest.

'She still there?' Demionscuk asked.

'Snug as a bug,' Tarrant replied.

'We move in on her tonight.'

'Good. I'm sure she would like some company. She is definitely looking lonely down there.'

'No point in waiting. Come back to the house now. Let's keep out of sight.'

Tarrant started to pick up the sacks. The snow underneath had mostly melted and some flattened blades of green grass could be seen. He changed his mind, leaving them where they lay on the ground as he followed Demionscuk down the slope. He was disappointed that the time had finally come. He had kept hoping something would happen to prevent them going through with the plan. He had grown to admire and respect Andrew Wallace after reading so much about him. And, in the last few hours, watching her, he felt he had somehow got a lot closer to Helen Wallace. He liked her. He didn't want to hurt her, to embarrass her, to ruin her. He didn't want to tell lies about her. He didn't want to cause her any problems whatsoever. Still, like the Demon said, it was nothing personal. They were just another force of nature to be reckoned with. You should have taken out insurance against us, Tarrant thought. Too late, though. No one is going to sell you a policy now.

Demionscuk went straight into the main room and stood beside the fire. Opening up his anorak, he pulled off his gloves and warmed his hands at the flames. Tarrant copied him. Almost at once his skin began to itch as the heat made his veins expand and his blood flow faster.

'Christ, this is a bloody cold country,' he said. 'Wallace would be welcome to it if it was anything to do with me.'

'Wallace isn't going to get it. That is why we're here, Murray.'

'Silly me. How could I forget.'

'Just you follow orders, Murray, and you'll be back home before you know it.'

'When do we go?' Tarrant asked.

'Soon.'

'What does that mean?'

'Soon.'

They sat by the fire as they had done on their first night in the house. There was no alcohol this time, and no conversation. Demionscuk sat silently with the firelight, tugging and kneading at the lines of his face, his Demon's face. Tarrant tried not to look at him. He rested his head on the back of his chair and tried to ignore him, thinking how he would cope with all the publicity that would result from their little bit of deception. Everybody in the world would hear about him. It would not last, of course. A few days, a week maybe, and then he would be a forgotten man. So would Andrew Wallace.

The darkness closed in rapidly. The wind strengthened. Sleet pattered against the windows. The fire seemed to burn more fiercely. Demionscuk did not move a muscle. He could have been carved from stone. When he spoke the voice did not seem to be connected with the figure seated in front of Tarrant.

'Time to go,' it said.

Helen Wallace danced to the music, spiralling across the floor with her imaginary partner. She was in high spirits, too excited to do any work. Andrew had just phoned her from New York, and she had been able to confirm that the Prime Minister, Peregrine Edwards, had resigned after his son was charged with conspiracy, and that a general election was likely to be called for the beginning of March. He had said he would be home as soon as possible and to keep his side of the bed warm until he got there. She was glad she had resisted the temptation to go to New York, because that now meant their reunion would be all the sweeter. It would all have been too public on the other side of the Atlantic, and there was going to be plenty of that after the election. They needed to snatch as many private moments as they could before the ultimate success meant them becoming public property. In the future, she suspected, the present time would seem all too fleeting. So many people were already clamouring for her husband's attention, but he was coming home to her. Tomorrow night they would be alone together, here in their own cottage in glorious isolation, and the rest of the world would just have to wait until she was ready to share him once more.

She went to the window and looked out into the darkness on the bleak, frozen landscape, with individual shafts of pale light piercing the grey-black clouds like flying buttresses holding up the louring sky. She thought how there was a particular beauty in the glen in every season of the year. In spring everything was new and fresh, then in summer it was all in full bloom, with the growth of purple heather like spilled wine flowing down the hills. Autumn continued the process of inevitable change as the grass and heather gradually lost their colouring and passed through into winter with its own special, austere beauty, when the land spun its chrysalis of snow around itself in preparation for the emergence of the butterfly spring again.

The lights of an approaching car appeared in the murk at the other end of the glen. Mrs MacPherson always phoned before she came out, so it couldn't be her. Who could it be, then? The lights vanished as the car ran into a dip and then reappeared after a few seconds. She glanced back at Breck, lying asleep on the rug beside the fire with his head resting on his front paws. If it was a reporter or a magazine writer they would get short shrift. She was not in the mood for anything like that.

She watched the car all the way. It was moving relatively slowly, probably because the driver was unfamiliar with the narrow road and its twists and turns. It turned unhesitatingly onto the slope of the drive and stopped right behind her own car. The headlights were switched off, enriching the darkness for a moment, and then she caught a glimpse of a man behind the steering-wheel when the door opened and the interior light went on automatically. She stepped back from the window and let the curtain fall into place. Behind her Breck rose to his feet with a questioning bark and padded over to the door.

Helen held the dog by the collar as she answered the loud knocking. Breck growled threateningly when he saw the young man standing on the threshhold holding out a wine bottle. Tarrant's first thought was that the way the dog's lip curled back from its teeth reminded him of Demionscuk.

'G'day. I'm your new neighbour,' he said. 'I thought I'd come over and introduce myself.'

Tarrant shivered in a blast of wind. He was wearing only jeans and a shirt and thin jersey. No coat or anorak. That way, Demionscuk had said, she can hardly refuse to let you in.

'This is unexpected,' Helen said. 'Mrs MacPherson said somebody had rented the Fowlers' house. You'd better come in before you catch your death of cold.'

She dragged Breck back from the door, his claws scraping on the carpet, as Tarrant stepped inside and closed it behind him. Helen crouched down in front of Breck and forcibly told him to sit still, holding his jaws to stop him growling. Not once did the dog's eyes leave the newcomer.

'Good boy. Good boy,' Tarrant said. Demionscuk had not told him there would be a bloody great guard-dog on the premises.

'Don't worry about Breck. He's very obedient and I wouldn't feel safe out here on my own without him. He actually belongs to Mrs MacPherson.'

'The lady with the supplies of scones and jam?'

'That's her. Anyway, I'm Helen Wallace. It's nice to meet you.'

They shook hands and Tarrant handed over the bottle of wine. 'Murray Tarrant,' he said. 'I should really have dressed properly but I thought I'd be all right in the car. I'm still acclimatising to your country.'

'You'll learn quickly or you'll freeze. Warm yourself at the fire. I'll open the bottle. You sound like an Australian. Am I right?'

'Right first time. All the way from Adelaide.'

'Oh? I was in Adelaide last summer with my husband.'

'Really? What a coincidence. Maybe we saw each other then.'

'I doubt it,' Helen said. 'I think I would remember.'

'Of course. I'm sure I would remember if we had.'

Helen levered out the cork and wiped a few stray pieces from the neck of the bottle. 'So what brings you to this part of the world at this time of the year?'

Tarrant accepted the glass of wine. She was actually more attractive in the flesh than in her photographs. Her eyes were bright and sparkling. Her hands were small and delicate. Her skin seemed satin smooth and he wanted to reach out and stroke it. I've already done that though, he told himself regretfully. Pity I can't remember anything about it. Breck started to growl again and she silenced him with a curt command.

'Cheers,' he said. 'Health and happiness.'

'*Slainte.*'

The wine was a little sweet for Tarrant's taste, but then Demionscuk had chosen it. Ten minutes, he had said. Take ten minutes inside and then make your excuses and come back out to the car so that we can work out how we're going to do the pictures. Get your fingerprints on things as evidence you've been there. Tarrant didn't see the point of that. The police weren't going to dust the place for fingerprints in a sex scandal. They weren't doing anything criminal. Well, not strictly criminal, anyway. It would be a case of her word against his. Kiss me nicely, Helen, and I'll tell the truth. Bugger the Demon and his mates.

'My wife and kids are arriving tomorrow,' he explained, anxious to impress her and knowing that he could make up any story he liked. 'I thought we would have a change from the usual Australian heatwave. Perhaps we could arrange to have a meal together sometime this week? You and your husband could come across. We should have figured out how the cooker works by then.'

'It's very good of you to ask, but Andrew is probably going to be too busy this week. We'll be heading back to Edinburgh either tomorrow or the next day.'

'Oh. Duty calls. I understand.' Tarrant picked up a framed photograph from the shelf beside the fire and pressed his thumb on the glass. 'Is this your husband?'

'That's him. He's out of the country at the moment but I'm expecting him back tomorrow night.'

'What is it he does?'

'He's a politician.'

'Really?' Tarrant said, feigning surprise. 'He's not Andrew Wallace, that Nationalist bloke who is trying to set up his own country, is he?'

'As a matter of fact he is, but he's not trying to set up a country — just a government in a country that already exists.'

Tarrant grinned. She wasn't annoyed. She was amused by him. He could see that they would have got on well together if they had met under different circumstances. She sat down and indicated that he should do the same. Her tight jeans moulded themselves even more closely to the shape of her legs and thighs. He felt an easy rapport between them that was relatively unaffected by the big dog sitting at the side of the room looking as if it was about to go for his throat at any moment.

'Pardon a foreigner's misconceptions,' he said, remaining on his feet. 'Scotland's far older than dear old Oz, so I reckon

230

it's entitled to its own government. We're across here looking for our ancestors. We've both got Scots blood, you know, me and the wife. She can go right back to the eighteenth century — to a baker in Glasgow. I hit a dead-end when my great-grandfather stepped off the boat in Botany Bay.'

'What business are you in yourself, Mr Tarrant?'

'Please, call me Murray. I have a truck company.'

She nodded and sipped her drink elegantly.

What a shame, he thought, that he was in the business of ruining her life. Still, it was nothing personal. Here they were, occupying the same space at the same time, and him having come all the way from the other side of the world. There she was, sitting hypnotised in the middle of the road, and he was bearing down on her in his truck. Sorry, sport, he thought sadly. Can't stop.

'I brought a present for you,' he said, laying down his wine glass. 'It's just a little thing, a belated first-footing gift. I left it in the car.'

'You shouldn't have bothered,' she protested.

'No bother at all, I assure you. I know all about these traditions you have over here. I insist you have it.'

'Well, if you insist.'

He moved towards the door. Breck stood up and his shaggy coat bristled all down his back. He snarled silently, showing his teeth until Helen ordered him to sit again. Tarrant went outside into the cold and the wind tore viciously at his clothes. He hurried over to his car to collect the box of chocolates from the glove compartment. The camera gear was on the passenger seat, but Demionscuk had gone. Nor was he in the back. Tarrant withdrew his head from the car — and turned to come face to face with Demionscuk with his anorak hood pulled up, and a scarf over his nose so that only his eyes were visible.

'Bloody hell, Renzo,' he said, stepping back. 'You didn't half give me a fright there.'

'How is it going, Murray?' Demionscuk asked, speaking in a stage whisper above the sound of the wind.

'She's a nice lady. We're just getting to know each other.'

'Any problems?'

'I can't think of any,' Tarrant said, thinking about the dog

231

and deciding Demionscuk could find out about that for himself. 'I don't know how you're going to get your pictures, though. All the curtains are drawn.'

'Don't worry about that. Just make sure the door is left unlocked and I'll burst in at some point.'

'It might take me a while to get her knickers off.'

'Get in there and get on with it, then.'

Under the scarf Tarrant knew the Demon's mouth would be twisted in its mirthless smile, just like the dog's snarl. 'If you insist,' he said, walking past him, wondering what his reaction would be when the Alsation greeted him on his dramatic entrance. Afterwards he would claim she had had the dog hidden away.

Tarrant thought he heard him say something else, like 'Good Luck', and caught a glimpse of a rapid movement against the light of the cottage window. He felt a sharp thump on his back and he was blinded by two bursts of glaring white light. He imagined that the Demon was slapping him on the back to encourage him. But if that was what had happened why was he sinking to his knees and why had it suddenly become so painful to breathe? Why was he unable to stand up? Why was his face pressing into the ground and his tongue against the wet soil? Why was the wind suddenly warm on his face, and even warmer on his back as if boiling water was being poured over it? Why? What was happening to him? Why was he rolling over onto his side? Why were two people looking down at him with the sky silently exploding behind their heads?

Tarrant thought he must be dying but he couldn't understand why. If this was what it felt like to die, it was not so bad really. There was no pain, and there was music, soft music. His favourite, Beethoven's Seventh, carrying him along. His lips were moving. He was saying something but he didn't know what. He couldn't hear the words. He was very tired. He thought about all the times he had turned over in bed and gone to sleep. Dying seemed to be as simple as that, and as comfortable and easy. He was turning over now, rolling onto his face. He was very tired. The warm covers were wrapped tightly around him, as warm and dry as the desert air. If people got to know that dying was so pleasant they would be queueing up to try it. The music boomed in his ears as he lost consciousness. Sorry, sport, he thought wearily. Can't stop.

Andrew Wallace could hardly contain his excitement. Helen would get such a surprise. He had phoned her from Glasgow, pretending he was still in New York and saying how he couldn't sleep properly without her beside him. Hurry home, she had said. I'll get there just as quick as I can, darling, he had replied. He saw himself in the rear-view mirror, grinning broadly. Beyond the mirror the small square windows of the cottage wavered like candle flames in the wind.

He was driving without lights because he knew they could be seen the length of the glen and he wanted to save the surprise for the very last second. He was driving much too fast. As he came round a tight bend the big Jaguar side-swiped an almost invisible bank of snow at the roadside. There was an angry hissing sound as he sawed at the wheel to straighten up. The moonlight suddenly illuminated the road ahead, making the surface shine wetly. He eased his foot down on the accelerator and the powerful car surged forward. The light disappeared just as suddenly and the darkness snapped shut in front of him. He pumped the brake and slowed to a crawl. There was no point in being outrageous. He wanted to get there in one piece, after all.

Not only was he getting to be alone with Helen, but a general election was a virtual certainty. With Christopher Edwards under arrest and apparently ready to give a full confession, he and the Party had been cleared absolutely of any blame for last week's fatal bombings. The circumstances would probably mean a significant swing in his favour. Things were working out extremely well. He didn't want to be too much of a pessimist, but it seemed like it was almost too well. Behind his elation, behind his air of supreme confidence, there was a nagging worry that just wouldn't go away. It was tiny and unfocused but it was there all right, like a shadow on an X-ray. Maybe it meant something, maybe it didn't. Time would tell. He had come a long way but he knew he wasn't home free yet.

Wallace slowed the car almost to a standstill as he negotiated the double bend in front of the turn-off to the cottage in pitch blackness. Then as he swung onto the bumpy driveway he saw the silhouettes of two people move across the lighted window. Oh no, he thought sadly. His surprise was ruined. Helen must have invited a friend to stay the night because he wasn't due back officially until tomorrow. He hadn't bargained for this. So much for the idea of a passionate and romantic reunion. Now they would have to sit and make polite conversation. This was going to be embarrassing.

In a bad-tempered gesture of frustration he stabbed at the dashboard and the car's headlights flooded the darkness ahead. He reached for his jacket and coat and in that instant he saw two people in front of the whitewashed cottage wall, throwing giant shadows that stretched up onto the roof. He saw the curve of a striking arm and the flash of a blade of a knife before it was buried in the back of the leading figure which fell forward onto its knees, and then more slowly onto its face. The standing figure half-turned, holding up an arm to shade its eyes from the glaring lights and then it stepped to one side, moving out of the sharply-defined area, merging with the darkness, disappearing like a ghost passing through a solid wall.

Wallace sat staring in shock, trying to make sense of what he had just seen. He was unable to move for several long seconds, and then the thought of Helen made him burst into action. Where was she? He scrambled out of the car, leaving the engine running, the door wide open and the light-on alarm squawking loudly. It couldn't be her lying on the ground. The figure was too tall. The other person had been too stocky, the wrong shape. As he ran up the slope, he saw her emerge from the door of the cottage and he shouted to her. She frowned back, screwing up her eyes. Then she recognised him and smiled and waved and came forward and saw the body on the ground and stopped again with the puzzled frown back on her face.

'Who is it?' Wallace said, kneeling down and rolling the body gently onto its side.

'M–M–Murray,' she stammered. 'Murray something. He was living in the Fowlers' house. Came over to introduce himself. I saw your lights.'

'Alone?'

'He said he was alone.'

She was shivering with fright and with the cold. So was he. She crouched down beside Wallace and clutched his arm tightly. The wind hit them both in the face as if it was slapping them deliberately. A groan came from the body on the ground and the lips trembled. The eyes snapped open and then fluttered shut. The body tensed and gradually relaxed. Wallace had his fingertips on the pulse at the neck. He could not prevent it rolling over onto its front again. He was surprised there was so little blood around the entry wound.

Helen gasped, jumping up and almost pulling Wallace over .onto his back. 'That's the knife I couldn't find. That's my carving knife.'

The moment she said it, Wallace recognised the brown wood grain of the handle and the ribbed moulding of the finger-grip.

'What's going on, Andrew?' Helen screamed, pressing her fists against her cheeks. 'Why are you here? You should be in New York,' she added.

Wallace was shaking his head in bewilderment when there was a loud thump and they both twisted round to face the car he had left at the foot of the drive. The deep-throated Jaguar engine roared above the noise of the wind and the beams of light lifted into the air and swung away as the car reversed out onto the road and drove away.

'What's going on?' Helen screamed again, close to hysteria.

'In the house,' Wallace ordered, snatching an arm and starting to drag the limp body unceremoniously over the ground. Helen took the other arm to help.

'Is he dead?' she asked reasonably.

'He's about as close as you can get,' Wallace replied.

They staggered to the house. Breck was barking furiously behind the door and Wallace tried to fend him off with a leg to stop him biting but the dog managed to get a mouthful of shirt and joined in the efforts to pull the body inside into the calm and the warmth.

'I must get the phone,' he said and grabbed the receiver from its cradle.

The line was silent and as he angrily threw it down

the electric lights blinked out, leaving only the orange glow of the fire. Wallace stood stock-still, swallowing hard and breathing rapidly. He recalled the events of the last few minutes in his mind. He had no time to analyse them and try to make sense of them. It had all happened so quickly. Now he had to think and act fast, trust to his instincts if they were to survive. He reached out and pulled the curtain aside. Through the bars, he could see that the glen was in darkness. The road was invisible. There were no lights to be seen on it. That meant his car was not being driven away. Whoever had stolen it had not gone far.

Helen called to him. 'He's coming round. Should we take the knife out?'

Wallace went over. Breck sat by the head of the injured man, who was face-down on the floor. A low, menacing growl rumbled continuously in the dog's throat.'

'Murray,' Helen said with her head down beside his. 'What happened? What happened to you?'

She leaned even closer, turning her head to try and make out what he was trying to say in an agonised whisper. Wallace picked up a towel and prepared to remove the knife, deciding that he would have more of a chance of surviving if they could clean the wound.

'What's he saying?'

Helen looked up. Her large, frightened eyes were luminous in the uncertain darkness. 'He says I came right through the windscreen,' she answered, finishing the sentence with a little nervous laugh. 'He keeps talking about the demon setting a trap for him.'

'He's delirious,' Wallace said, tearing open the shirt around the wound. 'Get ready. He may start thrashing about.'

Wallace gripped the handle of the knife and pulled, gritting his teeth and gradually increasing the pressure when there was no immediate physical reaction. The blade seem to be stuck, and then it started slide out slowly and came away altogether. Blood bubbled after it and he mopped it up with the towel.

'He's passed out again,' Helen announced.

She stood up and embraced Wallace as tightly as she could. He held the bloodstained knife away from her and kissed the top of her head.

'What about us, Andrew?' she breathed. 'What are we going to do? Do you think he's coming for us next?'

'Who? Murray's demon? I doubt it,' he lied. 'What would he want with us?'

'Maybe he will come back to finish the job on Murray?'

Wallace assessed the alternatives open to him. Helen's car was parked outside but it was jammed in by the other car. Even if they got it out and tried to get away, the powerful Jaguar could easily run them off the road if that was what the man outside wanted to do. The cottage, on the other hand, was well protected. There were bars on the windows and only one entrance, through the front door. They could withstand a siege by a whole army if necessary.

'We'll stay put,' he said, stroking her hair. 'We'll be safe until morning. He can't touch us in here.'

Renzo Demionscuk had been blinded by the headlights. The shock made him hesitate in confusion for a split second, the knife held at the top of the arc. Then he delivered the blow to Tarrant's back, losing his grip on the handle as the blade sank in and Tarrant fell forward. Demionscuk hesitated again. The strong light burned into his eyes. The plan was to kill Tarrant in a frenzy of stabbing to make it look like the work of a jealous lover, before making Helen Wallace's death appear to be suicide. After that, the trail that had been laid from Adelaide through London to the Highlands would tell its own story of scandal and adultery and Wallace would be left disgraced and humiliated. That was the plan, but it had now been blown apart. Demionscuk had been ultra-careful. There was only one approach to the croft and he had watched it carefully. Nothing had come that way. There should have been no one in the glen but the three of them, and yet here he was, picked out in a spotlight, pinned against the wall, fully expecting to be mercilessly gunned down. He fled into the safe haven of the surrounding darkness.

No fusillade of shots were aimed at him. No gang of bodyguards came running after him. He fell awkwardly over some boulders and lay where he was, looking back over his shoulder, watching a lone man hurry along the path of the beams of light as if he was moving along a tunnel. The woman came out of the house and they met over Tarrant's body. The man looked round. The wind whipped his hair from side to side and Demionscuk recognised the features of Andrew Wallace.

He did not waste time wondering why Wallace had returned from New York a day early, or how he had managed to get so close without revealing his presence. He started thinking how best he could complete the task he was contracted to carry out. There were two logical options open to him as far as he could see: he could leave things as they stood; or he could go back and finish the job properly. The first option meant they still had the difficulty of explaining away Tarrant, and why he was there. However, the second option was the only realistic one. He had not been able to ensure that Tarrant was dead, nor did he now have the time to walk back along the glen to collect his own car. They would all have to die now, Wallace included. He could make it seem as if there had been a fight to the death between Tarrant and Wallace. More spice to the scandal. That would be even better than the original plan.

Demionscuk got to his feet. He was less than fifty yards from Wallace but hidden in the darkness, and any sound he made was masked by the wind. He had already cut the phone wires in case the woman had tried to call for help before he could get to her. But there would probably be a phone in Wallace's car. He ran towards it, only realising the engine was running when he got right beside it. He slid into the driving seat and found reverse gear. The Jaguar's big engine almost stalled as he let the clutch out too quickly. The car jerked back. Ahead of him Demionscuk saw the group of three head for the door of the cottage. Tarrant was dragged roughly over the ground. The giant shadows on the wall followed them into the entrance, disappearing like smoke sucked into a ventilation shaft.

He turned the car round and drove back down the glen, stopping a few hundred yards away beside one of the poles supporting the electricity cable. He allowed it to roll back on the slight incline as he fixed the seat-belt over his chest. Then he pushed the accelerator to the floor. The car leaped forward. Its bonnet bulldozed into the waist-high bank of snow and came to an abrupt half after breaking the pole at the base and causing it to topple to one side. The cable scraped against the rear windscreen. Demionscuk revved the engine savagely and tried to reverse out but the car would not move. The snow was jamming the door shut. He had to open the window and climb out that way, wading through the thick snow to reach the road surface.

The wind was at his back as he jogged back to the darkened cottage. The windows had a faint red tinge, like bloodshot eyes. The two cars were still there. Wallace had not tried to make a run for it. The place was well fortified, with bars on all the windows. It would have been difficult for anyone to break in, but Demionscuk knew a way because he had faced the possibility of Wallace's wife barricading herself inside if she saw what was happening to Tarrant. He was confident he was a physical match for Wallace. There was no problem there. He would strangle him with his bare hands. It was the most common method of killing he used.

He sat under the window at the front but could not hear anything. He adjusted the scarf round his face. Once the curtains moved and somebody looked out and he ducked out of sight. Soon after that he went round the rear to where the half-built toilet was swathed in polythene sheeting. He tried to be as quiet as he could as he removed the anchor pegs and huge stones that were holding it in place, but the looser it got the more violently the wind slapped it against the wooden walls. He decided that they must have heard him inside, so he gave up trying to be quiet and instead moved as quickly as he could, clambering onto the roof and jumping down through the hole where the skylight would eventually be installed. Delaying only to pull off his gloves, he crashed through the interior door and stumbled on the step that led into the main room. He saw Wallace and his wife rushing for the door and was about to go after them when a dark shape launched itself at him from the floor. He heard the wicked growl and smelled the animal scent as the dog went for this throat.

Demionscuk got his arm up just in time as Breck hit him with enough force to drive the wind out of him. He was saved by the thick padding of his soaking wet anorak. The dog's muscular jaws clamped onto the material, knocking him onto his back in the toilet cubicle, but its momentum carried it right over his head so that it ended up beyond him on its side. He twisted round, feet scrambling for a hold, as the dog twisted round, claws scratching wildly at the wooden walls, until they faced each other. Saliva dripped from the torn sleeve. The dog watched him and snarled. Demionscuk stared back, never blinking, as he unzipped the anorak and slipped it off one shoulder. He could feel the pressure of the dog's teeth on his arm. He leaned forward and threw the anorak over its head, using his weight to shove it into the far corner. The moment the dog released its grip he snatched his arm free and slammed the door on it.

Demionscuk left the dog throwing itself against the walls in the tiny cubicle and barking furiously. He ran out the front through the open door, and a flurry of sleet hit him in the face. He wiped his eyes and looked round. The cars were both still parked there, so Wallace had to be on foot. In that instant he caught a glimpse of somebody's legs disappearing round the side of the building. Beneath the scarf his mouth twitched as he went after them.

They had cleaned and dressed the knife wound and put the injured man to bed in the furthest bedroom. He kept slipping in and out of consciousness and raving about demons and kangaroos and the sun rising on the horizon. Finally he settled to sleep peacefully. He had lost a considerable amount of blood and his breathing was shallow and wheezy, but his pulse was strong and there seemed a good chance that he would survive. They had locked the bedroom door as an extra precaution.

Wallace and Helen comforted each other, embracing in front of the fire with its heat stinging their cheeks. He stared over her shoulder and coloured shapes floated in and out of his field of vision, drawing and redrawing themselves into different patterns. The peat fire burned with a muted crackling, and outside the wind rose to a crescendo of shrieking. Breck prowled about the room restlessly.

'What is going to happen, Andrew?' Helen asked, sobbing quietly.

'We'll be all right,' he replied, squeezing her tightly to him. 'We're safe here. We'll be all right till the morning.'

'Do you think they've gone?'

'Yes. Why else would they take my car?'

'Then why have they cut off the power?'

He did not answer. Nausea gathered at the base of his throat. He could feel her body trembling against his. Why indeed had they cut off the power? If there was more than one of them outside, they could just batter down the door and come straight in. Or they might just sit patiently and wait to see if anybody would come out to try and get the car, and pick them off then. If there was only one person he might not be able to break in. That evened the odds a little, but he would have the upper hand if they tried to get out. In the circumstances the best option was to stay inside. Daylight would rescue them. News of his unscheduled early trip across the Atlantic would have broken by then, and droves of reporters would descend on the cottage.

'I was supposed to surprise you tonight — not the other way round.'

His attempt at humour failed. Helen released him and sat down in an armchair with her head bowed forward onto her knees. He went to the window and pushed the curtain aside. The entire glen was swamped in pervasive darkness except for shifting bands of watery moonlight on the hillsides. Above, the large gouts of cloud were like ice-floes caught in a swift-moving current. Breck joined him at the window and put his paws up on the sill, sniffing at the air. He patted the dog's big head and went back to the fire. Helen was still sitting in the same position. He was about to speak to her when she rose from the chair and said she was going to check if their visitor was all right. He watched her go, thinking that it could be no coincidence that the stabbing had been done with their missing carving knife. Murray, whoever he was, was not just an innocent bystander. Or perhaps he was unwittingly part of it all. It was a deliberate act, aimed at implicating him, or more likely Helen, in a murder. It was another plot against Andrew himself, to discredit him and ruin him following the failure to fix the blame for the bombings on him. Perhaps this was the CIA plot Sheahan had warned him about, and he had foiled it by sheer good fortune and his sudden, unexpected arrival. Nothing and nobody, he reminded himself. Nothing and nobody were going to stop him now.

He suddenly heard the noise from outside — at the same time as Helen who was coming back from the bedroom. His flesh crawled and every nerve in his body buzzed with heightened tension. He had completely forgotten about the unfinished toilet, the single weak spot in the cottage's defences. They were coming in that way.

'What will we do?' Helen screamed. 'What about Murray?'

'It's not Murray they're after. It's us!'

She stared at him dumbly, not fully understanding. The sound came again, louder this time. It was a clattering, rushing sound. A strange sound. A man-made sound. The wind howled as though trying to drown it out, but there was no disguising it. Breck whined as he padded over and began to claw at the toilet door. Wallace grabbed the dog by the collar and pulled him back. There was a heavy thump from inside the toilet cubicle. Somebody jumping down from the ceiling. After a few seconds the door burst open.

'Get him, boy,' Wallace ordered, releasing his collar.

The dog launched itself at the intruder, springing at his throat. Wallace shoved Helen over to the front door, and they stood with their backs to the wall, watching the battle until it became obvious that the man was getting the better of the animal.

'Out. Out,' Wallace shouted.

They charged outside into the drenching sleet and storm. Wallace braced himself for an attack that did not come. Only the wind trying to knock them over. There was only one man then, just one demon to deal with. He wished he had put something on over his shirt.

'You hide here and I'll lure him away into the hills,' he told Helen, pushing her towards the corner of the cottage.

'I'm not leaving you,' she protested.

'No choice,' he gasped. 'Take the car and Murray when we're a decent distance away. Bring back help quick. Quick, now. Move. I can lose him on the hills. Trust me. There's no time to argue.'

She hesitated for a moment, then went to hide, watching

him all the way with tear-stained eyes. He ran to the opposite corner of the cottage and stood waiting there. When the demon appeared at the door he started running for his life.

Wallace followed the course of the swollen burn, uphill. Once, the rough path gave way beneath him, and he splashed into the torrent. The freezing water sucked and tugged at his ankles and swirled round his knees. The stony bed of the burn tore at his feet through his thin shoes. He climbed back out and kept running, feeling his muscles grow rapidly weaker. He tripped and fell, and hardly had the strength to get up again. But somehow he dragged himself to his feet and stumbled on for another fifty yards or so. Then he tripped again and landed on his hands and knees. He looked back down the hill and could see nothing but the long needles of sleet flashing in front of him. The glen below him was black and featureless except for a tiny square of disconnected white and red lights that appeared and disappeared, following what must have been the dips in the road. Helen has got away, he thought with relief, as a broad band of moonlight swept over him and suddenly he could see everything laid out before him, right down to patches of moss on the roof of the cottage. He was aware of the veins on the back of his hand, and each individual hair on his forearm standing out on its little mound and bending in the wind. He saw snow crystals clinging to the clumps of heather and to the tangle of stems growing out of the earth. He saw his pursuer about one hundred yards down the hill, standing motionless, gazing after the departing car. No point in coming after me now, Wallace thought, but the man was already turning, throwing away his scarf and beginning to climb the slope.

The moonlight passed over and it was pitch-dark again when Wallace began running. He had to keep moving. There was no place to hide on the empty hillside, and the moonlight kept washing over him at regular intervals and revealing his position, showing that the demon behind him was gaining relentlessly. In the dark he ran into a stunted tree, and the branches scratched his face and ripped his shirt before they snapped like brittle bones as he thrashed in panic to free himself. Every time he looked back, the demon was a few yards closer. He fell across a sleeping sheep and was left clutching handfuls of coarse, wet wool. The creature lumbered off, bleating plaintively.

He changed direction and ran at right-angles to the burn, finding it easier for a while to bounce over the snow-encrusted heather, blundering along, no longer certain of where he was in relation to the cottage. His lungs grew red-hot inside his shivering body as the cruel game of cat and mouse continued. One brief scrap of moonlight showed that the gap had been reduced to barely twenty yards. He tripped again and crashed into the ground. He lay there helplessly, gasping for breath, resigned to the fact that he was not going to outrun the demon behind him. He would have to be ready to fight. Animal instinct had taken over. It would be a fight to the death, man to man — kill or be killed. Only one of them would come out of it alive.

He got up slowly and found himself standing on a small hump, with the land falling away on every side. The darkness was thick around him. He tilted his head back to drink the sleet. He saw the next shaft of moonlight racing towards him, a narrow band hugging the undulating contours of the hillside. Only a few seconds more before it hit him — and, in that small space of time, reason imposed itself over instinct. Fear returned. He was not dead yet. He could run a long way yet.

The moonlight arrived — showing Wallace that he was now about a quarter of a mile above the cottage, standing at the top of a near-vertical scree slope that fanned out like a colourless peacock's tail. But the chasing demon was right beside him — standing still, head slightly raised, looking straight at him; so close he could almost have reached out and touched him. They both moved as the darkness swooped down again.

Wallace jumped like a parachutist leaving a plane. He hit the ground heels first, but the ground shifted under his weight and he landed on his back and began to slide. Beneath the crisp covering of snow, thousands of small stones poured down the slope with him, producing a sound like running water. His legs touched solid ground and he was pushed into a standing position ... but his momentum was too much, and he fell forward onto his face and then tumbled over onto his back. Over and over he went, down the hill, completely out of control. When he finally came to a halt, he was dazed and sore and scratched all over. The salty taste of blood was in his mouth. There was a terrible pain on the side of his head that made him wince when he tried to touch it. He staggered to his feet, disorientated and off balance. A passing flash of moonlight revealed another person descending the slope, but more slowly and some distance behind.

The croft was quite close on his right. Wallace headed for it, believing he had gained a brief respite from the chase. He seemed to be walking very slowly, yet somehow got even slower if he tried to hurry. The pain in his head throbbed viciously. When he reached the cottage he saw that Helen's car was gone — and that she had smashed the window of the other car, presumably to get access to release the handbrake to shift it out of the way. The axe lay there on the ground, beside the front wheel. She must have used it to break the window. Now he needed a weapon, he thought calmly. The darkness fell again just as he bent down to pick it up and he had to feel around with cold-numbed fingers before he located it. The roaring wind died and he heard footsteps behind him, and he turned round in time to see a bulky shadow a few yards off. Even in the darkness he had an impression of outstretched arms, the running feet and hard breathing — a solid figure rushing straight at him. He swung the axe as he rose, bringing it up and over in a long arc and then down with all the force he could muster, grunting with the effort as it struck home with a heavy smack that jarred his arm. The shaft splintered and broke, and was suddenly weightless in his hand.

The white walls of the cottage appeared as though someone had thrown a switch. The blade of the axe was buried in the demon's forehead, above the bridge of the nose — between the eyes that were still fixed on Wallace. Blood trickled down the expressionless face. The wounded man took an awkward step backwards and leaned against the wall. His eyes rolled upwards, exposing the whites. His head dropped and his cheek rested on the rough stone, pulling the corner of his mouth up in a parody of a smile as he slid to the ground.

Wallace stood where he was, fascinated by the scene. Momentarily the darkness would hide the motionless body, and then the alternating rushes of moonlight would uncover it again — as if flicking over the pages of a book, but always to find the same picture.

Finally the chill of the air and the savage wind became unbearable and forced him inside the cottage for warmth while he waited for help to arrive. He freed the barking dog and stood shivering over the fire, poking at it with the broken axe handle to encourage the flames, till he felt its heat begin to nip at his frozen flesh.

The golden lion rampant rested on his bare, blood-smeared chest. The moving flames were reflected in its diamond eye. He clutched the lion in his fist and smiled weakly. 'Nothing and nobody,' he murmured. 'Nothing and nobody.'

CHAPTER TWENTY-ONE

All the interest in today's UK general election is focused on
the performance of the Scottish Nationalists who are seek-
ing a mandate for independence.

Opinion polls predict that the party will take more
than thirty of the fifty Westminster seats being contested
north of the border this time, and if that happens SNP
leader Andrew Wallace will immediately demand that
constitutional negotiations begin on the handover of power.

Support for Mr Andrew Wallace (48) and his party
has soared since January when a wave of bombings by
supposedly Nationalist sympathisers was discovered to
be the work of English political extremists trying to
discredit him. The former Prime Minister's son was
implicated in the plot, contributing directly to his
father's resignation and the calling of the election.

Mr Wallace also survived an assassination attempt at
his remote Highland cottage in Argyll, fighting off the
assassin with his bare hands.

Afterwards it was found that the incident was
connected to a false trail of events set up to try and
involve his young wife in a bizarre sex scandal. Although
the CIA were named as possible instigators, that has never
been substantiated.

Caledonian Press Agency

Dave Sheahan waited more than two hours before he was
summoned into Barrett Coleman's private office. He left the
reception area with its rows of shiny-leaved hot-house plants
defying the torrential rain that blotted out any view from the
full-length windows, and he followed the swaying hips of the
dark-haired secretary and the flowing creases of her tightly-

stretched skirt. She led him into a small, windowless ante-room which had two identical world maps in marquetry relief facing each other from opposite walls. Stopping in front of a door with an unilluminated, rectangular light panel beside it, she removed the false, red-painted fingernail from the index finger of her right hand and pressed a button. After a few seconds the green section of the panel lit up revealing the word ENTER. She stepped to one side as the door quietly hissed open to allow Sheahan to enter.

Coleman was sitting behind a big wooden desk. There was nothing at all on the leather-inlaid top. A dramatic American eagle was carved into the front panel. The CIA director was cleaning his spectacles with a tissue as he looked across and waved a hand in the direction of a straight-backed chair. Sheahan sat down, his knee inches from the eagle's beak, thinking how the apparent lack of any neck made the man look like a well-dressed snowman with the smaller ball of his head connected directly to the larger ball of his body. The rain cascaded in waves down the window behind him. The snow was long gone. It would soon be spring. Next week, in fact.

'What's this I hear about you resigning, Dave?' Coleman said.

Sheahan shrugged. He had expected to be more nervous about the interview but now that it was happening he was confident that he was doing the right thing. If the long wait had been meant to somehow intimidate him, it hadn't worked. Coleman didn't frighten him at all.

'That's right, sir. I have resigned,' he said.

Coleman held his glasses up and inspected them for smears. He found one and began to polish again. 'You should change your mind,' he said.

'I've thought about it very carefully. It was not a spur of the moment decision, sir. I need to get out of Government service altogether. I've lost the taste for it.'

'You were a good operator, Dave. We don't want to lose you.'

'Thank you, sir.'

'What will you do?'

'I don't know. My brother owns a bar in Houston. He wants to open a restaurant. I may join him.'

Coleman slipped his glasses on, hiding the red mark on the

248

bridge of his flat nose. Sheahan saw two tiny reflections of himself and the room around him in the lenses. They sat in silence for several moments staring fixedly at each other, communicating more effectively than by the spoken word.

'You could have a fine career with us, Dave, if you chose to stay,' Coleman said finally. 'The work you did in Scotland was excellent. Everything you said would happen there already has, or is about to happen. Accurate analysis like that on a first posting is pretty rare.'

Sheahan looked at his watch. 'The election will be starting over there soon.'

'Are you still predicting a victory of your friend Wallace?'

'Undoubtedly.'

'He has done well, but success in this election does not guarantee him full independence. Far from it.'

'Of course not. There are never any guarantees, just possibilities. Wallace is a survivor.'

'Oh yes, he's a survivor all right.' Coleman smiled and licked his top lip. 'It's foolish to resign, you know, Dave. It's oldfashioned to take these things personally, as a matter of honour.'

'Not a matter of honour, sir.'

'No?'

'No, sir. A matter of independence.'

Coleman smiled and nodded. Sheahan looked past him and smiled at his own ghostly image reflected on the rain-silvered glass of the window.

Sandy McInnes stood at the rail of the big car ferry as she swung round to the south in a long, easy curve to enter the mouth of Loch Ryan. The morning sea haar was being blown like smoke from the surface of the water and the land as the wind rose and the first rays of the sun broke through. The water was a dirty grey, waves flecked with white behind, but calmer in the sheltered loch. The fields on either side were an irregular pattern of green and white. Escorting seagulls matched the ferry's speed so that they seemed to be hovering around it. He tossed the remains of a sandwich out over the side and a bird dipped from its flight path to snatch it in mid-air and gulp it down.

McInnes was taking a chance by coming back to Scotland so soon, less than three months after carrying out Major Magic's final tricks. He had decided it was worth the risk. According to his mates in Glasgow, nobody was looking for him. He was not a wanted man. The police investigation had no evidence and no apparent direction. There seemed to be nothing to prevent him resuming his old life. Besides, he needed to cure his morbid homesickness. If he didn't he would soon be drinking too much again, and he didn't want to lose control. He had not been drunk for at least a month.

The door of the passenger lounge opened and an elderly woman came out, all wrapped up like him in a thick anorak. She was much shorter than him, and when she stood beside him at the rail her face was hidden by the hood.

'I always like to see our arrival at Stranraer after a crossing,' she said in an accent very like his own. 'You'll be glad to get back yourself.'

'Oh yes,' he replied. 'It will be good to be home again.'

Murray Tarrant had been back in Adelaide for two days when he got his first visitor. The loud, insistent ringing of the bell penetrated the rolling waves of music that surrounded him where he lay face-down on a bed of cushions on the floor. It was Beethoven's Seventh Symphony — his favourite. He had listened to virtually nothing else since recovering consciousness in hospital after that fateful night in the remote glen in Scotland. He kept playing it over and over again as if there was some meaning in it, some clue that he was overlooking, some message that he was failing to understand. The same music, the same part of the music approaching the climax of the final movement, had been playing just before Luigi Fachetti had beckoned him over at that rusty old wind-wheel in the outback north of Alice Springs less than three months ago. It was Fachetti behind the door now, waiting for him again as he had waited for him before. The music ended suddenly as if its throat had been cut.

Tarrant whistled noiselessly while he got to his feet. He rewound the tape to the beginning of the last movement. The bandage over his back and shoulder felt incredibly heavy, and he had to hold his arm out from his body at a slight angle. It was uncomfortable rather than painful, but it was frequently seized by a stiffness that made him feel as if he was made of stone. It would take time to heal completely, the doctors said, but he was young and strong and should recover rapidly. The knife had torn right through a lung and just missed the heart. The shock had made him pass out. His pain threshold had always been very low. A few days later he found streaks of grey in his hair.

The bell rang again, a short angry burst. Tarrant had been wary of coming back to Australia but he didn't really have anywhere else to go. Besides, he had kept the faith, surprising himself by his objective thinking at such a time of crisis. Fachetti should be grateful to him. He had feigned serious illness until he discovered that Demionscuk was dead. Then he was free to make up whatever story he liked, demanding immunity in return for telling all. Fachetti's name had never arisen. It was Demionscuk who took all the blame for the sex scandal idea, and for the last-minute change of plan which made Tarrant a victim instead of a perpetrator. When his sympathetic interrogators happened to suggest that Demionscuk might have been working for the CIA, Tarrant invented a mysterious American he had encountered only briefly in Luxembourg. That was exactly what they wanted to hear. Soon after that they let him go.

'G'day, Mr Fachetti,' Tarrant said when he opened the door and saw the old man standing there in the familiar wide-brimmed hat. 'Long time no see.'

Fachetti appeared to be alone, but his henchmen would not be very far away. It was dark on the landing but Tarrant didn't know what time it was, or even what day it was. He had not been outside since his return.

'Murray, my son,' Fachetti said through a wide grin that crowded the wrinkles on his face into tight bunches. 'Welcome home.'

'It's good to be back. I missed the warmth.'

Tarrant stood back and the old man shuffled inside, leaving the door ajar. He took off his hat in a strangely submissive gesture.

'They let you go, then?' he said.

251

'I reckon they felt sorry for me,' Tarrant replied.

'How is your arm?'

'It affects my shoulder more than my arm. He stabbed me in the back.'

'A nasty wound, I hear, Murray.' He tut-tutted and shook his head and frowned. 'I want to apologise for what happened over there, Murray. The Demon wasn't acting on orders when he attacked you. I just cannot understand what he thought he was doing.'

Tarrant nodded. Of course Demionscuk had been acting on orders. He was a force of nature. That was what he called himself. Forces of nature did not think for themselves, they acted according to strict laws. Fachetti had known full well what the plan was; lay the scandal trail and then the body right at the feet of Helen Wallace. He had set it up for whoever was paying the bill. And if Andrew Wallace had not unexpectedly returned at that exact second, and if the shining lights had not broken up the sequence of events, it would all have worked perfectly. He would have been murdered and Demionscuk would have then either murdered the woman or simply disappeared. Either way Wallace would have been ruined. Instead, the outcome meant that Wallace had emerged as an even bigger hero than before.

Fachetti clicked his tongue again and brushed at the lapel of his thin, white jacket. 'What can I say, Murray? It was not meant to happen like that.'

'He was a crazy man. Everything was going so well until he went haywire.'

Fachetti stared at him for a long time. Then he smiled. 'Yes. Yes, it was. That was why they called him the Demon,' he said.

Tarrant shrugged to demonstrate his stoical acceptance of the situation, and winced at a twinge of pain in his shoulder. He had worked it all out lying in his hospital bed. Fachetti had pushed him forward as a sacrifice, and Demionscuk had wielded the knife. By rights he should be dead, viciously slashed by his supposed lover in the frenzy of a crime of passion. But he wasn't and, as far as he could see, the best way to remain alive was to conform to a few other natural laws. Demionscuk could take the blame because he was dead.

252

Fachetti need not be implicated because he was alive and life had to go on. Even if they had managed to put Fachetti away, he had a lot of friends and a lot of influence. No point in trying to hide and start fresh somewhere else. They would find him wherever he went if they really wanted to.

'Sorry we didn't manage to do the job,' Tarrant said.

'No problem there, Murray my son. You win some, you lose some. You've been paid anyway.'

'I know. Reckon I've been paid for achieving exactly the opposite of what we set out to achieve.'

'What's that?'

'Everybody says Wallace will get what he wants in the British election. A national hero he is now. Nothing can stop him.'

'Well, good luck to him.' Fachetti flapped his hat to chase a fly away from his face. 'It's his country, after all. You ready to go back to truck driving?'

'I couldn't handle it yet, Mr Fachetti. My shoulder couldn't take the trip.'

'No hurry. Let me know when you're ready. Until then, rest up, enjoy yourself.'

'I don't know if I want to be a truckie again anyway.'

'We might be able to find you another job, Murray my son. A better job. I'll put out the word. I have to go now, but it's been good to see you.' Fachetti walked to the door and opened it. He turned and touched Tarrant's arm lightly with his hat, frowning as an indication of sincerity. 'Keeping my name out of this is much appreciated, Murray. You'll be all right. Don't worry. You did the right thing.'

'Thanks, Mr Fachetti. I hope so.'

Tarrant watched the old man go down the stairs. Dim figures emerged from the corridors of the landing to act as escorts, following a few steps behind. Tarrant closed the door and went back into the room to lie face-down on the pile of cushions. He stretched a hand out to switch on the music. It played at full volume and he felt the vibration of it coming through the hard floor and through the soft cushions to gently massage the wound on his back. *Allegro con brio.*

Sir Archibald Ballantyne finished reading the *Scotsman* and folded it carefully before placing it on the table beside the other papers and the unopened mail. His wife Audrey had filled the toast-rack and the teapot and was now standing with her back to him at the kitchen worktop fixing breakfast for the two dogs. Jill the shiny black Labrador and Jack the rough-coated retriever sat behind her watching the tins being opened. Ballantyne patted Jill's head and she twisted quickly to lick his hand before resuming her rapt observation of the preparation of her food.

He grinned and poured himself a cup of tea and spread a little honey on a piece of toast. He had already had the dogs out for a brisk early walk down by the woods, startling a couple of rabbits and disturbing the roosting pigeons. It was a beautiful morning, clear and crisp, with the sun sparkling on the calm sea around the rocky lump of the Isle of May, the seabirds constantly rising from it, making it look as if the edges were crumbling away. It was the kind of morning that made him feel good to be alive. He had held his hand over his heart to feel its steady, powerful beat as he strode along swinging his walking stick at long grasses and overhanging branches.

He ate one piece of toast and spread more honey on another. The dogs squealed with excitement as their food was put down on the floor in two dishes, and then snorted noisily as they wolfed into it. Ballantyne sipped his tea and picked up the weekly property section that came with the paper as a separate supplement. He always checked it to see how land prices were faring.

'Good God,' he said. 'Isn't that one of Suds's estates up for sale?'

'Who?' his wife said, leaning over his shoulder to look at the half-page advertisement.

'Suds. You know — Sembawa. My rich Arab pal from school.'

'Oh, him.'

'I'm sure this is one of his estates up in Invernesshire. Two thousand acres.' Ballantyne laughed. 'I wouldn't be surprised if the rest were up for sale as well soon.'

'Why do you say that?'

'Just a feeling I have. I don't think Suds fancies having Andrew Wallace running the country round land he owns.'

His wife sat down opposite him and opened her copy of the

Daily Mail. 'Speaking of Andrew Wallace, are we going to vote this morning?' she asked.

'Oh, yes indeed,' Ballantyne said firmly. 'We're going to vote.'

The polling booths were arranged in two groups of three on either side of the primary-school classroom. They were made from old sheets of plywood that had been rather carelessly assembled so that the joints did not fit together properly and the pieces looked like they were just leaning on each other to stay upright.

The walls of the classroom were decorated with colourful children's paintings. It had been designated for voters from the second half of the alphabet, and was empty apart from the two officials sitting behind a table in the centre, when Mrs Kirsty MacPherson arrived, leaving her shopping trolley by the door. They checked her name on their list and stamped her ballot paper before handing it to her. She moved across to the booths and rubbed against the makeshift partition walls with her shoulders because the alcove was so narrow. The whole thing rocked and for one awful moment she thought it was going to collapse. When she realised it wasn't, she hurriedly laid her paper on the shelf and picked up the short pencil secured by a length of string and a nail. There were three candidates to choose from. She didn't like the Nationalist man, Cunningham, at all. He was a rude person who was divorced and had once been banned for drink driving. And his eyes were too close together. Still, she wasn't really voting for him. It was Mr Wallace she was really voting for. After all he had been through, it was the least she could do. She made her cross.

Andrew Wallace raised the glass of whisky high and tapped it lightly against the ones held up by Helen and Hamish Henryson.

'Here's tae us,' he said.

'Wha's like us?' Helen said.

'Damn few,' Henryson said.

'And they're a' deid,' Wallace concluded.

They drank to each other and looked out the window over

the rooftops in the centre of Edinburgh. It was a bright, sunny March day. The statue of the Golden Boy on top of its dome sparkled like a swimmer just emerged from the water. The sky was light blue and two planes had left vapour trails over the city, forming a vast St Andrew's cross.

The campaigning was over at last and their fate was in the hands of the voters. Wallace had spent a good thirty minutes holding his voting paper over the slot in the ballot box in the local school while troops of photographers queued up to take his picture. Nothing more to be done now, he thought contentedly, until the votes were counted and the result announced.

Murray Tarrant was back in Australia, more a victim than anybody else involved in the recent series of events. There was probably enough evidence to convict him on a charge of conspiracy, but the general feeling was that he had suffered enough. He had confessed the whole story of how he was recruited and brought over to Luxembourg by the man Demionscuk and an American he assumed to be the controller of the operation. From there he told how he was to claim he had had a sexual relationship with Helen. Being stabbed in the back wasn't part of the plan as he knew it. Demionscuk had covered his tracks well. It was thought unlikely that any hard evidence would ever be uncovered to reveal the mystery American who had recruited him. The CIA, naturally, denied any role in the affair but were universally condemned anyway.

In prison, Christopher Edwards also made a full confession of his role in the fatal bombings and was charged with conspiracy to cause death by explosions. His father had died of a heart attack two weeks into the election campaign. The trial was scheduled for the end of April.

'Remember, Andrew,' Henryson said, his ancient, lined face creasing into a grin, 'once you take over here, your troubles are only just beginning.'

Wallace closed his eyes and tried to look into the future. He had absolutely no reservations about what he was doing and how it was happening. He had never felt more confident in his life. The way ahead was clear. Nothing and nobody was in his way. He winked at Helen.

'Let's make a start, then,' he said.